# RESORTING

# TO

# MURDER

Gail Hulnick

GAIL HULNICK

From Sirocco Press, an Imprint of

The WindWord Group Publishing & Media, LLC
#200, 100 Bull Street
Savannah, Georgia  31401
www.windwordgroup.com

This is a work of fiction. Names, characters, businesses, places, events and incidents are either the products of the author's imagination or used in a fictitious manner. Any resemblance to actual persons, living or dead, or actual events is purely coincidental. The publisher does not have any control over and does not assume any responsibility for author or third-party websites or their content.



ISBN-10:  0-9983990-0-0
ISBN-13:  978-0-9983990-0-3

Library of Congress Control Number: 2017901360

www.windwordgroup.com
Email admin@windwordgroup.com

Cover design by David Stone

Printed in the United States of America

*To my parents, with thanks for everything!*

*Especially the recipes*

GAIL HULNICK

# PROLOGUE

It was just past eleven p.m. when it hit the water, sounding like a tree falling in a hurricane or a non-swimmer show-off doing a belly-flop dive. By day, this dark water sparkled and shone in stripes of cobalt, turquoise and sometimes royal or navy blue. By night, only matte black.

About two hundred feet away from the marina, a brightly lit restaurant with a packed outdoor patio played 1970s classic rock. The sound was cranked up loud so that even the residents of the extended care home across the street could hear it—and no one noticed the splash the long box made. No one looked up—not over toward the dock, and not farther, toward the half dozen yachts at anchor. Not one of the deeply tanned, fashionably tattooed and dreadlocked teenagers, not the friendly waitress, not the bored ex-fisherman behind the bar—no one looked, no one saw, no one heard.

Every restaurant on the boardwalk was almost full and the aroma of delicious meals being prepared saturated the night air. Dozens of vivid posters announcing the upcoming *KweeZeenArtZ Food Festival St. Croix* hung in lines covering a fence in front of one of the waterfront hotels on the boardwalk.

If anyone had looked, they might have seen a dark figure hurrying toward the Fort, silhouetted against the advertising tapestry.

But no one was looking. The figure evaporated into the crowd celebrating a Friday night downtown and a very inconvenient item was hidden. Permanently.

# CHAPTER ONE

I knew, as soon as I saw her walk through my lobby and up to my registration desk. Exquisitely cut blonde hair, white-china skin, small feet in red shoes with towering heels, and huge sunglasses that she hid behind, even after coming indoors from the minivan taxi that had carried her and five others from the airport.

"I'll take this one," I muttered to Eleni, sitting beside me.

"Thanks, Nola," she replied.

But this newest guest didn't approach the desk after all. She hung back, a sneer curling her perfectly made-up mouth (Russian Red, I was guessing). Every two minutes the sneer was replaced by an icy stare, for a brief change of face. She was vigorously thumbing her phone.

Her traveling companion, a slightly built, dark-haired man with a right hand covered in silver rings and bangles, came up to my desk and dropped into the chair across from me.

"Hello and welcome to the Pitaya Beach Resort," I said, adding my best professional smile. Some people believe in meeting tourist bad manners with intense passive aggression but I don't. It doesn't help.

"Thank you, dearie," he replied. "Y'all think we can get through this right away?"

His accent made me think of biscuits and honey. "Yes, of course, Mr.——?"

"Lee. Park Lee. Two rooms, reservation under Maureen O'Hara."

"Mr. Lee and Ms. O'Hara." A good hotel reservations staffer is never ironic and never surprised. I located the reservation in the system and pulled it up to be printed.

On this June day in 2016, our resort was almost full. Many people think the Caribbean is a good place to avoid during hurricane season, from June to November, but many people would be wrong. We hadn't had a hurricane since 1995. Storms, yes, and sometimes some inconvenience, but if you ask me, that's more than balanced out by the good news—cheaper prices, smaller crowds, better tables available in the best restaurants. You have more hurricane concern in the fall than summer, anyway. Lots of people, including this batch, called the U.S. Virgin Islands a terrific choice this time of year and we were rarely empty. Buy your trip insurance, yes, but after that, get your weary self over here to paradise.

Ha. There's a travel poster slogan.

The real travel posters that were on our office walls this month were all about our imminent *KweeZeenArtZ Food Festival.* More than just a food festival, a chefs' competition. More than just a chefs' competition, an international, celebrity chefs' competition. In just a few weeks they'd be showing up from Italy, France, New York, Japan and Canada. Yes, Canada. You may not crave poutine but many people do.

St. Croix had become this firepit for foodie dreams quite gradually over decades. Every year something special stoked KweeZeenArtZ just a little bit more. But this year would be the ultimate because for the first time ever we had a local chef who had qualified to compete with the world's best.

"While we wait for the bell captain to take your bags to your suite, could I offer you each a rum punch?" I passed the reservation forms across to Mr. Lee and he handed his driver's license and a credit card to me.

"Wait? What did she mean, wait?" The stuck-up guest had been hovering, listening in on our conversation, but she wouldn't speak to me. A good thing, too, because I would have been tempted to answer her hiss of a question with one of my own—"You don't understand 'wait'? How about 'take your turn'?"

"I tell you, Park, the minute I get a signal, I'm texting that assistant of mine that she is gone! Gone like yesterday's fresh bread. I *asked* her, loud and clear, to get me a place to relax and chill. This is *not* going to work for me."

"We have just one bell man working this afternoon, Ms. O'Hara," I explained. "He'll take you as soon as he's back from assisting some of our other newly arrived guests."

"Other guests? This gets worse by the minute. I can't remember the last time I had to have strangers around me like this. *Do something.*" She reached for both the rum punches that Eleni had brought over on a tray, as we always do for guests who've just arrived. "Has Simon called?"

"No, but George has been emailing all day."

She rolled her eyes and stomped off toward the walkway through to the beach. Eleni didn't seem to notice how rude this guest was—too busy looking at the designer leather jacket over summer dress outfit. Two thousand dollars, I'm guessing.

"Don't you recognize her?" Eleni whispered.

"No! No, you do not recognize her!" Mr. Lee glared at my co-worker, then signed the forms, put away his ID and held out his hand for their key cards.

Mr. Lee had ignored the other four guests in their group who were also waiting to check in, as well as the five others who had come over in the hotel shuttle bus. None of them seemed to have their shorts in a twist, like his … his what? Girlfriend? BFF? Employer? Client? Their happy vibe meant that I could ignore them, too, but I wouldn't do it for long. Didn't want any of them to turn into offended divas as well, but it seemed safe to focus on getting Ms. O'Hara and Mr. Lee and their bad energy out of this small space before they turned it toxic.

It was a nice space, usually just the thing to make incoming guests feel that their time on St. Croix had really begun, if they hadn't quite been able to find that island feel at the airport with its lineups at the baggage carousel and the rental car counters. The colors were a soothing brown, gold and cream, the free drinks we brought them had little umbrellas in them and the air conditioning was turned up high. We even had an office dog, as a sort of homey touch. Eleni couldn't stand to leave Flash at home alone all day long, so she was allowed to bring him in with her as long as none of the guests complained. He was narcoleptic, she said—fell asleep constantly and instantly, and spent pretty much every minute asleep. Nobody even knew he was there.

Unfortunately it took another ten minutes before Isaac came back on the golf cart to take Miss O'Hara and her eight suitcases to her room. Ten minutes that the annoying woman insisted were 20. I was ready to blow up at her, so I took a deep breath and went to my 'happy place', as my mother would say. A charming restaurant with a carefully set table, snowy white linens, well-polished silverware, offering a plate of coconut chicken, blackened sea bass, carrots, pearl onions, spinach and an exquisite sauce with Bombay spice, cilantro and lime juice. Hmmm.

I had expected that the views the nasty guest had

of the Caribbean Sea as she gulped her rum punches would help. It looked heavenly. Sugar sand beach, gorgeous palm trees swaying with the trade winds, turquoise water mixing with azure blue then giving way to a carpet of almost royal purple, all the way to the horizon. How could she not be entranced by all this? I had been, since the moment I'd arrived here on vacation, four years earlier. Arrived and never left, despite the Olympic-level concern beamed at me by my mother, all the way from Seattle, Washington.

Miss O'Hara came storming back into the office and Mr. Lee's voice could be heard from behind her, as he followed. "Liz, please! It doesn't do any good…"

"How much longer will this take? I want to get into my room." The serenity of the sea hadn't helped her mood. Yet it was odd, but as angry as she seemed, there was more of a pathetic vibe to her than a scary one—if anybody deserves to be pathetic while wearing a two-thousand-dollar jacket.

The other nine incoming guests had had enough of her racket by the time Isaac showed up and they pretended to be busy, too busy to rush to the golf cart to get to their rooms. One of the couples who'd arrived in the hotel shuttle bus chatted quietly together in a chill way that made it seem like they were probably long-married. The other couple looked like newlyweds, draped over one another like damp towels on a beach chair. An elderly man on his own read a book that he had pulled out of his duffle bag. One of the men who'd come in the same taxi as Miss Noisy was hanging around the desk, trying to chat with Eleni, while his wife stood by a wall, reading the hotel restaurant menus mounted there. The other two had their smartphones out. None of them made a move or said a word when she marched over to the golf cart. We loaded her pile of luggage, then Mr. Lee climbed in behind her, and off they went on their way toward their beachfront suites.

Moments later, a car pulled up, filled with what turned out to be her pursuers. It was a dusty old Toyota, a left-side drive, as were most of the cars here, despite the fact that you'd expect a right-side drive in a country where the traffic runs in the left lane. Not sure how that came about, maybe some island planner spent too much time across the water in the British Virgin Islands and brought back their motoring habits, once upon a time. There's a story there, somewhere. Also not sure how these guys got past our gate, where the uniform and a confident manner were supposed to keep away anybody who wasn't supposed to be here.

These people definitely weren't supposed to be here. They didn't look like guests or tourists—no colorful shirts, no sandals, no hats protecting them from the sun— and they were carrying cameras that looked as though a small animal could crawl into the barrel of the lens and live for a year. There were four of them—three men and a woman—each with two, even three cameras slung around their necks. They started to focus and shoot the minute they got out of the car, taking pictures of the resort doorway, the grounds, the parking lot across the road, even the bench beside the front door. This was weirder than many of the weird things I'd seen in Seattle, and I'd seen a few. I pressed the button under my desk to call Isaac, who also doubled as our security guard, and Rico, our bartender, who wasn't trained in security but was strong like The Rock and was the mental twin of a deranged rabid dog if his protective instincts were aroused. Rico, not the dog. Keep up.

When Jason had traveled in the past, in the days before hitting bottom, as he liked to think of it, he was always in a rush. Moving fast, watching the blur, feeling pride in how quickly he could take things in. The youngest reporter ever hired at the Times, the first one on social media and the last person you'd expect to get his tires stuck in the mud. Forward motion was what he was about.

That was why, despite the incredible beauty of his surroundings, Jason was finding it hard to settle in for his stay on this island. Ever since he'd arrived on St. Croix the day before, he felt that he'd been hopping from one foot to another, just itching to move, like a six-year-old trapped on his grandmother's couch for a visit, with no TV or any kind of entertainment anywhere in sight. He walked around the resort four times in the first half hour, scoping out the restaurants, the bar, the dive shop, the entrance to the hiking trail and the pool.

Today he was back to doing the same. Maybe another guy would have found the place exceptionally appealing. There did seem to be quite a few unattached females lounging around the pool—the pretty one with the orange bathing suit who was helping to look after that group of toddlers who seemed to be everywhere, she looked interesting. A nanny, maybe, or an au pair? Maybe a younger sister to that one who looked like the mom? Jason tried to suck in his gut each time he walked by their encampment of pool noodles, water wings and towels strewn around five lounger chairs. Nobody looked at him. He was only 30 but he was kind of an old 30, he thought. Five years since college graduation, five years of sitting in front of a computer, five years of the once thick dark brown hair going a little thinner, the middle going a little thicker. His friends told him he hadn't changed a bit but that's why they were his friends. He could look in a mirror and see that he didn't look 22 any more, but so what? He might not have the same face but he had better clothes.

Yeah, Jason knew how to dress. He'd had the knack for cool when he turned 14 and those things started to matter at his school, and he had it still. While other guys would go out to buy a jacket and wander back with something acceptable, Jason would come in with something leather, zippers, collar, stitching, everything just right and that jacket would change him from plain Jason Palmateer into Jason that hot guy. Same with jeans, suits, even T-shirts. Oh sure, every once in a while some woman who knew how to pay attention to detail would sort out the difference between her attraction to Jason and her attraction to his jacket or his jeans but most looked at Jason and saw the clothes, not the man. That all meant he didn't have to be too concerned about his actual looks, just his style.

And his wallet, which was pretty thin these days.

When he left New York the people in black were coping with an unseasonal cold snap. Here in the U.S. Virgin Islands, the thermometer was nudging 90° and everyone was wearing shorts or bathing suits. The walkway that ran from the circular drive in front of the resort, past the gift store and the Barbacoa Restaurant, was like a magical tunnel, with a wide-plank mahogany floor and wispy white curtains that gently stirred in the breeze.

The pool deck here was very nice. Lounge chairs, umbrellas, a little basketball hoop at one end, a giant chessboard and a four-foot jenga game, in case you needed a few other options for passing the time or had some junior members to entertain. The red roofs on the resort buildings matched the shade umbrellas around the pool and on the beach. A larger-than-life mural on the side of one of the restaurant buildings put Caribbean culture pool-side, showing a performer wearing a colorful costume of yellow, blue, orange and red checks. The dancing character's costume was trimmed with white lace on the long sleeves, at the waist, hips and in three rows around the Capri-length pants that dangled down over the stilts that he was rocking in the painting. A straw hat and sunglasses covered most of his face. Blue skies, fluffy clouds and a rainforest mountain filled out the upper half of the painting. In the lower half, a water line hit the stilts just above the knee. Below the line, Jason had a view of Underwater World with purple coral, an octopus, green fish, a conch and a sea turtle whose mottled face was dominated by eyes that seemed strangely wise.

Sea turtles didn't have to worry about careers or locating second chances. Jason rolled his eyes at himself— who knew what turtles worried about or thought or if they did anything, at all, besides swim, eat, and get really old. He headed for the bar and the comfort of another drink.

He *had* hit bottom, there was no avoiding the conclusion. As he'd walked along the hallway linking the Kingfisher Bar to the front of the resort, Jason watched his reflection in the gift shop door. Unshaven, and not in a good way. Unsteady, thanks to the rum, and wearing a pair of jeans that probably pre-dated this hotel. A T-shirt even older, that he'd inherited from his dad. He wasn't able to bring a lot of his clothes, once the locks were changed and he couldn't get in to get his stuff. He'd boarded the Saturday flight that his brother Anthony's frequent flier points got him, carrying just his college basketball duffle bag, stuffed with all his worldly goods. He had a little borrowing power left on a credit card, too, but that was it.

He settled in to spend the rest of the afternoon on a bar stool, nursing Captain Morgan, and wondering if he'd made a terrible mistake, coming here. He'd used up the last of Anthony's reward points to score a (relatively) free three nights here, and the idea was to lick his wounds and try to pull himself together enough to start over.

He felt exhausted, and ready to sleep for a week. This resort at Pitaya Beach looked like the ideal place to take a break and figure out his life. A bed, a beach, a bar—what more did a disgraced reporter need?

The photographers piled into the hotel registration office, cameras only inches from their noses, ready to start shooting at any second. In fact, the burly one in the cargo pants came in pumping off shots as he walked around the room, causing one of the guests, an elderly woman with a bad haircut and a cane, to raise her purse in front of her face.

"Good afternoon," I said.

"Has she checked in?" The man demanding an answer had a scorpion tattoo on his neck and Ray-Ban sunglasses that he didn't remove. "Miss… Stewart?"

I instinctively wanted to cover my name badge with my hand, but managed to hold back the impulse. A small woman who needed a serious coating of after-sun moisturizer aimed her camera long lens at my laptop and I slapped it shut. "I have no idea what you're talking about, but if you aren't guests, you didn't stop at the gate and you don't have permission to be in here."

"She's probably here under another name. Betty Flintstone, maybe?"

"Ha. How about Bonnie Parker?" Another of the photographers was sizing up the other guests and seemed particularly interested in those tropical drinks we always give them to say 'welcome to the island' and 'please don't get mad if everything doesn't go as fast as it does in New York'.

"I have no idea what you're talking about," I repeated. "If you're not registered, you're trespassing and I'll have to call the police."

"Alright, register me." He removed his sunglasses and tried smiling at me, but it was too late.

"We're full." I got up from my chair and leaned over my desk to screw with Sunburned Sarah's attempts to frame a shot of the items on it.

"Hey, we're off on the wrong foot, I'm sorry. I'm just trying to do my job," he said, again trying with the smiling and the charm.

"And what is your job, exactly?" I asked.

"Liz Barga was seen heading this way from the airport. I have an assignment from a major magazine to get photographs of her while she's visiting St. Croix."

"Why don't you just ask her to meet you somewhere and pose?" I asked innocently.

"Well, she wouldn't do that."

"No kidding." Eleni had been bursting for at least 30 seconds and finally couldn't hold it back. "You really don't know who she is, Nola?"

I shrugged. "Beats me. But all our guests get the same treatment and have a right to have us protect their privacy." I crossed my arms and tried to look intimidating. "You photographers have to leave. Now."

"I saw her picture all over the cover of the tabs this week and USA Today, and last month she was on Conan. She's some kind of business rock star."

Scorpion Neck looked at us both as if we were Martians. "She's the CEO of Portrush Inc., the food conglomerate, and she just took a $300-million pay-out to leave the company."

"Three hundred million dollars? And she's here?" Eleni liked the obvious.

"Shh. Eleni. Professional, remember? Filters. Come on." I tried to rein her in but she seemed barely aware that I was still in the room.

"What magazine are you with?"

"Eleni. Stop. Look, mister, I'll have to ask you once again to leave."

He was staring at his smartphone, then heading for the door. "We'll find somewhere else to stay." The woman photographer put out a lobster-red arm, held the door open for the rest of them and they were gone as strangely as they'd arrived.

I looked around the suddenly empty room. "Alright, Eleni. Tell me again. Liz who?"

# CHAPTER TWO

Hotel St. Croix Pitaya Beach was a resort with all of the fittings of an upscale vacation environment mixed with something of the atmosphere of a mountain cabin, thrown in—for what? For contrast, maybe? Or maybe it was just Jason's bent way of looking at things. No, but still. There was dark mahogany wood everywhere—the cabinets, the tables, the window shutters and the doors. Then, the screened porch, shaded by trees—ok, you just had to keep your focus on the porch and not raise your chin. If you did, you'd see the waves of the Caribbean Sea pounding on a sandy beach and you'd know it was just silly to think about mountain cabins.

And pound, those waves did. Man, it was noisy. Jason rolled over in the four-poster king-sized bed onto his right side and watched the sunrise light filtering through the louvered French doors. The sound of the surf was like the rumble of New York traffic, but without the sirens and the honking. Just as loud, but soothing, somehow.

The room was bigger than he'd expected. It had a sort of Raffles/Singapore or Graham Greene/Havana or maybe Downton Abbey kind of quality—vanilla walls, dark chocolate wood, not a frill in sight. The bed was set up to look out through three sets of double windows, covered with Venetian blinds. An industrious ceiling fan kept him from feeling too drowsy with the heat, and he liked that better than meat-locker-style air conditioning, anyway.

The sun was at a low simmer just below the eastern horizon and the wispy clouds reflected a tinge of yellow. As he watched, the lemon shade warmed to gold and then caught fire in a blaze of orange as the sun moved up to full boiling point.

He flopped onto his back and stared at the ceiling fan. The breeze it sent over his legs was about as sweet as the trade winds that caressed this island. He knew he had to do something soon, take action, step up, but he was damned if he could figure out what it should be. It was weeks since the magazine had let him go. He had tried every contact he had, brainstormed every possible new career path. Public relations, political speechwriting, non-profits, publishing, even advertising—fields that he had no training for, and probably even less aptitude. No one would take him and he was beginning to get it—that nobody was taking anybody on. He was on the outside now, on his own with no job and no co-workers, in a world where everybody was willing to do what he did, for free and for fun. How could anybody make a living writing any more?

You go solo, Anthony said, as they huddled over beers in the rooftop lounge at the Marriott Marquis in New York. Beers that Anthony would have to be the one paying for, since he was still employed while Jason was not, a situation he didn't make fun of, even though Jason expected it. They'd been teasing each other about absolutely everything since they were kids. His brother got the six-pack abs, the long legs setting him up at a good three inches over six feet and the hands the size of dinner plates, making a basketball court his second home. But Jason liked to claim that he got the brains and the personality. That was usually in the midst of some lame wrestling match that let two grown men pretend to be ten years old again.

"Go solo? I'm already gone," Jason had said as he downed his gift beer. He had exactly $65 left in his bank account and his credit cards were so close to incinerated that they practically smoked. He'd applied for a new one and been turned down.

"Look, man, you gotta get your head back in the game." Anthony loved his sports metaphors. "I've got some frequent flier points, hotel points, take them and go somewhere to think things over."

So here he was, and he owed it to Anthony to come back with some sort of result. His strongest urge was to lie there all day, but he had to shake that off and make a move. Breakfast, maybe. That would be a start.

The buffet in the restaurant was good value. He gorged on the eggs and baked goods, then sampled fruit from guava to strawberries. The a la carte menu was a little less appealing, he gathered from watching the family of five nearby as the dad protested the $6 charge for his cup of ordinary coffee.

Pleasantly stuffed, Jason strolled down to the water. The Sweet Bottom Dive Shop occupied a prime spot, beachfront. Might be nice to take in some snorkeling later on. He settled himself on a lounge chair to soak up some sun. Nice not to have to try to stake out territory with towels left on a chair in the pre-dawn hours or compete to claim a lounging spot the second that somebody else decided he was done for the day.

He watched the waves roll in for a while then headed back up to the pool deck. Man, he was going to have to find a good book somewhere! The Wi-Fi was spotty and his usual method of filling the boring moments with absent-minded thumb-scrolling of his social media didn't seem to be an option. Maybe he should try to learn to meditate.

A small group of fully equipped scuba divers arrived at the side of the pool and climbed in. In a few minutes it was clear that they were beginners, practicing with masks and air tanks, and trying to absorb all the information the instructor was passing on. Maybe he should stay here forever and become a scuba instructor? First, he'd have to learn to dive. Small detail.

Yeah, it was funny, but it wouldn't be so funny when the time came to pay his bill. Jason watched the scuba lesson, then the family arguing over whether the dad should get off his chair and go in the water to play pool basketball with his young son. A tiny girl marched around shrieking at her mother and her nanny. He closed his eyes. Was he actually tired? How could he be, he'd just slept for 12 hours. But yes, he was. At some point, he promised himself (and Anthony), he would get out his laptop and start looking at job websites. Just not right now.

In the restaurant on the patio, the hotel clerk who had checked him in his first day was sitting having lunch, alone. She was hunched over a laptop, staring at the screen. What a waste. Really. But she probably had a boyfriend and a huge circle of friends that surrounded her on every weekend night; here at work, if she was alone for a little while, it was probably a matter of choice. She was brunette, willowy in that way that drove him nuts, and her tan was a nice cinnamon, not that leathery-looking shade. Her lunch was a sandwich, a tall glass of what looked like milk and a side dish brimming with strawberries. Geez, it made him feel healthier just to look at her. Jason smirked at himself and closed his eyes. Om.

I squinted at the website for the Cornell School of Hotel Administration. How much money?!! Are you even kidding me? Why did college programs have to be so expensive? My grandma Ruby told me stories of the 60s when college was about a tenth of what it is today. There was even a time when there was a lot of push to make it free. Free tuition. Free education. Because a civilized society makes sure everyone who is capable is educated. I definitely didn't spend 45 minutes absolutely stunned by such a generous idea, by the way.

Hah.

Here in the hotel restaurant on my lunch break it was easy to give myself permission to get a little worked up. It's a never-ending circle, isn't it? You can't get ahead and make more money if you don't have more education, and you can't get more education if you don't have more money.

This is a good sandwich, definitely a good sandwich. I feel like it's the best one I've had all month. I'll have to remember to mention it to Pascal. He really is one of the best chefs on the island.

Thank God I can eat whatever I wanted without having to count every calorie or run three miles for every piece of pie. Eleni says it's evil, how much I can eat, but was it my fault that they gave me this metabolism?

It was a stroke of employer genius to make meals available to all the staff here. I wondered how I could get them to go another step and offer free college tuition?

Probably ain't gonna happen. So. My options were: A: to try to borrow for tuition and living expenses and spend my next ten working years, trying to pay off the student loan debt. Assuming I could get a job. My cousin had finished medical school a few years back and still hadn't found work as a doctor. Sure, he said, he could open up his own office somewhere but he felt he needed to get a lot more real-world experience before he was ready to do that. He still talked about the grad speech and all the other careers the speaker said that their medical training would equip them for.

Yeah.

Not.

Life—and employment—these days, was like a game of musical chairs, with six chairs and about six million players.

Plan B. Don't go. Stay here on St. Croix, checking guests into and out of the hotel. Maybe move over to a place like The Buccaneer. Or deal cards at Divi Carina Bay Casino.

Not judging. Friends of mine did that, but it wasn't for me. I didn't want to work in a place, I wanted to run it. And not just any place, a hotel place. A five-star.

So, Plan C. Get a scholarship and get to hotel school that way. No point kidding myself that I could work hard here, get noticed and wake up a hotel vice president one day. I didn't know much about how these things worked but I knew I didn't want to wake up one day and be like Sally, the fifty-something woman who was often on the same shift and made me so crazy with her negativity that I was ready to jump off a boat and be fish food.

I typed in a few notes, then looked up from my laptop. The man who was staying by himself in building 17 was at a table near the deck railing. He caught my eye and nodded. Kind of cute, not my usual type, but for some reason I wanted to hug him. He looked so tired, so defeated. And appealing as hell, with that retro Stones T-shirt and the jeans.

But. I had more important things to do—not to mention the hotel rules against staff fraternization with the guests. I packed up and headed back toward the office.

Just outside the gift shop Eleni came out of the restroom and fell into step with me.

"So, tell me again why this Liz guest is famous."

Eleni grinned at me. "It's so much fun when I know something you don't."

"Never happens."

"Happening right now. Okay, she's the head of this big company but she's also a celebrity chef. She started with a small restaurant in Boston, then did a cookbook, then a reality TV show, then she got hired to head up this company."

"It wasn't a company she started on her own, and built up?"

"No, it was already a big deal, but they wanted her name and her contacts. Sort of like the Mayo Clinic hiring Dr. Oz to run the place." Eleni's references were often medical, for some reason.

"Is she still a chef?"

"Oh yeah, still has her restaurant, still turns up on awards shows, special foodie occasions, stuff like that. But she's in the news right now because something went wrong with some new product her company developed and there are stories that she knew all about it beforehand."

"Cover-ups and so on," I thought out loud.

Eleni nodded. "Cover-ups, payoffs, stock price fiddling."

"No wonder she didn't want anyone recognizing her."

"Who didn't want anyone recognizing who?" The question came from behind me and I turned around to the unwelcome sight of Bondi Shepherd following closely.

Bondi is not a bad guy, just a pain a lot of the time. As the chief dive instructor he was in and out of the hotel all day long, and most of the guests thought he was just terrific. He kept them all safe, was a treasure chest of information about tropical fish, coral reefs and ocean weather, and his blond hair, broad shoulders and Australian accent sealed the deal on his popularity. I just thought he was kind of snoopy a lot of the time. And lacking in manners. Accents never have done anything for me, either.

"Good day, Bondi," I said.

"Good day. How are the girls today?"

"Liz Barga, a celebrity chef, is here with her assistant! They're trying to keep a low profile." Eleni was a Bondi fan.

"How do you know he's an assistant?" I asked her. This was something I didn't have sorted out yet.

"I asked him," Eleni said. "He's worked for her for two months and been to five new countries. Hey, Bondi, what's that you're carrying?"

He offered the paper bag to her. "Cookies. My cousin Sarah sent them. She's the one who works over town at the old folks' home across from the harbor, you know? She likes to bake and she always gives me way too much."

"How does she like it, working over there?" Eleni asked, as she pulled out a cookie. "My sister's looking for something new."

"Good, I think. There's been some commotion lately, with one of the residents roaming out by herself at night and getting lost. There's another one who's really loud, and sings Christmas carols all day and night long." Bondi smiled. "Just sounds like a house I shared with a bunch of mates when I was at the uni and we had a bit too much of the amber fluid."

When we got back to the registration desk, everyone was clearly in the midafternoon slump. They attacked the bag of cookies and they were almost all gone in minutes.

"Hey."

I looked up and there was Park Lee. Unlike most of the second day guests, with their beach clothes, straw fedoras, flip flops and sunburned chests, he was dressed for the club: sharp shirt, cool jeans, shades in his right hand, hair spiked with product.

"Good morning. Would you like a cookie, Mr. Lee?" I held out the bag but he just wrinkled his nose at it. Yes, it probably would be better if they were on a plate but somehow I think even then he probably would have passed. He didn't look like a cookies kind of guy— probably more like caviar.

"So, we're going to be checking out. Nola, that's right, Nola?" he said, reading the nametag on my top. "Could we have the final bill, please?"

"Of course, Mr. Lee. Was something not quite right?"

"No, the place is great. I'd be happy here, for the vacay or whatever. But she's used to something bigger— and we need more private."

"That reminds me, Mr. Lee. There were photographers here right after she went to her suite."

He stiffened. "Where are they now?"

"We threw them out. We didn't disclose any information about your ... boss?"

"Yes, she is my employer."

"But they were going to try out other resorts and come back to try to stake out this one. We do have the gate staffed round the clock, but..."

"That's okay, we're going somewhere private. What we should have done in the first place. The news this time is so big that they're spending whatever it takes to follow her around and try to get that ambush cover photo.

And they think she might be meeting Simon Humberton somewhere, which is even more marketable."

"Simon… I beg your pardon?"

"My God, don't you read the news? Simon Humberton, the billionaire computer guy." He tossed the key cards across the desk to me. "Who she's dating isn't the main reason, though. Those vultures are only interested because the SEC is investigating her and it could mean the company is going down." He looked grim. "But it won't, if Miss Barga has anything to say about it." He seemed about to say more, then caught himself and remembered his surroundings. "Well. That's enough. Thank you, Nola, for your hospitality here at the Hotel Pitaya Beach. We'll give you a good review online." He saw my surprise and grinned. "Yeah, I'm just joking, I don't think she'll have time for that. She doesn't do that."

"Do you need me to call you a taxi, Mr. Lee?"

"No, thanks, we've got our arrangements made."

Five seconds after I saw the back of him I was on my browser, looking her up.

# CHAPTER THREE

When I walked through the bar and restaurant that afternoon, I was still frustrated with the circle my mind insisted on following: to kick-start my career I needed to do something exceptional for the Hotel St. Croix Pitaya Beach resort. But to do something exceptional, I needed a job with more authority and scope than the one I had. To get that job I needed a college degree… the right college degree…and to get that, I needed money. To get more money I needed to get promoted to a better job, and to get promoted I needed to do something exceptional.

I stopped in at the kitchen to watch Pascal make pasta for one of the dinner entrées. The egg dropped into the hole at the bottom of the tower of flour, salt, and water, and immediately began to sizzle on the heat. Freshly made pasta is an art form, a mouthful of paradise that makes any Italian dish taste of Tuscany, olive trees and Mediterranean sunshine. I intended to go to Tuscany someday, to Florence, to Venice, and to Rome. But first I needed a career that could carry me and plans for a future that didn't involved a minimum wage job at a fast-food joint.

An award. That might be the golden ticket. I sat down with my laptop in a quiet spot and went online. I knew I should probably wait until I got home to start searching this, but I was used to taking action when I had a thought, and right here, near the restaurants and the pool, the Wi-Fi was almost always good.

I jumped from site to site and then—ah-right! There it was. The Professional Hospitality Awards website. The categories were numerous and complicated. Best hotel restaurant. Best guest response record. Best 5-star experience.

What could we do here? What could I do or start that wasn't already running elsewhere on the island or at some other resort in the Caribbean? Creativity had to be built right into the mix. A copycat thing, with a little local style thrown in, wasn't good enough.

What about a music festival? Or something more upscale? Maybe a speaker program or something about history?

OMG, I was getting drowsy just thinking about it.

I looked up as a small family of three passed me and waved a 'hello'. The little boy, about 10 years old, carried a skim board to the beach. Mom and Dad had heads down, with sunburned shoulders and arms, ending in fists that clutched smartphones. No question, they would be texting furiously the minute they all found beach chairs, the little kid playing by himself. Quality time—ha! You had to wonder why some people bothered to have children.

I combed over the Professional Hospitality Awards website for almost an hour, trying to come up with a strategy. There didn't seem to be any kind of pattern to the list of winners from the previous ten years: big chain hotels, small boutique hotels, major cities, tiny towns in fly-over states. But there had to be. I re-read the entry criteria, the descriptions of the award categories, the glowing testimonials to the various winners. "Incomparable customer service". "Customization". That seemed to be as specific a signal as they gave.

Seemed to me that the key to hotel success was

making each guest feel that the place had been built and was running just for his or her personal satisfaction. Seemed to be what many of them expected, anyway, especially the cranky ones. I stared at the Awards application form, trying to will the solution to find its way into my brain.

Yesterday's experience with the carload of photographers and the food company CEO started a faint blip on my radar. What if we created and offered a program to provide the celebrity or newsmaker guest the ultimate in privacy?

I could feel my excitement level rising with this idea. We are secluded. Quiet, remote, with only one road in. Security at the gatehouse. Maybe we could add a kennel, with dogs friendly to the guests but guard dogs, nonetheless.

These special guests could go somewhat off the grid here. Well, not really off the grid, they'd be connected 24/7 as everyone wanted to be, but with the connection going in the direction they wanted. Plus the very best in food, beverages and coconut water.

The sun was about an hour away from setting. A silvery path rolled out over the water, spreading wider as the minutes passed and the sun sank closer to the horizon. Every few moments, a wave and a curl of whitecap broke the surface near the shoreline. To the far west end of the beach the waves crashed against a wall of rock. When I first came to St. Croix people predicted I would get used to the pounding pulse but four years on, I still hadn't. This was the thing about the Caribbean that I loved the most, more than the sun, more than the trade winds, more than the white sands. Better than a symphony, that sound of the waves.

A small group of scuba divers had gathered at the water's edge. Just offshore, the Cane Bay Wall was a magnet for every diver and every novice who had ever picked up a copy of *National Geographic*. Bondi had them lined up and practicing their mouth breathing, among them the newlywed couple who had checked in yesterday and the youngster who'd been trying to get his father's attention at the pool. A few other guests were wading in for a sunset swim. I watched for a few minutes, stood up and stretched, straightened my nametag and headed up to the restaurant patio.

That night, clouds filled the horizon. The sunset became just an orb sliding down and quickly disappearing into a pocket. The surf crashed into the rocky breakwater, curling then hitting the rock at the lowest point, then leapt upward in an explosion of white foam. Jason sat on the sand and pondered his current mess. Not the only one he'd ever been in, of course, but the current one, and by far, the sloppiest one so far.

It had a lot to do with the newspaper world's frenzy to cut costs and downsize staff, but he didn't like to make excuses. It also had a lot to do with the mistakes he'd made. Yes, they were burning through cash like a forest fire jumping highways but they hadn't let *everybody* go. Some of the people they kept, but his boss insisted, 'It's not personal, Jason, don't take it personally'. It was hard not to. Plus he was pretty much convinced it had to do with his investigation of the food business story.

The birds at sunset were putting up a song that sounded like cooing doves or pigeons but he hadn't actually seen any of those around here. They were elusive and quick, much like the furry little creatures he'd seen scurrying across the paths, seeking safety in the thick shrubs. Looked a bit like an anteater. A mongoose, one of the housekeeping staff had told him when he asked

The blue hour had arrived, that gorgeous time of soft twilight just before the dark. Where did that name come from? His ex-girlfriend, Marie, would tell him the effect was caused by differences between short blue wavelengths of light versus the longer red wavelengths. During the blue "hour" (about 40 minutes in length, actually), red light passes straight into space while blue light is scattered in the atmosphere and therefore reaches the earth's surface, where we all could see it. Marie could kill the magic in just about anything.

The blue hour certainly suited his mood. Maybe he should wander over to the Kingfisher Bar and find something blue to drink. Or just drink an ocean, because he was blue. Speaking of names and wondering where they came from, he had asked earlier today about the source of the name of the bar, and the server had pointed out the birds. The Kingfisher Bar...very memorable, as was the name 'blue hour.' The blue water, the sky, the darkened beach with the occasional couple or solitary figure moving slowly in the distance. He watched a woman pull her hair back into a ponytail then wade into the surf for a short dip in the last minutes of light.

In half an hour, the sky would be midnight blue, approaching black. Stars would come out, looking like small holes in the black cloth above them, showing the light on the other side.

Jason shook his head. He was letting himself get absolutely wack. Time to get over to the bar and clear his head. The dive class was breaking up and as he walked across the sand toward the resort, a young couple fell into step beside him. A few minutes of conversation about the diving, the weather, the island and the glories of vacation time and then the man was extending his hand to introduce himself.

"Bjorn Vester. This is my girlfriend, Natalya. Oh, yeah, oops." He grinned as she glared at him, then sidestepped as she pretended to hit him. "Wife, Natalya. New wife."

"Three days, so far," Natalya supplied, as she smiled and stuck out her hand to Jason. "Nice to meet you."

"Jason Palmateer. No wife, new or old."

"You should try it. It's not bad." Bjorn seemed to be intent on spending a lot of time instigating play fights with his new spouse. She took another mock swing at him and he grabbed and held her wrists. These two should get a room.

"Maybe I will, one of these days. Nice to meet you both, I'm going this way." And Jason speeded up, turned right into the bar and left them to their games.


I was breezing my way through the restaurant when a person eating alone caught my attention, mainly because of the enormous hat she wore. You see a lot of hats at a vacation resort but this one was memorable. Brilliant white, broad brim, candy-apple red ribbon. The woman was wearing it to cover her face but below it I could see a long neck, well-toned arms in a sleeveless dress, then, farther down, great legs and killer heels. I'd like to dress that well. She made it look effortless and unique. That's what I needed, some way to make my hotel uniform of blazer and sensible shirt look effortless and unique.

She definitely was not one of the middle-aged mom types. Maybe one of the underage teenagers-on-vacation-with-parents types? If so, judging by the Lime in the Coconut piña colada drink on the table in front of her, a precocious one.

She drained the glass then signaled the server for another one. Her right hand was still in the air when she lifted the left one—wait, what, did she want two more?

Then I saw that she was beckoning to me. Huh. I walked over to her, she raised her chin and beneath the hat I could see that it was the grouchy witch from the other day. The one that her assistant, Park Lee, had checked out of the resort. Liz Barga, that was the name. My internet search on her name had turned up about 800,000 hits. Liz Barga was a celebrity chef, one of those psychotic, despotic ranting fools who seemed to be required for any Michelin-starred restaurant's success. She had started as a 12 year-old child (had any of them not?) in a kitchen in Tuscany, then emigrated with her family to New York in the mid 60s. She had trained with the best, at Elaine's and Sardi's, then gone off to find herself in France, Japan and Spain. When a California wine country restaurant had put her in charge, put up her name alongside the dining room's and helped her establish her reputation as a source of unspeakably exquisite mouthfuls, she was on her way.

Strategy seemed to be her second, and equally important, talent. Cooking, at the exalted and high-risk levels involved in a top-end restaurant, was a man's game in the 1970s, 1980s, and 1990s, but Liz Barga got in and played to win. She cemented her reputation with a series of cookbooks and a culinary school. She worked night and day, studied, invested. Despite her snobbery about television and popularity, she let herself be cast in a reality TV show and while she might argue, among friends, that the kind of people who watched that TV show would never be the people she would feed in the restaurant of her dreams, she couldn't deny that the platform and the exposure built her brand in a way that nothing else had, not the social media posts, not the cookbooks, not the word of mouth.

The initial feelers from Portrush Inc. had seemed like a joke and Liz probably looked over her shoulder to try to determine whether a 'gotcha' was coming from some direction. What did she know about running a corporation, even one having to do with food? But George Corelli, the man who aspired to be her boss, insisted that her natural smarts, her passion for exceptional food and her attention to the finest detail were what was needed in the situation and that he would back her all the way. It meant more coming from a person who had been a chef himself, and quite a significant one, winning international competitions and founding successful restaurants in three major cities. So she shook George's hand and brought her knives to Portrush.

Liz's career swelled like the crown of a soufflé and so did her fame. In addition to Simon Humberton, her current boyfriend, there were the past romances with various movie, TV and business stars. Vacations in exotic places with hundreds of photos taken with long lenses. Magazines and online articles probing her company, her life, her decisions, her illnesses, her new clothes.

If it were me, I'd go insane.

Corporate bosses don't usually draw that kind of attention, but her next TV stint as one of the investors on *Venture Lust* had given her that crossover success. When she and one of the other hosts of the show fell in love and ran off together, the headlines grew to 26-point font. Even CNN, which was up to dedicating about 20 percent of its daily space to gossip and invasion-of-privacy stories, raised its quota that week. The liaison hadn't lasted but Liz's fame did, and she used it to position herself to be headhunted for the chief executive officer position of one of the country's largest food production companies.

Her business fame grew and her personal notoriety kept pace. One article said that if you added all her husbands' names she was Liz Barga Fitzgerald Tellier Pratt. I wonder if she has to sign all that when she's in front of a legal document? I laughed at my own silliness. Of course not, and no one but a tabloid writer or reader probably knew all those names or kept records like that. Records of every mistake, choice of partner, lover or domicile, every reversal of decision or fortune. Again, I would go absolutely insane, if it were me and my life.

Liz Barga was pointing for the third time at the high white chair across the table from her. "Please join me."

I smiled at her and climbed up onto the chair.

"We met yesterday in the office." Her words were friendly but her face wasn't.

"I'm surprised to see you still here, Ms. O'Hara."

She shot me a sharp glance. "Why, was there some kind of problem with my bill, or something?"

I think she was winking or grinning or something, to try to signal a gentle joke. But maybe I was completely wrong. "It's just that Mr. Lee told us you'd be checking out."

Her peach cocktail with its maraschino cherry arrived and she gave the server a nod. "I've decided to stay on at least one more night. Park is scouting a good villa rental for me and my friend Jennifer in L.A. says she might be able to lend me her house, so I won't be here long." She put away a third of the cocktail in one swallow. "It will do for now."

"I've been thinking, there might be ways we could make it even more ideal for someone like you, even for a night or two—" I began but she waved me off. 'Shut up', her hand movement said, and not in a nice way. Why did she call me over here if she didn't want to talk to me?

I tried again. "Have you decided to stay to see our KweeZeenArtZ Food Festival later this month? Anybody with the connection you have to outstanding food would find it fascinating, I'm sure." Who was this talking? Why couldn't I just sound like myself?

"What are you talking about?" Her nose screwed up tight and the pale complexion of her face reminded me of skim milk.

I tried again. "We are a small island, it's true, but we have a lot of traditions that go back many years, particularly when it comes to food. And I know that's one of your… that you are an expert in… that you…"

Liz Barga took a long swallow of her cocktail. "What can you tell me about the man in 172?"

*Ah, there you go.*

I took a moment and pondered the view out to the horizon. "Not a thing, Ms. O'Hara. I'm sure you can appreciate, our policy is not to say anything about any of our guests."

"Oh, come on." She pulled off her hat and blasted me with full-on, green-eyed contact. "Cut the Ms. O'Hara crap. You know who I am. I'm here by mistake, but maybe it won't turn out to be so bad." She took another gulp of her tropical drink. "I met him on the path this afternoon and I think he might be what I need for a driver/security guy while I'm on St. Croix. But I don't have time for résumés and references and all that. What do you know about him?"

"I think he mentioned that he is a writer," I said. "Not a driver or a security guard."

"Skill sets every guy has. I'm sure he can manage." She peered across the restaurant toward the sea. "I got a good vibe from him. Trustworthy, solid type. And cute, in a normal kind of way. I'm sort of done with the Greek God type for now."

This conversation was so outside my job description and so bizarre for someone her age and position that I didn't know what to say. I didn't want to offend her but I so did not want this to continue. I grabbed my phone and looked at the screen.

"Hey, someone in the office is texting me. I have to go. I hope you have a lovely stay in St. Croix, Ms. Barga, um, Miss O'Hara." I slid off the stool, practically ran out, and passed Jason Palmateer on his way in. I couldn't help it; I turned around to take another look at him. Just in time to see Ms. Barga lift a finger to beckon to him.

# CHAPTER FOUR

Jason still wasn't entirely sure what he'd gotten himself into. Liz Barga had offered him significant bucks to drive her around for a few days and stay on the alert for any photographer or other intrusion that might threaten her getaway week in the Caribbean. He felt about as torn as he had ever been, his reporter instincts on high alert yet his wallet and his need for self-preservation urging him to ignore those instincts. Got to keep the snoop impulse under control, he coached himself silently. Just the sort of self-talk he should have had in gear two months ago when some extreme urge had shoved him into writing the business piece that got him fired. Let's call it what it was. He wasn't downsized and he wasn't the victim of the magazine "going in a different direction." He was fired.

And he needed money. Man, did he need money. So here he was, taking this temporary gig with this corporate queen. He'd made it clear to Liz that he wouldn't be a security guard or an assistant, but somehow 'driver' seemed to have some dignity. She'd made it clear that the day was confidential, off-the-record, and he'd signed a non-disclosure agreement. They had pulled away from the Hotel St. Croix Pitaya Beach just after sunrise with the twisty road to themselves.

Some of the other Caribbean islands Jason had visited in years gone by had been relatively flat, but not this one. Later, if he had time, before Anthony's points ran out, he could do some hiking. For now, it was driving, and they were headed to Frederiksted, one of the two towns on St. Croix and the farthest from the resort. As his first assignment, Liz had ordered that he take her around the circuit of the island and so he was behind the wheel of this rented Mercedes.

Less than 24 hours ago, he'd chatted with her in the hotel restaurant when she'd waved him over to her table. She looked like she didn't belong here; her clothing was too expensive, even though casual. Her manner was fidgety and indecisive at first. He asked if she was alright and she smiled at him and asked, "Where's the shining armor?" Then he recognized her. Well, shut the hell up. A flirt and a multinational CEO worth billions. How was he supposed to take a pass on that?

The first turn after leaving the resort was onto Highway 80. Calling it a highway was a bit ambitious. It was a standard paved two-lane road, but compared to some of the others Jason drove later that day it was in not bad condition. Hotel Resort Pitaya Beach was at the western end of a road that could ring the entire island but for a rocky outcropping that met the surf at the west end of the beach. If you wanted to see Hams Bay Lighthouse at the north end of St. Croix you couldn't come at it from this beach (no matter how much your new employer insisted from the back seat). You had to drive east, then south for about half the island, then north again. The long way around, but of course once Liz understood, that's what she wanted to do.

He made the right on Highway 69 and drove south. The turns were hairpin and the speed 50 mph, although every car that Jason met coming toward them seemed to be going at least 65. The map was cryptic— thank God for GPS. Whoever invented and marketed that genius piece of easy navigation equipment deserved an independently wealthy life in the south of France. He drove past the Carambola Golf Club, then the Ag Fair Grounds. Next, onto highway 70 past the St. George Botanical Garden and on to Frederiksted, a coastal town that dated back to the 18th century. Jason drove slowly through the streets that hugged the waterfront, along Prince, then Market, past groups of people hanging outside their front doors, passing the time. Strand Street was the main drag along the beach, tiny cafés sharing the sidewalk with hotels and souvenir shops. The Fort on the waterfront looked interesting, and a sign said there was a museum but Liz had as much interest in it as she had in the botanical garden they'd passed. Zero.

The beach area seemed pretty quiet but Jason could imagine the action picked up quite a bit when one of the cruise ships was in port. The pier was designed for the liners; maps on the walls of the souvenir shops showed photographs of the white floating hotels docked at the pier. But today the whole area was empty and forlorn. Just two yachts were at anchor, two catamarans—one called The Jolly Dad and one the Lonesome Lou. They should get together.

Jason tried to chat with Liz about the history of the place but she didn't seem interested. In anything, really. 'Preoccupied' was probably the best word to describe her. He did manage to get her out of the car to walk about half a block and she was polite enough to pretend interest in his comments about the historic buildings—the old stone foundations, the well-designed and carefully tended upper floors in Caribbean colors. Some were lovingly restored and some were dilapidated beyond repair. A story in every one. The Fort had a clock tower built of light golden rock, Victorian gaslight-style lampposts around the square in front, and a location that promised views out to an endless horizon. Jason stared at the promenade from the Fort to the pier and imagined long-ago soldiers, families and servants strolling in the evening air, enjoying the breezes after a day of trying to stay out of the heat of the sun. Beneath the pier and all along the rocky breakwater, the crystal clear turquoise water of the Caribbean Sea never let you forget for a second that you were in the tropics.

All this fascinated Jason but Liz seemed barely to realize where she was, except for the moment when they strolled in front of a café with half a dozen local people lounging in front, passing the steamy time of day. She paused to read the short menu posted outside but wanted to get back into the car almost immediately. The one bright moment came when he pointed out Cecilia's Souvenir and Gift Shop, with its sign "Mind Your Business. I Minds Mine." That got, if not quite a laugh, at least a tiny smile.

All of the tourist pamphlets that Jason had seen mentioned the beach at Frederiksted as one of the best on the island for snorkeling and this was his first chance to get anywhere near it. He suggested to Liz that they check it out and she winced. "Lord, no."

Okay, not snorkeling, not sightseeing in the historic district, any other possibilities?

Just keep driving, she said, and there was no information about where. Past Frederiksted they encountered a road with an impressive collection of potholes; farther along, they could choose to turn on 56 or 78, toward the rainforest and the mountains. After about ten minutes of potholes that grew larger by the mile, Jason convinced her that a 4 by 4 would be a better vehicle choice than this comparatively dainty luxury car, and they turned back.

Backtracking to the junction of 69 and 80, Jason recognized most of the landmarks along the way. It wasn't a big island, 26 miles end to end, and it was easy to get a feel for it. At the corner, he put his foot on the brake and waited patiently for Liz's instructions. She'd been backseat driving the whole day, no reason to change the pattern now. To the left and west would be a return to the resort, and to the right and east would be more exploration.

"Keep going," she said, and he obediently turned right.

The north shore road led them past Cane Bay, hugging the water's edge to Salt River Bay, where Jason pointed out to Liz that Columbus had landed on a point of land just north of there, in 1493, on his second voyage from Spain.

"Given that he explored all over the Caribbean, wouldn't you think there would be a lot of places that could claim he put his Spanish foot down there?" she asked in a seriously bored voice.

"Do you know why St. Croix has a French name now and so many Danish place names all over?" he asked.

"Tell me." Her tone was barely civil.

"Seven other countries explored it and took it over at various points, after the indigenous Arawak met the Spaniards, who renamed it Santa Cruz. The French just translated that to St. Croix. The Danes took over in 1733, when they bought it from France, and then Denmark sold it to the United States in 1917, along with St. Thomas, St. John and a few smaller ones."

"Sold it? Really." Her manner was a little more engaged now, probably because now they were talking about some commercial transaction. "For how much?"

"Don't know."

"I could look it up on my phone, if I could get a decent signal." And she was back in her miserable mood again. She didn't speak to Jason for the next five miles, until they were on the edge of Christiansted.

My phone rang about 10 a.m., which meant that my mother, back in Seattle, was up before the dawn. I stared at her name on the call display and picked up the call almost before the second ring. Thank you, thank you, thank you.

"Hey Mom, how are you?"

"Nola, dear, I'm fine. How are you?"

"Just fine." It wouldn't do to spill all my problems at her too fast. "Nice to hear your voice."

"I know, cookie, yours, too." I heard a long pause and a very quiet slurping sound. She did love her tea, and found a way to insert it into almost every activity, even a phone call. "What's going on with you these days?"

"Not much. Same-old, same-old."

"How's work?"

"Okay, I guess. I've applied for a promotion and I've even started looking at maybe a transfer to another hotel…although I love it here and I don't really want to move."

"You're going to get that promotion, I'm just sure of it."

"Thanks for the confidence, Mom, but I'm not feeling it. I don't have the credentials."

"Credentials, what does that mean?"

"The education, Mom. I need a degree in hotel management."

"How long does that take?"

"Two years or so. But that's not the big issue. The thing is I don't have the money to go."

"Scholarships?"

"I'm looking at that, yeah."

Another long pause, a long swallow of orange pekoe. "Have you tried going at it in a different way? Something creative, something that doesn't take so much time or money?"

"Yup, I'm on it, Mom. If I could find a way to stand out here, be a tall poppy—" The various options and ideas started swirling around in my head and I got distracted, almost forgetting she was on the other end of the call.

"So, the weather here in Seattle is just brutal right now, nothing but non-stop rain."

"Was there a particular reason you called?" I asked. Something was up, I could just sense it with her.

"So, I'm thinking of taking a vacation."

*She was on permanent vacation, retired from her job at the hospital, what was she talking about?* "What do you mean, Mom? Are you planning to travel?"

"I was thinking that I haven't seen you and your sister in almost a year, not since she decided to stay and live there with you."

*She was talking about coming here. Ever since my dad had died from a massive heart attack ten years ago, she didn't hesitate much about anything.* "Dana doesn't live with me, Mom. She has her own job and her own place."

"I meant, ever since she moved to St. Croix. Which I have never seen. And I would like to."

That's a wonderful idea, Mom. Let's all three of us get on the phone soon to talk about that."

"Nola, you like to talk things to death. I've got my ticket."

"Wait, what now?"

"I said, I've got my ticket, cookie. I'll be there on the weekend. Can you pick me up at the airport or should I ask your sister?"

*Okay, this was a little brash. But in the same moment, I'm not gonna lie, I was feeling relieved. It would be wonderful to see her.*

I mumbled something about coordinating a ride

for her and got her flight details. Arriving Saturday at 5 p.m. With a one-way ticket. Just for now, she said. She didn't have a job or a business she had to return to right away and so she thought she'd play it by ear and decide later when to return to Seattle.

Somehow, my weekend was suddenly looking a lot brighter.

Wait till Dana heard about this.


Jason parked the Mercedes and took a minute to brush off a clump of mud that clung to the vivid turquoise and yellow license plate. *U.S. Virgin Islands. America's Caribbean*, it read. The four fish in the corners and the hibiscus flower adorning the lower middle spot on the plate all carried a layer of road dust. He walked around to the passenger side and opened the door for Liz.

"My God, that took you long enough."

Had this woman dedicated her life to being toxic? Jason gritted his teeth and concentrated on getting through to the end of the day. He'd suggested stopping somewhere to eat, maybe *The Turtle Nest*, which he'd heard was one of the best places on St Croix. He'd had to suggest it twice because she didn't answer him and he had to look into the rear view mirror to get a response. She shook her head 'no' while she stared at her phone, reading whatever it was she was reading.

All along the road heading east Jason saw strange stone structures that looked like the bottom half of a windmill. A windmill from the 16th century, with a shallow roof and a round foundation. In some places, modern homes had been built around them, using what appeared to be ancient walls as a side of a new building. What were those about? He tried to make conversation with Liz about them but she wasn't interested so he turned his concentration to finding his way in through Christiansted to the waterfront.

This harbor was a highlight for boaters all over the Caribbean. It was full of sail and powerboats at anchor. No super-yachts—Jason saw more of the 'life-time dream, saved up for 15 years' type of boats. He watched an older couple walk along the sidewalk in front of them, her long gray hair hanging to her waist and caught back in a ponytail, his hair silver and his left ear pierced with a gold hoop. They held hands and were striding along at a pace that had them overtaking everybody ahead of them; obviously neither one of them was bothered by even a twinge of arthritis in those slim hips.

He drove slowly past the Fort, taking in the yellow shade chosen for the walls—what was the story there, Jason wondered. It had a gold pergola with a weathervane and in front, a stately palm tree, almost regal, dominated the approach. The design reminded him vaguely of a farmhouse, oddly unmilitary for a building with cannons all around.

The boardwalk across the street was a cluster of cafés, restaurants, hotels and bars, shimmering in the Caribbean sun. Lots of fun after dark, too, he'd bet. The colors were bright and confident—blue, yellow, tangerine—so vivid and yet never looking garish in the tropical sun. Carefully, he maneuvered the car through the narrow streets and when a parking space opened up just a block from the Boardwalk he pulled into it, parked, and turned to ask Liz over the back seat—

"Would you like to stop and take a look around?"

She shrugged and he took that for a 'yes', jumping out of the driver's seat and coming around to open her door. As they walked he hung back a little so that she could lead the way toward whatever caught her interest to investigate, and she showed no hesitation in leading the exploration.

It wasn't a huge historic district, but there was plenty to see that was quaint and unique. A turn down any of the streets or alleyways led to shops that might or might not be open. Signs proclaimed the owner or the clerk's intention. "Returning at 1:30. Ish." That was the announcement on one hand-lettered piece of paper taped to a glass door. A more permanent sign declared "Probable Hours. Open when we're here, closed when we're not." Couldn't get more obvious—and true—than that. That one was lettered right on the door. Next spot over told the reader "Summer hours. Closed Tuesday, Wednesday, Thursday, Sunday. Open Monday, Friday, Saturday, 8 to 3." Early risers, Jason thought. A spirit of independence showing here; he or she was not ready to sit there, day after day, hoping to have a single customer on a Tuesday who might make the entire wait worthwhile. Better to go snorkeling or diving and just show up, part-time. Maybe they even had the locals trained to come by only on the reliable Monday, Friday and Saturdays.

There were many buildings in the historic district that were still waiting for someone with the money and the interest to bring them back to their former glory. A few had been thoroughly done, though, with gorgeous yellow marble, white columns, green shutters—looking just like the movies he'd seen that were set in the Caribbean. He pointed out the elegance and charm of some of them to Liz but she just rolled her eyes and sighed.

On the waterfront she stopped briefly to take in the harbor view. A pack of elderly men and women, some with canes or walkers, some arm-in-arm with a caregiver dressed in a uniform, passed between them and the boats, and Liz had some difficulty in controlling her impatience. Jason felt the need to speak up, just to smooth the mood.

"Hello, please excuse us, we're just going to go 'round you here, just in a bit of a hurry, you know…" He made apologies as Liz worked her way past the crowd, taking advantage of any gaps in the traffic that opened up.

"Getting worse down here, every day," said one old woman wearing a bathrobe and a woolen cap.

"Crowds, crowds and more crowds," another agreed. "That's why I do my walks on my own, late at night. Not so many tourists."

Liz looked at them as if she'd stumbled on hyenas in her Jacuzzi and tried to do a fast 180° turn. Didn't work, there were too many of them.

"Now, Esther, you know no one is allowed to go out walking alone late at night," said a caregiver wearing light blue pants, polo shirt and a nametag reading *Sarah.* "You also know you haven't been doing that. You're just telling us stories."

"If that's true, how did I know about the splashing and the other noises I heard?"

"Through your window, just like I did." Jeannie spoke contemptuously and Jason got a hint that the two old ladies were about to mix it up with one another.

Sarah stepped in smoothly. "Who wants ice cream?"

And the battle was averted, as a happy discussion of the merits of vanilla versus pistachio broke out.

Jason turned back to Liz, expecting to find her agitated beyond belief by the delay. Instead, she was quiet and preoccupied. "Thank you, Jason. I'd like to go back to the car now."

They drove east from Christiansted and the surroundings became much more prosperous. The west end has the rain forest, rugged roads and lower income, Jason thought. The east end was dry to the point where there even were cacti every few dozen feet. The road was still two-lane, but now with very good blacktop.

They rounded a curve and then could see breath-taking mansions spotted along a hillside like beautiful women sitting side by side in the most exclusive day or nightclub in the biggest city. Breath-taking for those driving by and probably breath-taking for those inside, looking out toward the view of the sea. No doubt this was the sort of place that Liz expected, and was heading for, when the new assistant's mistake had landed her at the Hotel St. Croix Pitaya Beach.

Just a few miles out of Christiansted, Jason saw a structure that made all the others look like yurts squatting on a Mongolian plain.

It looked like a palace, a royal residence of some sort—but without any of the familiar features of something European or even Asian. Jason slowed down and tried to keep one eye on the road ahead while the other squinted at the architectural vision in the distance. Much more than a mansion or a castle, it reminded him of something. Something exotic, fantastic, but real. Jason tussled with the memory that teased at the edge of his mind and suddenly it flashed in. The Alhambra.

Five years ago an assignment for a national business magazine had taken him to Malaga in southern Spain. He'd grabbed the opportunity for a side trip to Granada and a tour of the ancient Moorish palace. Its fountains, its galleries, its towers and its intricate carvings had overwhelmed and impressed him. He thought he'd never see anything like it anywhere, again.

But there, on a gentle hill on St. Croix, was something that was certainly similar. If he could have whistled, he would have whistled. "What the heck is that?"

Liz wasn't the slightest bit curious. "No idea," she snapped, still furiously working her phone. "Are you getting any sort of signal out here?"

"I'm driving," Jason pointed out.

At the end of the road, they came to Point Udall, the easternmost point of the U.S. Virgin Islands, and, actually, the easternmost point of the United States. Its significance was indicated by the Millennium Marker, four massive stone triangles set to form a sundial. As Jason drove slowly around it, they saw a couple walking past, their car parked a few hundred feet down the road. Well, hey now. Bjorn and Natalya, from the resort. Natalya wore a red bikini, the kind that lives on in the dreams of men who were old enough to remember fast times at high school. Bjorn was probably also a picture of fantasy flesh, with his six-pack, sculpted pecs and solid biceps. Each had tattoos curling up their arms, across their backs and over to their collarbones, like snakes of ink.

They were doing their own private photo shoot, posing for one another next to the giant sundial. Then they noticed Jason and Liz noticing them, and moved to a wall farther away. Liz was staring at them intently and Jason had a sudden thought.

"Do you know them?"

"I think maybe." She looked at him a beat too long, her mouth twisting slightly. "It's Jeremy and Jennifer Washington."

"Who are they?"

"Do you live under a rock? They own the hottest restaurant in Chicago right now."

*Uh, really?*

Jason parked the car, nose out to the circle. It was the end of the road, U.S.-wise. Kind of a cool thought. "Are you connected to your cell service now?"

Liz didn't look up. "Which one? I'm signed up with all of them. Something's got to work."

"Isn't that major expensive?"

He turned to look toward the back seat and met

her eyes as she let her sunglasses slip down her nose. The icy stare. Right. Expensive didn't matter.

"I think you've got it wrong, anyway. In case you're interested." That got her attention. A short glare, at least. "Their names are Bjorn and Natalya, I met them yesterday. They're just a regular couple. I've seen them a few times at the resort. "

They drove the next few miles in silence, which suited each of them just fine. He admired the beauty of Grapevine Point, Red Bay and Robin Bay; he spotted the casino, the mini-golf and the pizza joint and didn't even think of pointing them out to her. She had her shades on, her phone out, and she was in another world: her own world, which encompassed an area about six inches around her own body.

It would have suited him fine if she hadn't said another word, but unfortunately his preference didn't matter. About half an hour before they reached the resort gate, she suddenly revealed that she knew who he was, and that he was much more than a random stranger at the resort.

It had been a long enough drive and day already, but now it felt like an eternity. When Jason pulled up at the resort gate he was so ready to get away from her he could taste it.

# CHAPTER FIVE

Jason signaled the bartender for another. Out past the sidewalk, under the palms he could see the sun shooting its last sparks at the planet as it rotated and turned its face away. Yellow sphere, dropping into clouds hugging the horizon, palm trees in silhouette. It looked to Jason as though the last rays were hands, reaching upward, trying to hold on. And then they were gone. Get a grip, son. He reached for his glass.

Sunset this late in June happened around 7 p.m., and across the way in the Barbacoa Room, the Pirates' Feast was in full swing. Jason had seen the posters around the resort, advertising this Friday night party, with a huge seafood feast, Moko Jumbies and fire dancers promised, He was almost lonesome enough this evening to cross the patio and take it in. Probably cost too much, though.

Rico showed up with a tall, frosty glass of beer.

"Thanks." Jason was all out of conversation. His day with Liz had used it up.

"You going to the feast tonight? It's pretty good."

"Looks good. But it's not in the budget, man."

Rico grinned in a slightly insane way. "You want to go? I'll sneak you in."

Jason raised his glass in a toast. Something to look forward to.

I couldn't help but notice that the man from Building 17 was one of the few resort guests who hadn't changed color even slightly today. Not freckled, like the mom who'd chased the toddler all morning, trying to keep his hat on and his little body sun-screened, then had taken him off to his coma-like nap in the suite all afternoon. Not lobster pink, like the know-it-all teenager who had parked poolside with a novel. Not bronzed like the scuba instructors, who knew how to manage their sun exposure. He looked pretty much the same way he had when he checked in—which was pretty damn good.

He smiled at me as I walked by the chair he had taken near the railing. Out toward the beach you could see a thousand stars in the sky—the Big Dipper and Orion showing off tonight. Jason, was that his name? I smiled back and stopped.

"Good evening. Are you looking forward to the show?"

"Moko Jumbies." He tested out the words. "Cool name. What is that, a reggae group?"

I laughed. "No, although they're certainly performers and you will hear some reggae music. They're the ones who come in on stilts, in costume. They dance. It's a tradition that goes back more than 200 years... comes from Africa, I think. Has something to do with ancestral spirits or ghosts."

"Scary, then? Menacing or disturbing?"

"No, no. They're seen as protective, sort of blessing or honoring a place by being there. You've seen the mural painting down by the pool deck? That's a Moko Jumbie. I think you'll be impressed when they come in. It's very exciting and seems to make everyone very happy.

Amazing physical demonstration too, the way they dance on those stilts."

I kept an eye on Jason, during the feast, and he didn't line up like the other guests, didn't pile a plate (or two) high with the spicy clams, ceviche, breaded shrimp and coq au vin. Maybe he didn't like to eat? I shook my head. Now there was a concept that I just couldn't get.

Jason strolled past the buffet table, taking inventory, before taking up the spot by the railing that Rico had indicated ("Just keep out of the way, man.") It all looked delicious—the fresh mussels and shrimp, the paella station, the salad station with exotic greens, potato salad, spicy bean salad, cole slaw and then mac and cheese (not sure how that qualified as salad, maybe because it was cold?). The rest of the tables were covered with platters of grilled mahi mahi, roasted chicken, expertly carved roast beef and four kinds of coconut cake and chocolate pie.

How could anyone consume so much? Yet he watched as people went back and forth two or three times, replenishing their plates to the edges each time.

Over by the open door to the patio he saw Liz and Park Lee. My, my. Still here, and going out to mingle with the masses? Interesting. On the patio, he noticed another couple that looked familiar. It was Bjorn and Natalya, the newlyweds.

As Jason scanned the tables on the patio, wondering whether there was reserved seating and not wanting to draw attention to himself in any way by doing the wrong thing, he saw Bondi motioning to him from across the room.

"Join us, mate," Bondi said. "Lots of room here."

Jason dropped into the one empty chair at their table. Surveying the crowd around them, he saw a long table with about two dozen members of what looked like a family: two pair of gray-haired, somewhat bulky folks, numerous thirty and forty-somethings, a few teenagers and youngsters and one toddler determined to escape from his high chair. To their right was a round table with nothing but women, dressed to impress, hair extensions and long fingernails announcing their dedication to glamor. To their left, another round table of women, each of them wearing a T-shirt that declared "Team Bride". Those were the large groups; he also saw a few foursomes and quite a few couples.

"We were just getting some first impressions of St. Croix," Bondi said as he eased Jason into their group. "Everybody, this is Jason, he's from New York. Jason, this is the VIP guest table at the resort this week." He scanned the circle of faces and grinned.

"Then who let you in?" With an answering grin, a very relaxed-looking man with 1970s length hair and a moustache challenged Bondi.

"Usually they don't let staff sit with the guests, Sam, but they identified you lot as up for a big night and thought you might need some supervision." Bondi took a big gulp of his beer. "And I'm just the bloke for the job."

He got the round of laughs he expected, as well as a warm smile from the woman sitting next to Sam, holding his hand. "Chelsea and Sam Harmon," she told Jason. "From Boston. We won't go too wild, we're taking the kids snorkeling early tomorrow."

Sam released her hand to pick up his highball glass and take a swallow. "Unless we decide to delegate that to the nanny and sleep in."

She matched his drink with her own. "We'll see."

Sam picked up the previous conversation. "Let's face it, St. Croix isn't Ocean City," he commented.

"Or Martha's Vineyard," A fiftyish, extremely well-dressed woman seated beside Bondi was eager to get in on this. "Even Christiansted, which is supposed to be so charming, isn't much more than decaying old buildings and an 18th century fort." Her tone was sneering. "Isn't that right, Gregory?"

The man sitting next to her was wearing a plaid shirt, jeans, and a ball cap. Jason guessed him to be her husband, but an absentee, passive-aggressive one, staring intently at the phone in his hands.

"Isn't that right, Gregory?" she repeated. Her voice was sandpaper on glass.

No wonder her husband won't put his phone down, Jason thought. "If you want 12 miles of skyscraper condos, you go to a place that has that," he said. "And if you want Martha's Vineyard or the Hamptons, you go there. Seems to me St. Croix is its own creature. You don't say 'Hey, duck, why don't you run like a horse?' You don't tell a dog it should learn to purr." He added a smile for the society lady in the designer dress and a bro to bro nod for Joe Six-Pack, and had them both grinning back at him.

"Alright, you have a point, Jason," she said. "Doesn't he have a point, Gregory?"

"Yes, he has a point, Gloria."

"What's so amusing?" Someone was in the space behind him and he realized it was Liz. Her voice had an unmistakable tone of authority; Jason could imagine her chairing a meeting or speaking to a roomful of hundreds of employees. Maybe just as she was telling them they were all laid off.

"Nothing much." Jason tried to curb his instinct to make a face. And then his instinct to use the word 'ma'am'.

"Could I speak with you for a moment, Jason?" She smiled at the others at his table with as much friendliness as she was capable of and waited confidently for him to stand up and follow her away from the table. When he didn't make a move, she leaned toward him and tried to speak privately.

"It's important."

"What's up?"

"I've run into a problem. There are some people here who have been following me around for a few days and I really don't want to run into them tonight. I don't know how they got in, but they did."

He followed her gaze around the patio but couldn't figure out which people she was speaking of. There were quite a few there who might be the ones she'd noted. He shook his head blankly and she responded with an irritated clenching of her mouth. She glanced at the table and he could tell she wasn't happy discussing this with so many interested listeners nearby.

"It's photographers. Over there."

Jason followed the direction of her quick gesture and saw a table filled with people who looked pretty much like everyone else there. Cell phones in their hands, snapping pictures around the room, some taking video as they panned across, recording visuals of the decorations, the plates of food on their table and at the buffet, with the night sky beyond the patio railing.

"If there are professional photographers here, maybe it's for some other reason? Maybe the hotel has them here for PR purposes? Or some other celebrity invited them?"

"I spoke with that hotel staffer, Lola, Anna, whatever her name was. No photographers were invited here tonight." Liz pinned him with full eye contact. "It just doesn't feel safe here, to me. Would you mind escorting me back to my suite?" It was a question but it didn't sound like a question.

"No problem, Liz, sure."

"Oh, Park. There you are." Her assistant had quietly appeared at her left elbow; no doubt he would now get the job. "Jason is going to walk me back to the room. I can't stay here any longer."

Apparently not.

"Of course, Liz. I'm going to speak with the hotel staff about some of the arrangements for tomorrow."

"And then stay to take in the show, will you? When the group is here at the end of next week, we'll want to set up a few local experiences for them and this show might be a good one to bring in."

"You got it." Park took a step backward and turned toward the buffet table. "See you later, Jason."

Jason followed Liz out of the room, wondering how quickly he was going to get paid for all this and whether it was appropriate to send some sort of invoice.

I saw Otto, the Pirates' Feast boss, give a signal to John, the DJ. All evening he'd been playing a mixture of reggae, hiphop and Calypso, plus some soca tunes. It was almost time for the show.

"Ladies and gentlemen!" John announced. "In just 20 minutes you're gonna see the Moko Jumbies, the best on the island, and you're all gonna dance, trust me! And in about 10 minutes, you're gonna see Blaze and the Fire Leapers. So get ready! It's almost party time!"

Exactly as promised, 10 minutes later, the Fire Leapers appeared. Their performance, as usual, was amazing. I'd seen it two or three dozen times now—the fire eating, the bottle dancing on crushed glass, the snake dancing, the limbo—and each time I cheered along with the crowd, feeling just as much enthusiasm as the time before. Nobody did anything quite this energetic back home in laidback Seattle.

And as if there weren't enough excitement from the combined energy of the performers and all these dinner guests, there was a rumor going around that Tim Duncan might be showing up here tonight. I had never met him, but apparently he was a frequent visitor to the island where he grew up before going on to pro basketball fame with the NBA. My sister Dana says she spotted him once at a bar on the boardwalk and had submitted about a dozen requests to his people for an interview for the USVI Times, the newspaper where she worked.

A short break and then the music took a turn for the exciting once again. All eyes turned toward the patio entrance. The Moko Jumbies. The first man, in a dark purple suit, his stilts painted in glittery red, white and blue thirds, came out dancing to a driving beat, his body hitting the exact rhythm he needed to stay in balance. His forehead was covered by a white scarf, as were his nose and mouth, leaving only his eyes to be seen, hot and somehow expressive, even though they were 12 feet above me. The man (and I had to keep reminding myself that he was a man and not some magical puppet or creature from another world) towered over the tables, the dance floor and the laughing, clapping audience. He danced from end to end of the patio, stopping each time a guest approached him, dollar bill in hand, and either held it up to him immediately or danced with him first. Quite a few of tonight's guests wanted to dance between his legs and within minutes there was a raucous, celebratory tone throughout the patio. Some Friday nights things were quieter, maybe due to a more reserved crowd of guests. But tonight we had quite a few long tables set up for large groups, families celebrating birthdays, off-islanders here to celebrate weddings. These people were here to party.

My gaze was drawn away from the Moko Jumbie by a young woman in one of the nicest outfits I'd seen so far tonight, even in the midst of a very stylish crowd. Long skirt, at least that's what it looked like from the back, but when she twirled around I could see that it was cut as a miniskirt in front. Made of some sort of shiny, twinkly, shimmery gold fabric that flashed and moved as she danced. Sleeveless, low-cut, designed against overheating, as most clothes are in a tropical climate. But most clothes weren't being worn on a body that would fit in on a Miss Universe runway. She really was a beautiful girl but unfortunately, she was a little too familiar with the fact, it seemed. Just something about her way of dancing—it was as if she were competing with the Moko Jumbie for the crowd's attention. She was the first, but certainly not the only one to leap up to dance with him, and she offered money to him, just like the others did. But when she danced between his stilt-legs and turned back to face him and lean backward in a wide-armed shimmy, there was something just that much more suggestive.

I moved around the room, keeping an eye open for any guest who might signal me with some request. As I got closer to the dance floor, I got a better look at the enthusiastic guest-dancer and I recognized her: It was Natalya, the newlywed.

Ha. Hadn't thought of her name like that, before now. Where was Bjorn?

The first Moko Jumbie finished and danced back toward the entrance, nodding in a sort of handoff to the next one who took the floor. Natalya was in his orbit immediately, and this one played up to her much more than the first. She was dancing as if she planned to shimmy out of her dress at any moment, and when a group of overweight, middle-aged girlfriends danced up in front of the Moko Jumbie, arms spread and hips shaking, she joined their line, stared at the moves they were making, and in two minutes, copied the motion and added it to her repertoire.

They got tired out before Natalya did and headed back to their seats. She had the stilt dancer all to herself for the moment, and she moved between his legs again. But this time, instead of passing through, she stopped directly under his crotch, arms thrown upward, knees bending and straightening as she wriggled her hips.

This time, Bjorn lost it.

The angry man came roaring from a table somewhere toward the back of the room. He marched up to Natalya, grabbed her hand and pulled her away from the performer. I could hear his words—everyone could. "Hell, Natalya! Cut it out!"

They mixed it up for a few minutes, him trying to hold her wrists and her trying to pull away. The Moko Jumbie wisely danced away from them, toward the other end of the long dance floor, and pretty soon the crowd's attention was back on him, with other guests coming forward to join in the fun, including a pair of adorable twins who looked about six years old. I watched Bjorn and Natalya disappear toward the corner of the room he'd emerged from, back to their table, probably.

Then, seconds later, they were in the spotlight again. This time it was Bjorn in forward motion, with Natalya trying to stop him. "Baby, please, I'm sorry! I didn't mean it, I'm sorry! Don't be like this, come on, sit down, let's finish the wine, I won't dance any more, I promise…"

I could hear her voice as they went past me, saw her trying to grab his hands and saw him trying to shake her off. They were almost out of the room when suddenly something seemed to shift, like a high-performance car doing a 180° turn—maybe he called her a wrong name? She stopped pleading and started to stalk away from him. He went after her. She stopped, then took a swing at him. He ducked and she lost her balance, stepping backward—right into the path of the Moko Jumbie.

Have you ever heard that total silence that happens when time stands still, as they call it? Just before an accident, a fall, a change of heart? I held my breath—we all did, everyone who saw what was going on. Then he swayed, on those 8-foot stilts, lost his balance and fell.

People jumped up from their tables and almost everybody in the room rushed to him, it seemed. Then Otto the Feast manager got there and pushed everyone back.

"Jayden! Are you okay?"

The young man opened his eyes and slowly smiled. "Yeah, it's cool."

The entire room exhaled.

Otto took charge. "Okay, let's get you up. Somebody, unstrap those stilts. There you go, take it easy…"

A movement in my peripheral vision to the left—Bjorn and Natalya heading out the dining room door.

I turned my attention back to Jayden and John, and I didn't notice Park until he was right in front of me.

"Miss Nola, have you seen Liz anywhere?"

"I saw her about half an hour ago, stressing about cameras in the room. She told me she was going to ask Jason Palmateer to walk her back to her room," I replied.

"I knew about that, but I just knocked on her door and there's no answer. That's unusual."

"Have you tried phoning her or texting her?"

He looked at me with a total lack of respect. "Well, duh. No reply."

"Try again." The voice was Jason's and I turned to see him behind me. "Keep trying until she answers, if you're concerned."

Park bent over his phone, thumbs flying. We all waited for a few moments, listening for a tone or a buzz that would signal a reply. Nothing.

"Maybe she just went for a walk down the beach. Or maybe she's gone to sleep and didn't hear your knock."

"Not Liz. And not Liz." Park seemed almost paralyzed, zoning out for a moment, then dreamily coming to attention. "Alright. I just came over here to see if she'd come back to see more of the show. It was a long shot, not the sort of thing I'd expect her to do, but I just didn't have another idea."

"Let's all check out the various areas of the resort," I suggested. "Jason, could you please do the beach? Is Bondi still here? Ask him to go with you. Mr. Lee, take the pool and the other restaurants and I'll go over to the office and the lobby areas. Meet back here in five minutes."

Jason nodded and headed off down the steps to the beachfront, but Liz's assistant just stood there.

"Come on, Mr. Lee, go take a look around the pool. And circulate through the entire patio area, ok? She might have joined some group at a table that we're just not seeing."

"Not Liz," he repeated, but at least this time he made a move.

The office area was quiet and dim at this time of evening, and it was easy to see in a second that there was no one there. I checked behind the door to the inner office, just to be sure, then walked the corridors past the spa, the restrooms, the gift shop, the back of the bar, and did another sweep of the patio, where all three Moko

Jumbies, making a solid attempt to put the lovers' spat behind everyone, had the crowd up and dancing.

Five minutes later, when Jason, Park and I re-met at the restaurant entrance, things were a bit more intense. Park seemed to be on edge and ready to explode.

"She's missing! Oh my God, she's missing. Simon is gonna kill me. It was my job to protect her, and now she's gone. He's gonna kill me."

I thought this was quite a leap to make. "Simon, her boss?"

"Simon, her boyfriend." Park gazed at me with growing hysteria. "*And* George her boss. Holy monkey crap. This is terrible!"

"Now Mr. Lee, we don't know she's actually missing. Like, not in the serious sense of missing. She could be in any one of a dozen places in the resort, and she's a grown-up. She doesn't have to tell someone each time she goes somewhere…"

"Yes, she does, these days, and she wants to! We have security on her round the clock because of the SEC investigation of the company. All the bad press she's had personally has her so jumpy she barely wants to be alone for five minutes, anywhere!" Park was pacing from side to side like a caged tiger. "I have been in constant contact with her every minute since we got here and the entire time in Nantucket before that. She is not just *taking some private time*, she doesn't want any private time. She's missing."

I stared at him as if I were seeing him for the first time. "Alright, Mr. Lee, I think it would be best if you calmed down a little."

"Calm down! You don't seem to get the importance of this. If she's missing, hundreds of people— no, thousands of people are going to be affected. She was supposed to stay here, out of sight, safe, until we could get the strategy in place, and now she's gone!"

He stopped his pacing right in front of me, six inches in front of my nose, invading my personal space. "It's your fault, too, you know. She told me that you persuaded her to stay on, after she'd already decided she didn't like it here, didn't think it was the right place for her to be, in the midst of all this crap."

"I did not! I did not persuade her to do anything, I didn't discuss that with her!" I was shocked—how had I suddenly become a part of this?

"She told me you did, and it's easy to see why you'd rather not own that right now," Park almost spat the words at me. I felt Jason stepping forward.

"Hey now. We're all getting way ahead of ourselves here. We don't even know for sure that she's gone anywhere, how, or why. Let's take it one step at a time." He was speaking in a low, calming, cadence, like someone trying to settle a hysterically barking dog.

Park turned on him. "Don't you tell me what I'm supposed to be doing! You're in as much trouble as she is."

"What do you mean by that?" Jason's voice took on a warning tone.

"You're the last one who was with her."

"So what?"

"So, what do we know about you? Who are you, anyway?" Park stepped back into my face. "Call the police. Assuming you have any, on this tiny island." He pulled his phone out of his pocket. "Never mind, I'm calling someone I know in New York."

# CHAPTER SIX

Sofrania and Jean-Claude pulled up to the hotel gate and were waved through without stopping. They didn't have any kind of siren or flashing light going on their police car but all of the guests and staff milling around the resort entrance knew exactly who they were and that there was something going on. We party late in St. Croix sometimes, but 3 a.m. was still a bit unusual. A police arrival, on any island, in any city, in any country of the world usually turns into a disruptive event.

At the resort doorway, I met them and starting spilling like an overfilled pot. Maybe it was the stress build up, maybe the excitement of having something like this happen, maybe because I'd known Sofrania quite well for two years, through my Saturday morning running group—whatever it was, I wanted to talk to her. I was just so shocked and the situation seemed to require action. Talking was action.

Sofrania and Jean-Claude followed me down the hall to the manager's office, murmuring questions as we went.

"Where was she last seen?"

"When was that?"

"Who reported her missing?"

"What can you tell us about her?"

They reminded me of a litter of puppies, falling over each other trying to get from point A to point B. They kept on spitting out these questions as they looked around the room, then each chose the seat they wanted, and took out interview equipment: pens, notebooks, recorders. Looked like they were settling in for a while. My face ached from smiling at the guests and I just wanted to get home to my bed.

"Any idea how long we'll be here, Sofe?"

She had her professional's face on and I could tell she didn't appreciate the familiarity. "Might take a while, Nola. Please make sure no one leaves until we allow them to."

I nodded. "Of course. But you will keep in mind that it's 3 a.m. and a lot of these people have been here more than 18 hours?"

Jean-Claude smiled at me. "We will. Including you, I'm guessing?"

I nodded.

"Here we go." Jean-Claude got everything that I had to say out of me in about ten minutes. As I talked, I realized that besides being upset there was one detail buzzing around the edges of my mind, like a gnat. Park Lee had mentioned that Liz had round-the-clock security. Who would that be, him? I doubted it. Where or who else was this 'security' he was talking about?

They left me while they went off for their first walk through the grounds and the buildings, the first of what might be many. When they came back, about an hour later, they told me that half a dozen other cops had arrived and were hunting through everything and everywhere, paying particular attention to the beach and the shore. They were ready to talk to the staff now and asked me to show them to the meeting room.

When we walked in, we found a quiet, sleepy group, who were happy to answer the questions as best they could. Hadn't seen her, didn't know her, heard nothing unusual, saw nothing unusual. Sofe released them to go home or back to their jobs, but I stayed on to hear whatever they might tell me about their interviews with the guests. After I'd hugged and squeezed hands with most of the other staff and seen them go off toward the parking lot and home, I went into the front office to wait until all the guest interviews were done. We had a high-end coffeemaker in there, and I put it to work, grinding fresh from beans and scooping just the perfect amount into the filter. I might not be much of a chef, fated to play the role of appreciative eater rather than cook, but I knew how to make an exceptional cup of coffee.

The reaction the cops got from the vacationers was a bit less cooperative, Jean-Claude told me later, even though that crowd hadn't been required to put in their waiting time in a hotel staff room. They'd been allowed to go back to their rooms, but asked to stay up until he and Sofrania could meet with them there.

"That Gloria Flynn, she's quite a handful," Jean-Claude commented. "Loud."

"And not used to being asked questions." Sofrania dropped into a chair behind the manager's desk. She was showing her fatigue.

I passed them each a cup of coffee.

"The husband was okay, though. Not like that other guy, what was his name?" He consulted his notebook, flipping back through many pages covered with handwriting.

"Sam? Mr. Harmon?"

"Yeah, the one who looked like a refugee from the 1970s, the long hair and the tie-dyed shirt." Jean-Claude stopped to read a page. "Wife Chelsea. Vacationing from Boston." He looked up. "I don't know why, I just had a feeling about those two. As if they were hiding some piece of information. Him more than her, I think… maybe not, though. Maybe her. Maybe both of them."

"Hey, that's a lot to go on." Sofrania grinned.

"Yeah, whatever. Did we talk to everybody?"

"For a start. We also have the lists of all the Feast guests from Otto and we'll start on them tomorrow. Hotel guests, yeah, I think we saw them all. We knocked on every door, 150, apparently. Thanks for the registration roster, Nola."

"No problem. I talked to my boss, he's over on St. Thomas but he'll be on site tomorrow. He cleared me to give you guys total cooperation."

I took a sip of my coffee. "Can I ask you a question?" When Sofrania nodded, I pushed forward with something that had been teasing my curiosity for hours now. "Okay, this is kind of random, but would there have been a response that fast from you guys, all these interviews, all the personal information gathered on every guest, if it had been anybody else who disappeared?"

"Absolutely." Sofrania didn't hesitate. "We take everybody's safety seriously, but especially guests'."

Jean-Claude nodded. "If a resort got a reputation for guests disappearing, it would be kind of hard to get bookings!"

"No kidding," I agreed.

"But we have to think about the whole island." Sofrania added. "Any call we get from anybody any place, we go. Right now, right away. The media would be all over us if there was any trouble and we didn't jump, right away. Not to mention all the amateurs on social media. I'm actually kind of surprised that Dana didn't show up here yet. She's the night owl at the newspaper, I'm told." Sofrania looked intently at me in a way that she never did when we were just hanging out.

"I haven't called my sister." I promised "And I won't. If she shows up here, it will be because somebody else decided it was news."

"If we really do have a celebrity chef/CEO of a major American corporation gone missing on St. Croix, it's news. I'm just not sure we should be ready to conclude she's disappeared, after only five or six hours."

"Anybody have any idea where else she might be? Any of the guests with an idea or a suggestion?"

Sofrania and Jean-Claude looked at one another, then downed their coffees simultaneously. "Nothing to report, at this point," Jean-Claude said. "But if you hear anything, you'll call us, right?"

"I will," I confirmed as I walked them out to the entrance.

To everybody's surprise, Jason was standing there, waiting for them. "Could I speak with you, officers, before you leave? Are you leaving now?"

"We were going to," Jean-Claude said.

"What is it, Mr. Palmateer?"

If anything, Jason looked better rested than he had at the start of the evening, which was more than anyone could say about me. I'd been awake almost 24 hours—pale skin, circles under my eyes, hair gone frizzy from no attention since midnight.

"I'm a bit concerned about the way Ms. Barga's assistant is stressing the fact that I was the last person seen with her. As I told you, I walked her back to the door of her suite, saw her unlock it and go inside, and that was that."

Sofrania fixed him with full-on eye contact. "We have some concerns about the events, Mr. Palmateer. Liz Barga doesn't seem like the type of woman who would just go off for a drive or a walk by herself late on a Friday night. We're going to be investigating further—a lot further. And until she shows up again or we have some answers, we're calling this a suspicious incident."

Jean-Claude put out a hand. "Your passport, please."

Jason leaned back in shock. "My passport?"

"We don't want you to leave the island until we have a chance to clear all this up. You were the last one to see her, or be seen with her. Your passport, please."

Jason looked as though he might be sick. "I don't have any plans to go anywhere. I don't have any money to go anywhere. And even if I did, I wouldn't. I know how it looks if someone takes off at the wrong time. I gotta say, I don't much like being singled out this way, out of all these people, all the people she's talked to tonight, and since she got here. I think you're being way too quick to point a finger at me. I know there's always pressure to wrap these things up fast, especially in a tourist town, but if you're looking at me, you're looking in the wrong direction."

"Nobody's pointing a finger, Mr. Palmateer. We just want to make sure you're in a place where we can talk to you again, if we need to. Your passport please. " Again, with the hand extended.

"I don't have it on me."

Jean-Claude turned to me. "Is it in the hotel safe? Ms. Stewart can go and get it for us."

Jason shook his head. "It's in my room. On the desk, with my driver's license."

Jean-Claude turned to the door. "I'll go get it, you wait here. On the desk? You don't worry?"

"I've been leaving stuff out in my hotel room for years and never lost a thing. The only reason they give you all those warnings is for their own liability protection and so they can blame the guest, if anything actually does ever get taken. Which rarely happens."

"You're an optimistic sort, Mr. Palmateer."

"Well, I'm not a cop, Detective. And I hadn't expected to need my passport tonight or to be asked to hand it over to anyone."

Jean-Claude made a face and then disappeared through the door. I turned to Jason—he was the picture of misery. What could I say to make this not so bad?

# CHAPTER SEVEN

Jason had been on St. Croix for a week now and was starting to feel familiar about many things that had seemed so foreign when he first arrived. He now knew that the muggy jungle feel didn't last long, only until the next ocean breeze lightened the air and made you think of paradise. He knew the furry creature that skittered across the lawn first thing every morning was a mongoose and he'd discovered that he loved the crashing sound of the rollers and the waves beating against the rocks at either end of the beach.

It was a week since he'd fled New York and three days since the Pirates' Feast when Liz Barga disappeared. Many times in his life he'd had the ominous feeling that the other shoe was about to drop, to borrow one of his mother's strange clichés, and this was one of them. He'd surrendered his passport to the St. Croix police, had answered all their questions, and was helping as much as he was able, but it didn't seem to matter. He was under a cloud here, and he knew it.

As the days went by, it became clearer that more suspicion was falling on Jason Palmateer. The police interviewed him multiple times. The hotel staff were asked to be conscious of all of the comings and goings at the resort, but particularly Jason's. I couldn't help myself—I became very suspicious of him, too. Even though I had met him so recently and hadn't seen any signs that he was a liar or a criminal, the doubts about him seemed to hover in the air. Where there's smoke, there's fire, right? Right? Even though we talked a few times over those days and I'd imagined he might become a friend (and on some lonely evenings, in my thoughts, he became much more)—now I was filled with doubt, even though I had no proof that he was a liar or a cheat. Somehow, just the whiff of suspicion had me mistrusting him.

There was a shadow now on everything he said and did. Why was that? What happened to "innocent until proven guilty"? Yes, I did believe in that principle, on the face of it, yet there's something in the very accusation that seems to give weight to the allegation. It's not the first time I've ever seen or felt something like that. Even way back in high school, gossip had a way of turning into "everybody knows", as if it were fact. On the internet every day, I read information about people that was presented as truth, and I tended to believe it until shown otherwise—particularly if it was startling. Even if the person denied it—of course, they would deny it, right? So many reports of movie stars and other celebrities' bad behavior, even their deaths—must be true, it's online. Dead until proven alive. Guilty until proven innocent. That's what was happening with Jason. Well, maybe not guilty, exactly, but I didn't know him well enough to reject completely the possibility that he'd had something to do with Liz's disappearance. Didn't neighbors and bystanders always comment, in the aftermath of a tragedy or attack, that the bad guy had seemed like such an ordinary, trustworthy person? Trust nobody, seemed to be the wisest way; that's what our news, our movies, our TV shows all say. What a world we are living in.

Liz's absence was confirmed as an actual disappearance almost immediately. No one had caught sight of her anywhere since Friday night and all of the flights out of St. Croix were checked and double-checked. It's an island, after all, and there are only two ways out, by air and by sea. Sofe told me that they'd checked all the commercial and private flights for three days; all of the marine comings and goings had been documented, too.

Didn't mean someone couldn't have taken off or set sail surreptitiously, maybe in the void of night, but it did add up to a situation that was becoming more complicated for the police.

For the resort, too. Guests had been asking questions since Saturday morning and several of them had to make adjustments to their travel schedules to accommodate police questioning. All the rest had to leave personal information details with the cops; everybody was seen as a possible witness and nobody was happy about that.

Almost nobody, that is. Dana, my sister, was in her element, just delighted with all this. It's hard to be an investigative journalist in a place where hardly anything ever happens; that's why her editor insisted she take on half a dozen other jobs on the paper. Besides being the food and restaurant critic, she was the police reporter, the city affairs reporter, the business reporter and the movie reviewer. They would have given her education to cover, too, but she rebelled. What she really wanted to do was be the sort of independent investigative reporter that only the *New York Times* had resources for but her editor stubbornly resisted her efforts in that direction. He had been inclined to assign someone else to the Liz Barga disappearance, too, but Dana was leveraging her food critic knowledge to insert herself into that one.

I walked through the bar and was surprised to see

Frida Axelsen on a stool, chatting across a table for two with a man who looked as though he'd spent the past nine years on a boat deck. He was about fifty, mahogany tan, hair bleached blonde, jaunty yellow kerchief around his throat, cargo shorts with that lived-in look and a vintage Pink Floyd T-shirt. I didn't know him but she was unmistakable. Her mouse brown hair was held back with an elastic band and her bangs were cut just a bit too short and too unevenly to have been done by anybody but herself. She was wearing an Australian outback style hat, a safari shirt and a pair of blue jeans far too tight for a woman who must be in her sixties, maybe even seventies. Her fingernails were long and red, to match her earrings, and her belt buckle featured silver and turquoise that were probably real.

She was a duchess or a baroness or something, in ancient Danish nobility circles, someone told me once. She was rich enough to live anywhere, it was said, and she chose St. Croix, the very eastern edge, just before Point Udall. If you looked at her home from one angle, the mansion looked as if it was built in a screamingly modern style, with a tower that pierced about a hundred feet into the sky in the best possible imitation of any skyscraper in New York. If you looked at it from another angle, it was a symphony of middle Eastern history and fancy. It was the Alhambra West, built in an approximation of the red colors that had given the real thing the name "the red castle" back in the thirteenth century.

This more modern version was built when this wealthy Danish woman decided she wanted to build her dream residence on a prime piece of land on St. Croix, looking out over the water tower toward Buck Island. It took four years to build, and the stories about the construction phase were numerous and bizarre. Workers reported buffet lunches laid out one week and paychecks that bounced the next. Truck drivers delivered expensive and rare blocks of marble and slate that they were asked to stack in a corner of the property and cover with a tarp. Carpenters had to sign non-disclosure agreements before they were allowed inside, then were offered pieces of silver cutlery to take home as gifts. Frida supervised all day every day, despite the presence of her general contractor, according to stories told by tradesmen who'd been there or their sons and grandsons, who passed along the stories.

The day the construction was complete, Frida closed the doors and no one from the island had been allowed inside since, so the stories went. From time to time, guests arrived from off-island, either via the airport or the harbor, but the time they spent hanging out elsewhere on St. Croix was zero to none. The visits never lasted more than a few days and no photos of the place ever surfaced on social media.

While her guests and associates might have been extremely tight-lipped, Frida herself was friendly and outgoing. She talked a lot, I'd heard, with anybody about anything. But now the line was drawn at the front door of Alhambra West.

I watched Frida chat with her lunch companion and it occurred to me that I was watching a very accomplished flirt. I settled myself at a table just behind them and opened the menu.

"The problem here," she was saying in a very confidential sort of voice, "is that there is a dearth of suitable men."

He chuckled and leaned forward. "Oh, I'm suitable, Miss Frida, I'm suitable. Believe me."

She chuckled back and took a sip of something frothy and golden in a wine glass. "It was nice of Leona to introduce us. Have you been to St. Croix many times before, Ronald?"

"I've been cruising the Caribbean for quite a few years now," he said as he stroked the sides of his beer glass with his fingertips.

I saw him look over at me and quickly pulled the menu up higher in front of my eyes. Probably didn't matter anyway because it was my legs he had been looking at, not my face.

"I've been to almost every island," Frida said. "This was my favorite when I first came here, in the 1970s, and it still is. It's not as wealthy as some of the others and there isn't as much night life, but for sheer beauty, you can't beat it."

"I see Christiansted a lot of course, and I'm very familiar with the harbor and with Buck Island."

"Oh, you must spend some time inland, the views are sensational!" Frida's voice had not a hint of age and if you had to guess, without seeing her, you would not guess anything older than forty or fifty. "My house is on a hill and you can see as far as the British Virgin Islands, I swear."

"Well, the thing that appeals to me the most is that St. Croix is part of the U.S. of A.," Ronald said.

"Certainly makes it easier for you U.S. citizens, if you want to move and live here full-time."

"Are you here full-time, Frida?"

"No, I stay a month or two at a time, in the winter, but I have a few other places I like to be."

"Such as?"

"Cannes, St. Paul de Vence, Rome."

"You like to travel as much as I do," Ronald commented.

"But by land, not in a boat," she said with a laugh.. "Not enough space in a boat, if you ask me."

"And I would bet you have been asked, over and over, Miss Frida." I could hear the smile in his voice and picture it on his face. Two consenting flirts.

"What is the name of your yacht, Ronald? Do I have that correct, calling it a yacht?"

"Yes, a yacht is anything over a certain size that is a boat for personal uses, not business or commercial."

"What size is it?"

"About 120 feet. Name is *Seas the Day.*"

"I'd love to see it sometime."

"I'll show it to you. Two more of the same, please."

The server appeared at my table seconds later and I ordered the lobster mac and cheese. Eavesdropping is hungry work.

"Are you staying long?" Frida was asking.

"Depends. I am looking to stop somewhere for a while—the weather forecast is a bit stormy over the next week. But I might go over to St. Thomas, put in there. What do you think, what should I do?"

"Oh, I wouldn't have much advice for a mariner, Ronald."

"What about just comparing islands? I wonder about safety—are you concerned at all?"

"Up to now, I never have been. But did you hear about that disappearance from one of the hotels?"

"Yeah, I heard something about a woman, CEO of some company. Just gone, after dinner in the hotel restaurant."

"Her name is Liz Barga and she's also one of the best chefs in the world. She is a friend of mine."

My ears expanded and tuned in harder, at that point. Whose wouldn't? Maybe she was just a name-dropper, or someone who liked to feel 'in the loop' on what must be one of the biggest topics of conversation on the island today. But it could be true. Frida and Liz would be the types to travel in the same circles and it seemed quite plausible that they might be friends.

"You must be quite concerned."

"I am and I'm not." I waited, hoping that Frida might add to that. "She's a big girl and she can take care of herself."

"What's she like?" I was appreciating this Ronald somebody. He asked the same questions I would ask.

"Very confident, very imposing, as you'd expect from somebody running a major corporation. She's one of the most influential women in the world—I'd put her in the same category as Anna Wintour or Hilary Clinton, in their fields. But hers is cuisine, of course. She got her start as a chef, and even with the cookbooks, the restaurants, the TV shows, and then the multinational business, she still goes into a commercial kitchen from time to time and creates a meal that sets everybody talking."

"How did you meet her?"

"I approached her for a charity thing I was involved in—fund-raising for an arts organization in Denmark, it was. I asked her to donate something we could auction off, and she sent one of her sketchbooks. About 60 or 70 sketches of dishes she'd imagined and then created—a work of art, every single one of them!" Frida laughed. "You know, when I cook, I just start pulling out pans and pots, look in the refrigerator, get the spices lined up. But I guess the professionals, the great ones, start by drawing the way it will look on the plate—the shrimp cut into fifths or sixths and arranged in an arc, then a sprig of asparagus up in the right corner, a dab of mustard down in the left—is that correct, does asparagus come in sprigs? Anyway…"

Ronald laughed. "Beats me. But I have heard that really good cooks work on the colors, too. Wouldn't put pumpkin, carrots and cantaloupe all on the same plate."

"Unless it was Halloween."

"So, how much did the sketchbook go for, at the charity auction?"

"Two alpha types got into a bidding war over it and it ended up bringing in $300,000." Frida paused—probably taking a sip of her drink. She really was quite good at timing. "The committee was thrilled, the symphony and the art galleries were thrilled, and Liz and I have been friends ever since."

I paused to inhale the mouthwatering aroma of the lobster pasta dish just set in front of me. How many times have I said or thought—thank you for this rocket-fuel metabolism. I would hate to have to count calories or watch what I eat.

"So, what's your bet on where she is?"

"No idea. Might be that she just needed to drop out of sight for a while, for reasons of her own. Although somebody with those responsibilities isn't likely to just take off, like some unreliable, selfish teenager. I hate to say it, but I am worried. And I hear that the police are investigating, so…"

"I'm sure she'll turn up. Everything will be alright, Frida. I'd bet money on it. Serious money." The words were soothing and so was the voice. She must be looking upset.

"Thank you, Ronald. I think so, too." I heard them start to move. "Thank you so much for the drinks, too. It was nice to run into you."

"You're welcome, Frida. I enjoyed talking with you, too. Love to see inside your house sometime."

They moved past my table, without noticing me at all. I heard Frida ignore his hint and make some comment about the weather changing, and then they were gone. I sat for another ten minutes, savoring every mouthful of my mac and cheese, and wondering what bet I would make on where Liz was.

I hated to say it, or even think it, because what hotel wants anything bad happening on its premises, ever. But this didn't feel good, and it was very possible that wherever Liz was, she wasn't returning because she wasn't able to.

Jason sat on the sand, staring out at the incredible view of the Caribbean Sea. The demand for his passport had rattled him, he had to admit. He'd spent a significant portion of his life practicing being relaxed and unstressed about virtually any challenge that arose. Exams, athletics, workplace conflict, relationship drama, looming bankruptcy—he handled them all with a shrug. With many crises, he'd found, if you just waited a while, everything calmed down: the test was written, the game was won (or lost), the fight was avoided or the money was located. In fact, the less you concerned yourself with the problem, the more likely the good results and the solutions.

But this situation in St. Croix was new territory and he wasn't sure that his usual method was going to work. He didn't like the way those police officers looked at him and the questions they asked could definitely be called hostile. What did it mean, the request for his passport? He had other ID and he knew that everything would check out, once they looked into his answers to their questions, but still, it was disturbing. Were they collecting passports from everybody or was it just him? He wished he had thought to ask.

He had a feeling that losses were mounting, somehow, and that he should take action. His resources were scarce, but he was quite confident he could contact Anthony and arrange for a loan or something that would give him the funds he needed to leave the island.

Nobody had told him he couldn't. He hadn't been charged with anything, and he felt astonished that he was even thinking a thought like that—'I haven't been charged with anything.' The whole thing was starting to take on the vocabulary of a B-grade TV show and he tried to order himself to shake it off.

He was letting himself get cranked up over all this and blowing it up out of proportion in his mind. He was free to come and go as he pleased and if he wanted to, (and if Anthony sent him money and if the cop returned his passport), he could just get on a plane and go somewhere else.

But how would that appear? Would it look as though he was running away? As though he was guilty of something?

But if he waited too long, though, would his window close and would he be stuck here, caught up in something he couldn't escape?

# CHAPTER EIGHT

The weather changed dramatically that Tuesday morning. I got ready for work with darkness outside, as usual, but by the time the first glimmers of dawn were showing through the slats in my patio door I could tell it wouldn't be a blue-sky, eye-widening-sun kind of day. Something about the air—and when I opened the shutters there was the reason. A thunderstorm, rolling in from the north, bringing forks of lightning every few minutes. I stood and watched for a while, wondering how far off it was and appreciating the fact that I was not out on a boat. The rain began, and within seconds I could see it as a gray curtain across the lawn, as drips from the palm fronds grew into puddles around their bases. So many sounds, like instruments in a band—the steady, constant backbeat of the waves hitting the beach, the gush of the rain showers, the water dripping into puddles, the punctuation of thunder, the drops hitting leaves of various size and texture. I didn't want to leave for work in this downpour, so I made a second cup of coffee.

Jason watched the storm from the padded bench inside the screened porch of his suite. For a half an hour or so, it stopped and he thought it was over, then he saw another flash. A camera somewhere nearby? The drum roll of thunder, louder even than the waves pounding, updated him on the status of the storm—not over yet. A few seconds later, the clouds opened up and sheets of rain poured down. He canceled his plans to go out for a run and settled in with a book. The rain hadn't cut the humidity or the heaviness of the air at all; if you lived here and spent much time outdoors, away from the air-conditioned chill, you'd have to get used to a constant sensation of damp skin.

The power and sound of the rain picked up and for the next half hour he could barely see the 200 feet down to the beach. When the storm finally broke, he could hear, once again, the shrieking of the toddler staying in the suite above his. Even with all the garbage raining down on him right now, he was glad his life didn't include a little girl like that. Every morning before 7 o'clock, he could hear her screaming. He had noticed her and her family by the pool—an older sister about seven years old, the mom and the dad, usually hidden behind a newspaper or with nose down into a tablet, plus a beautiful young woman in her early twenties who was probably the nanny or an aunt.

Once the rain stopped Jason grabbed a towel and headed over to the pool for a swim. The same family was there, too, organized on five deck chairs with mountains of toys, bags and gear around them. The dad disappeared almost immediately. The toddler shrieked there, too, so he could see it wasn't fear of the storm earlier or pain or need of any kind, just pure spoiled toddler-iness, if there was such a word. Brattiness, that was it. He'd go nuts, if he had to put up with that.

"Hey, mate."

Bondi was poolside, preparing tanks and masks for a beginner lesson. No sign of his class members yet, but Jason wished a good group for him—no drama queens, no arrogant show-offs. He liked Bondi.

"Hey yourself." Jason got up and strolled over to watch Bondi's preparations.

"Do you dive?"

"Never have. Looks like fun, though."

"Come on along with me, sometime. I'll show you how it's done."

"You're on, Bondi. Where would we go?"

"Buck Island is the best, marine gardens you won't believe. And almost the whole island is surrounded by reef—sponges, sea turtles, coral, schools of tropical fish. If you're an underwater photographer you think you've died and gone to heaven. And we have to do The Wall." He fixed Jason with a spooky laser beam of eye contact. "If you can handle the stress."

"The Wall? What's that?"

"All serious scuba divers have heard of this one. It's in Cane Bay, and it's super-popular. But can be terrifying. If you're new. You swim along; you got gorgeous coral, amazing colors of fish, warm blue water. But then, just like that, it's frickin' freezing, black water, nothing to see." Bondi took a deep breath. "There's a drop-off and the floor is suddenly two miles down. Lots of hungry, fast creatures down there, dude. Lots of people are spooked by it. They say blue whales come back covered in wounds, scientists have found goblin sharks, sea-devils— what else lives down there, right?"

Jason realized he'd been sucked right in by Bondi's storytelling skills and he pulled back with a laugh. "Alright, watch out for the abyss and the Wall."

"Nah, I'm just messing with you, man. People who know what they're doing love to dive there. I'd take you there if you want to go. Lots of other great places to go, though."

"Such as?"

"Buck Island. It's off the eastern end of St. Croix,

and it's a national park."

"Yeah, you mentioned it. Good diving?"

"Great diving, great snorkeling, frickin' amazing, man. But access is limited, so if you want to see it, we'd have to make a plan."

"I'll let you know, thanks, Bondi."

The minute I saw the headline on the *St. Croix Times* I knew there would be trouble. *CELEBRITY GUEST GOES MISSING FROM PITAYA BEACH HOTEL.* The story had my sister's byline—*Dana Stewart, St. Croix Times staff.*

I picked up my phone.

"Hey, Nola!" Dana's voice was enthusiastic. She was a sunny day about to get hit by a typhoon.

"Don't you try to be nice to me now, Dana. Where did your information come from?"

"Information about what?"

"Today's front page."

"Ah." She got up and I could hear a door being closed. "Are you getting yelled at for that?"

"Not yet, but it's likely," I answered. "Mr. Winter has warned me about nine times about talking to you about anything going on at the resort."

"As if he has to," Dana muttered. "Trying to find out anything from you is like trying to talk to a statue. You've never given me so much as one lead in all the years you've been there. It's like Confidentiality Castle or something."

"I actually had an idea about that, but you've ruined it!" I blasted her. "Total confidentiality and privacy for the celebrity guest. Market the resort as an unbelievably secluded place for unbelievably prickly guests. I was going to present a strategic plan to Mr. Winter and see if we could take it to HQ. Not much chance of that now."

"You are totally shooting the frickin' messenger, girl," Dana blasted back. "I didn't make it up—you guys *did* have a celebrity guest disappear. And I didn't *take* her, I just reported on it."

"We would rather that news about this didn't get out."

"And I would rather that my landlord not cash my rent checks. But he does. Regular AF."

"Where did you get the story? We didn't put out a press release."

"Sources."

"Yeah, well, Mr. Winter thinks I'm your source."

"Give me his phone number. I'll talk to him, tell him it's not you."

"I will not."

I could hear her shrug. "Your call. Look, I gotta go, any minute here. Two celebrity chefs coming in at the airport and I have to get some photos."

"For the cooking competition?"

"Yes, Gennaro Bianchi from Italy and Hisashi Mizuno from Japan. Both staying at the Buccaneer."

"Hey, did you know that Mom is coming to town on the weekend?" I asked.

"Yeah, she called me. Can you pick her up at the airport? I'm scheduled to work Saturday."

"So am I."

"Could she take a cab?"

"A bit cold, don't you think?" I felt my shoulders tense up as I thought about the upcoming conversation with my boss. *Sorry somebody leaked the bad news about our hotel, it wasn't me, I swear, and by the way, could I have Saturday off?*

I wouldn't want to talk to me, either. *Oh, and by the*

*way, again, I'm trying to find a way to get a promotion with the hotel, can you suggest something?*

He probably has every second employee—no, every employee!—asking him for help. *I'm applying for a scholarship to get a master's in hospitality management; do you think you could write me a reference letter?*

I got tired of waiting for her to reply and I rushed in with my promise. "Yeah, Dana, I'll go get her. Somehow."

"Thanks. I'll be there if I can, but there's no predicting what kind of day it will be at the paper."

Oh yeah, very different from a hotel. Sure.

"And hey, Nola? They were going to run a headline saying HOTEL GUEST A VICTIM OF VIOLENCE? I stopped them, I want you to know that."

"Thanks, Dana."

What could I say?


A coconut fell from the tree outside Jason's screen porch and the thud on the ground woke him up. He had started napping. Not a good sign. Was it 5 o'clock yet?

No, only 4:30 p.m.

Early enough.

Jason headed for his favorite stool in the bar. Across the small room he saw that hotel desk clerk, the one who practically gave off sparks, she had so much energy.

She seemed a bit different today, a bit droopy. He ordered two Stellas and walked across the room to her.

"Hey, what's up, Nola? You look a little low." He put the beers down on the table.

"Oh, I'm fine." She managed a brief smile, one that looked more like pain than welcome. "Trying to avoid running into my boss."

"Whoa. Doesn't sound good." He took the chair across from her and waited for her to speak.

"There's a front page story in the local newspaper about Liz Barga's disappearance." She sipped from the bottle. "My sister wrote it."

He nodded. "I get it."

"I was just starting to get some traction with him, you know? I have a lot of ideas about things we could do to build up the resort—events, PR, messaging. Now, he won't listen to a thing I say." All of her attention was going to that beer. "I'm trying to move up, put my career on the high burner. I need him to write a recommendation for a scholarship for my master's, I need to get in line for an assistant manager job. This won't help."

Jason was familiar with this kind of no-win. "Can you talk to him, persuade him that you weren't the leak?"

"I'm going to try. But you know how old people are. They think they know everything."

"Is he that old?"

"Fifty, anyway. Maybe more. Doesn't matter. I'm hooped."

"Nola, Nola, don't give up. Geez. Look at where you are, what you've got. You live in one of the most beautiful parts of the world."

"And I can't afford to enjoy it because I have a crappy job with a tiny salary and no future."

"You work for a giant hotel chain with dozens, hundreds…thousands of opportunities!" His grin and wide sweep with open arms drew a bit of a smile from her.

"And I can't afford to get more education so I can get a better job within the company."

"The company is very supportive of leadership positions for women, and you are one."

"And I have great ideas for the resort that no one

will listen to."

"The island has lots of avenues for you to use to get the kind of attention you want."

"Name one."

Jason faltered, but only for a moment. "Alright. Events. You've mentioned that a few times. Let's lock on to this KweeZeenArtZ I've been hearing about. You could position the hotel to piggyback on whatever positive attention it's getting and generate more. Make everybody forget about the missing guest."

"Like how?"

Jason racked his brain. Although he had covered many public relations and marketing launches, this was not his area. "Contests! People love contests. Is there any kind of contest connected with KweeZeenArtZ? Hottest chili sauce? Best key lime pie? Or maybe something consumption? Most shrimp eaten in ten minutes? Gotta make sure they're not doing something similar with any of the other food festivals, though."

She glared at him. "So, are you being sarcastic? Or are you serious? Because those ideas are all so not-smart."

"Then let's hear you do better." Jason was pleased with himself for getting her head out of her... yeah.

"Maybe a contest." She was thinking. "Celebrities coming in, staying at our hotel, attending KweeZeenArtZ. Maybe a celebrity chef, cooking contest, menu contest... maybe a wine pairing challenge?"

"I was just going to say that."

"It would be so great if people were coming here because it was *the* hot place to go." Nola's face had a faraway look. "It is beautiful, but any island needs more than that."

"People coming here, but not too many," Jason agreed. "Just the right number, organized in the right way, so that the ecology stays in balance, the oceans continue to be cleansed, but the people living here can raise their standard of living."

"There are quite a few people working on that," Nola said. "Agriculture is geared to organic now. We have committees all over the Caribbean of people who care about the future of the planet and about the local economy."

"Big picture done."

"Medium focus, we've got St. Croix getting ready for another boom time. The oil refinery shut down about five years ago but they're making noises about new investment. Sugar was the basis of the economy for centuries—it might be coming back. Cruise ships, small ones that the wealthier people like, are going to be coming to Christiansted, as soon as the harbor is dredged to accommodate them."

Jason got in step with her. "And of course, this is the home of Captain Morgan. Rum, since the time of the buccaneers."

"Definitely an attraction for the tourists," Nola laughed. "Maybe we could get a famous alcoholic or two to endorse St. Croix."

"I think that's been done."

"What about you, Jason?" Nola was obviously feeling better. "What's your problem today?"

"You mean, other than the fact that the cops took my passport and people are thinking I might be involved in Liz Barga's disappearance?"

"No, I mean *real* problems," she laughed. "Like polluted oceans and climate change and economic recessions."

"Oh, well, I got nothing to compete with that," he said. "Let's have another beer, shall we?"

He waited until the bartender saw his signal and sent over two more. They sat in sociable quiet, looking out over the Caribbean Sea, until they each had another drink in hand, then Jason answered her question.

"I've got the cops' suspicion to deal with, top layer. And that missing woman, Liz. What happened to her, is she alright?

"Going a bit deeper, it's my career, and some stories I filed back in New York earlier this year. I've got to find a way to prove I didn't misquote somebody on purpose, didn't make up some stuff, to take the easy way out.

"Next layer down, I've got to figure out my life. I don't know where I want to live, what I want to do next, if they won't let me be a journalist any more. I lived in New York three years, San Francisco four years before that, Dallas before that. Twelve cities, I think it is, since I graduated college. I don't know where home is."

"Where did you grow up?"

"Columbus, Ohio."

"What place did you like the most?" Nola asked. "Go there."

"None of them. And all of them." Jason smiled at her. "I think you're over-simplifying."

"And I think you're making it more complicated than it is."

"Says the woman who wants to solve an entire island's economic problem and lift an entire resort to international prominence. That's too much responsibility for any one person."

Nola toasted him with her beer bottle. "Says the man who thinks he has to rescue a woman who was a stranger to him a week ago."

Jason laughed. Feeling good. Better than in days.

"What if there were a way we could sell things about a celebrity chef cook-off event at KweenZeenArtZ to people who don't even come here? A little taste of St.

Croix without the thousands of dollars for plane tickets and hotel bills? Something that became really cool and everyone wanted to have one?" Her excitement was all over her face, like fireworks on the Fourth.

"Yeah, well, let me know once you figure out exactly what that is."

He laughed, she laughed back and they had a moment that wiped out all the suspicions she'd been having about him and Liz's disappearance. For a few seconds only. Then her face darkened and she was gone. Her mistrust was back. He could feel it.

I had been listening to Sofrania for half an hour when it suddenly dawned on me that she was floating an idea and looking for my reaction. When she called up this morning, inviting me to go running, even though it was Thursday, not Saturday, and it was just the two of us, not the usual group, I had my suspicions that she might have something other than exercise in mind.

As we ran along the boardwalk, she didn't look at me once, while she asked her questions. Pretty interesting, the way she did it. She was speaking in short bursts, just able to get the words out, given the pace we were running, and although it sounded as though she was giving me her thoughts, she was really probing for mine.

"Nola, did you see that newlywed couple have that fight at the Pirates' Feast?"

"Bjorn and Natalya? I did."

"What did you think? Her fault?"

"Nothing is ever any one person's fault. She pushed him, some might say. He was not very chill, some others might say. He should have joined in with her and the Moko Jumbie."

"Any buzz about the two of them at the resort?"

"I'm not hearing much of anything about them. They're not socializing or even saying hello to the other guests much, I don't think."

"I wonder why she chose that time to stir up so much commotion? I mean, weren't there lots of other times she could have picked a fight with him? At their table, during dinner, maybe? During the DJ time, the dancing, before the show started?"

I slowed down a bit to look directly at Sofrania. "Are you saying you think she acted that way to get him riled up at that exact time? But why, Sofe?"

She grinned at me. "Hey, I ask the questions here."

We ran along in silence for a few more minutes, and then she went at it again. "When you have your husband all to yourself most of the time, why would you fight in public, in a noisy place like that?"

"Maybe she's just an impulsive type, doesn't think through a strategy or a timing. She got up to dance, he didn't like what she was doing, lost his temper, yelled at her, and she doesn't back down."

"Did you think he looked actually pissed off? I mean, really, like a guy does?"

I thought about it for a few hundred yards. "I have to say, I didn't see that truly angry thing, there wasn't that vibe. You know, when you know a guy is at the end of his string and he's pretty much going on testosterone in the situation?"

It was a rhetorical question and she didn't object to it. "Do you think maybe he was just putting on a show? They were both just putting on a show?"

"But why would they do that, Sofe?"

If she had an answer, she wasn't saying.

"Maybe they're just strange people who like to

have their conflicts in public," I imagined. "Maybe it cranks them up for a great time in bed, later."

"Or maybe?" Sofrania prompted.

I ran along, letting my mind go into scenario mode. "Maybe they wanted everybody to be looking at them."

"Why?"

"So they wouldn't look at anything or anybody else."

"Because?"

"Maybe there was something else going on that they didn't want everybody looking at."

"Like a distraction?"

"Yes, making a distraction. So we wouldn't notice…"

"What else went on that night?"

"Liz Barga's disappearance."

I stopped by a bench and she stopped with me. "You think Bjorn and Natalya put on a big show to cause a distraction while something happened to our celebrity guest?"

"It's a possibility. An abduction, maybe?"

"An abduction, maybe. But why?"

"Ransom money?"

"I haven't heard that anybody has demanded any. Have they?"

She didn't answer. "Revenge or payback for something she did?"

"Everything I've heard or read about her and her style points to quite a few enemies along the way."

"Random nutcase kidnapping in a paradise getaway place?"

"Every tourism business's nightmare."

"And what if it was more than just a kidnapping?"

"We wouldn't know that until her body turned up.

So far there's no body, and maybe she's just taken off without having the courtesy or the empathy to think of informing her employees or her colleagues." I started stretching because it seemed as though our run was done. "Or her family. Has anybody heard from her family?"

Sofrania shook her head.

"Do Bjorn and Natalya know anybody else at the resort? Who would they be providing a distraction for, anyway, Sofe?"

She had her forehead down over one knee and I couldn't see her face. "Could be all wrong, I know. Fights between newlyweds have been starting since forever."

"Yeah, well, I give that pair about two years. No, change that. Two months."

She laughed. I pivoted on my left foot and thought about the hints Sofe was dropping about this couple. I had watched them throughout the previous week and the cracks in the new paint were already showing. Humid heat can do that—but so can a growing feeling that you've married the wrong person, I bet. Natalya had a scowl on her face pretty much constantly and Bjorn had an anxious look that was just painful to see, in a newlywed. When she leaped to center stage on the dance floor with the Moko Jumbies, his facial expression had changed to anger and then to ice. Many men would have stalked off back toward their honeymoon suite and many women would have stopped their showing off, at that point, but not those two. They'd taken their fight right out onto the dance floor, not caring whether it spun out of control and who saw it. At least, that's the way it had all appeared, to me, last Friday night. But maybe it really was a hoax, to cover up what was really going on.

Like what?

"Maybe they're working with Jason. Or maybe with somebody else, somebody we haven't even thought of yet. We're going to go through all the guest names and all the people who bought tickets to the Feast. Search through everything we can find about her, too. Whatever it is, we'll be discovering the story."

As the afternoon wore on, I couldn't stop thinking about that scene on Friday night, with Natalya dancing between the Moko Jumbie's legs and Bjorn stalking up to grab her by the arm. Something just didn't seem right about it—is that what a new husband would do? Hard for me to say, since I wasn't a new husband, didn't have one, and didn't even know any, except for the ones I'd seen passing through the resort during my three years there.

But although I might not know much about being a new husband or a new wife, I did have a little bit of experience with being jealous. And that was not what this looked like.

# CHAPTER NINE

"Hey, Nola, can we catch a ride with you over to Jump Up tonight?" Eleni had four of the servers and Rico the bartender with her.

"I can't fit this entire crew in my car!" I was laughing and so were they. "And if you think I'm making more than one trip, you're wrong!"

Jump Up was an event that took place four times a year on the streets and the boardwalk in Christiansted. Company Street and Strand Street were closed to traffic, and the tourists and locals alike came together on a Friday night to celebrate life and fun. It felt like a mix of a carnival and a street party, a parade and a market. You're going to find Jump Up all over the Caribbean islands—it means 'dance' and it gave us all a good reason to drop our drama for a while.

I managed to fit four of them in my car and we'd arrived early enough to find a parking space fairly easily. The air was sweet and warm, the crowd excited. The man to my left had dreads so thick that the white stocking he was using for a cap was about two feet square. The woman to my right wore a batik dress in orange, purple, turquoise and red—just gorgeous. A colorful poster for the Caribbean lottery shared space near the sidewalk with a Ginger Thomas, its yellow flowers and green leaves as inspiring as a painting.

We were standing just a few feet away from a charming historic hotel painted in soft colors of turquoise and aqua. In another building across the way, walls in a soft yellow contrasted with forest green shutters by the windows. The oldest hotel on this part of the island was also nearby; black wrought-iron balconies, columns, and wicker chairs graced the exterior and porch. A small sign read *Hotel St. Marie, est. 1757.*

Jump Up was billed as a cultural carnival and it had that feel, although it was no Mardi Gras Parade. Much smaller, much lower cost. People strolled along, stopping to inspect the goods at small tables, many of them covered in vinyl cloths. I had been to Jump Up quite a few times and it really wasn't the island jewelry or crafts I was interested in. Two reasons I wouldn't miss it—the music and the food.

The band tonight featured a guitar, a banjo, steel drums, regular drums, bongo, keyboard and triangle. The beat was reggae, the tune vaguely familiar. I felt my head beginning to bop and my shoulders to shimmy—the rhythm was impossible to resist.

The other thing almost impossible to resist was the smell of open-air cooking. Freshly caught fish sizzled on a grill somewhere nearby and the aroma mingled with the scent of flowers. The temperature was probably around 90° but I never felt too hot here. Warm, yes, sometimes uncomfortable in the humidity for a few minutes, but it was never any longer than that before the breeze came in from the water and it all cooled off. Watching video of the islands, before I moved here, I'd seen the signs of the wind blowing—the palm tree branches lifting and shaking, and thought "Is it too windy there?" But once you were here you realized that the wind was one of the best things about the place.

I found a comfortable spot to lean against a doorway and got ready for the parade to start. Just in front of me the driver of a jeep was trying to park in what must have looked like an open space. Right beneath a *Do Not Park* sign.

"Look at that," Eleni said. "Takes a lot of nerve."

The cops were on it in two seconds. The driver of the jeep ignored the police officer standing in front of her front fender. The driver's side door opened and an unusually tall woman wearing a short red lace dress and knee high boots swung herself down to the ground. An enormous straw hat with a leopard skin ribbon covered her head and I could barely see her face. From the look of her mouth, though, she wasn't going to let these cops do their job.

"No parking on Company Street, Miss." The officer who had been in front of the jeep came around to the driver's door and planted himself in the way.

"I'm not leaving it long." It was Frida Axelsen, come down the hill from her tower. "I'm just picking up one of the performers to get him over to the west end for a private party at one of the villas. Along with this other one," she explained to the police officer, motioning past her right shoulder toward a person in the passenger seat.

As soon as I saw her lift her chin to show her full face under that hat and heard her speak, the entertainment value of the encounter went up a notch or two, for me.

"It's not far, you know that," she continued. "I'll be back with my other guy and the jeep will be moved before you know it."

I tried to peek past her at the passenger and the police officer made it easier by shining his flashlight into the vehicle. This was all drawing quite a crowd. We all looked—or tried to look—at Frida's passenger and he nodded at us. He was wearing the costume of a Moko Jumbie, including a white mask covering his forehead, mouth and chin. No stilts, though; were they in the back of the jeep?

"You'll have to circle the outer streets like everybody else," the cop ruled.

"What's going on here, there's no parking allowed here!" The woman's voice behind us was high but authoritative. Frida lost our attention for a moment and we turned to see who it was, the cop looking annoyed for a second, then changing his expression to a respectful one when he recognized one of his police department superiors.

"Yes, Captain, we know that, and Mrs. Axelsen is leaving right now."

Sofrania's face didn't soften when she recognized the famous and influential parking rule-breaker. "No exceptions."

Frida looked angry, and I could just imagine her pitching a fit—but then she seemed to decide to rein it in. She smiled at Sofrania, gave what might have been a sarcastic salute, although it passed so quickly it was impossible to tell, then climbed up behind the wheel of her jeep. The low growl of the engine when she started it drew the attention of people about a block in each direction. She backed up and drove away, going the wrong way on one of the open streets.

Sofrania was furious, too. "Officer, you can't make exceptions like that or it will be a free-for-all! One person allowed to park, then everybody parks, and our signs are a joke."

"She only took a minute, you could hardly call it parking."

"She should have got a ticket. You should have given her a ticket."

"Now, that's just using a hammer to kill a fly." Another voice I recognized— Sofe's partner, Jean-Claude.

"What would you do?" she demanded, as they did the cop version of toe-to-toe. How on earth did those two manage to work together?

"Just what Tyson here did. Speak to her. Politely. Get her moving along. Then go have a nice drink to take the edge off my feeling about this boring dead-end career that I have."

"No drinking on the job."

"A soda, Sofe, that's all. I know the rules."

"Why do you have to take the edge off your feeling?" asked a young, beautiful woman who was one of about half a dozen people who had stopped to watch the Frida show and stayed on to listen to the conversation.

"Ah, what can I say to that!" Jean-Claude gave her a big grin and I could see that he was about to draw a curtain around the truth. "I have a good job and I'm glad to have it. Lots here on this island who can't find jobs and I'm not ungrateful."

We all nodded and smiled along with him but we all knew what he meant. Or at least, I did. It was difficult, many times, to watch the way the tourists spent money and enjoyed themselves, knowing they were going home to even more, while we were staying here, repeating ourselves, day after day. Where was the ladder going up? I was still looking for it.

Looking across the street, I spotted the Harmons from #165 and the woman waved to me. It was my first choice that I get a break from the hotel guests when I went out to Jump Up, but if I had to bump into anybody, I wouldn't mind it being someone like Mrs. Harmon. She had introduced herself warmly when they checked in and had been friendly every encounter since. Over my three years at the resort, I'd noticed a lot of difference from one person to the next, when it came to socializing with strangers. Some people travel or go on vacation with a goal of meeting new people and making new friends; some are open to it, but don't go looking; some keep to themselves, and some are outright surly to others.

I hadn't been on enough vacations to even know what I'd be.

Up and down the street, police officers and hired security were watching all the guests. They were jolly and friendly with everyone but they were watching. Christiansted was to be kept safe, at all times. The sight of all those uniforms got me thinking about Liz and her disappearance. No one was ready to call it foul play yet, and most of those who were aware of her at all had convinced themselves over the past few days that she had just decided to leave the Pirates' Feast without telling her assistant. No big deal, and something many travelers do.

"Nola, how are you!" Mrs. Harmon was wearing a pretty yellow sundress and about a dozen silver bangles, plus a St. Croix bracelet on her right arm. Her earrings were huge hoops and her shoes were red flip flops, the kind that looked like costume jewelry, with glitter and sparkling designs all over the straps. Her blonde hair had lightened up even more in the tropical sun. Her three small children and her husband crowded around her.

"Mrs. Harmon, hello." I kept my eyes firmly on her, ignoring the eager look her husband directed my way. Whether he was just looking for a babysitter to watch their kids, or something else, it was always better to maintain eye contact with the wife.

"Please, call me Chelsea. So nice to see you here." She sounded genuine and I relaxed. I was off-duty and she recognized that.

"You've been so good to us at the hotel. Could we persuade you to join us for an ice cream? Maybe even some dinner?" All five sets of eyes stared at me, waiting, smiling. How could I say no?

"I'd be delighted, thank you. We can stop right over there," I said, pointing to a sidewalk café that I knew served outstanding coconut shrimp.

We settled in, with fresh cold water all around and a weak, bright orange rum punch for all of the adults.

"How are you enjoying your stay?" I asked.

"Just fine," Mr. Harmon said. "Nice hotel. 'Where the rainforest meets the beach.'

I smiled at him, and immediately saw my mistake. His smile back was warm and his eyes were dancing, in the seconds when he zapped me with some full-on eye contact. Next, his gaze was on my breasts and I realized I had one of those flirty ones to deal with.

Damn. And his wife seemed so nice, too. Why don't these boys get it, that they are being disrespectful, both to the woman they're giving the once-over and to the wives who are usually well aware of the roving eye. I had a boyfriend like that once; he tried to tell me it meant nothing, that he wasn't going anywhere. He needed to see that even in those few seconds of flirty connecting with some random woman he was in fact 'going somewhere', right now. He was going, and he'd already gone. Stop it, or find yourself another girl, I say. You don't get to decide whether you're going to get in the game or not. Stop it right now. Raise the bar high, ladies.

Ha. If my sister Dana were here, she would say 'raise the bar high, bitches.' Hard to believe anyone let her anywhere near a computer with a 'send' button.

I smirked into my rum punch glass and then noticed that Mrs. Harmon—Chelsea —was trying to get my attention. "I saw all the action over the parking at the curb over there. Who was that?"

"Yeah, she's pretty noticeable, isn't she? That's Frida Axelsen. She's been here about 40 years and apparently she once was some sort of Scandinavian aristocrat or baroness or something. Not sure if was her family or a family she married into, but the story goes that she came here alone in the mid 1970s and built a huge house, with a wall and a moat and an inner courtyard—practically like a small town. They call it the Alhambra West."

"Does she always dress like that?" Mr. Harmon wanted to know.

"You mean the miniskirt specifically?"

"No, just how costume-y it all looked," Mrs. Harmon said.

"She's usually in some sort of costume. I saw her last week and she looked like an Australian cowboy, with an outback hat. Last month, I saw her at the grocery store looking like a Spanish dancer, with one of those flat hats with the fringe, you know what I mean?"

"She likes hats," Chelsea commented and we both grinned.

"And big buildings," Mr. Harmon added. "We noticed that palace when we were driving around last week."

"It's famous, Mr. Harmon."

"Please call me Sam. I can imagine that it is. Do any of the neighbors complain about it?"

"Not that I've ever heard." What a strange question. "People on St. Croix don't complain much of the time, Sam. We just keep reminding ourselves that we live in paradise." The server came by and I signaled her for another rum punch. The Harmons glanced at their kids and shook their heads.

"Maybe there's some complaining from the ones who would like to get an invitation inside and never do," Chelsea said as she helped herself to a spoonful of her daughter's ice cream.

"It certainly dominates the view," Sam

commented. "Have you ever been inside?"

"Not personally, but my sister Dana might have."

"Did someone mention my name?"

My sister Dana is a babe, I ain't gonna lie. Legs up to her armpits, big brown eyes surrounded by the type of natural eyelashes that people paid hundreds of dollars to imitate with lash extensions and a smile so warm she could heat up a frozen pizza.

She also had a technique that involved sneaking up on people and surprising them, so their reaction to her was amplified. This was the device she was using this evening.

Sam Harmon perked up visibly but she skillfully avoided his efforts at zapping her with his charm and was pretty much totally focused on me. Hugs back and forth as if we hadn't seen each other in months. It was last week, but she's a demonstrative girl.

I did the introductions all around and she dropped into the chair that Sam held for her. She made friendly faces at the three little kids checking her out, but ignored their father. "We were just talking about the Alhambra West, and I told them you'd been inside."

"Well, yeah, once, technically. Almost. But I have met a couple of people who have seen a lot of it."

Dana came out from Santa Cruz, California to visit me a year ago and never left. The laidback, almost rural, vibe on St. Croix suited her the way chocolate-covered strawberries suited Valentine's Day.

"And what's it like?" Chelsea asked her.

"I interviewed this guy who was in the Axelsen social circle and he'd been there a few times. Palatial, I guess is the short answer. It is the Alhambra West, after all."

"What's the Alhambra East?" The Harmons' oldest child was eager to be included.

Dana turned to him and gave him her huge smile. "It's an ancient fortress that was built by the Moors in Granada, Spain. Princesses lived there… sultans, too. And King Ferdinand and Queen Isabella, in the 15th century. It has amazing fountains and gardens and statues, with rooms that have carvings and mosaic tiles and wall trimmings that look like lace. It's *the* Alhambra, the only one. This 'Alhambra West' nickname is just something some people made up here."

"Have you been there? Have you seen it?"

"Not yet." Dana said. "It's built on hills, with thick, stone walls, so that enemies' arrows couldn't get through, and so that anybody riding up could be seen for miles before they got there."

"I'm going to see it some day, too." The little boy was a firecracker, clearly. I gave him a thumbs-up, and his mom beamed at me.

"Of course, you are, Colby," Mrs. Harmon patted her son on the shoulder. "I wonder if it's as easy to get around Granada as it is the USVI?"

"I've heard that it is," Mr. Harmon threw in. "But, Dana, what details do you have about the Alhambra West?"

"Five foot tall floral centerpiece in the front hall, changed daily. Fine art everywhere—paintings, sculpture, stained glass windows. Amazing palms throughout the house and in the formal gardens. Arches everywhere, very Moorish, although there are lots of Danish touches, I'm told. Apparently, she likes a lot of different styles. Marble. Aqua and turquoise. Phenomenal aquariums in every room. Mirrors, too—she's known to be quite vain. But aren't we all?

"Is there a Mr. Axelsen?" Chelsea asked.

"He'd be the Baron, if she's a Baroness. Or a marquis, maybe?" Sam said.

"Not quite," Dana replied. "Her title came from some other guy, maybe as many as three husbands back, she's a bit vague about it apparently. Wikipedia and all the other usual sources don't help much either. It seems like she—or somebody—has gone out of their way to put out so many stories that it's hard to tell what's what. She married Oliver Axelsen about five years ago but he spends most of his time in Copenhagen and she likes it here."

Dana's piña colada arrived and she took a moment to appreciate it. "Lots of people know her. She's never been like some wealthy people, only mixing with people who have just as much money as she has."

"Maybe she's trying to make friends." Chelsea brought out computer tablets for each of the kids from her side bag and they happily dove into screen-world.

"No one knows why. Lonely? Finding security in knowing the locals? Needing fans? Could be anything."

"Could be just basic human nature. What are we talking about? Or should I say who?" The voice came from several feet above and behind my shoulders. Deep, smile-inducing. Swoon-worthy.

"Hello, there, Jason," Chelsea shifted her chair over a few inches.

Sam shifted in the other direction. "Lots of room. Just get another chair."

While Jason went off to find one, Dana looked at me with 'well, what have we here! He looks pretty great, who is he?' written all over her face.

"Dana, this is Jason Palmateer, one of our guests at the resort this week," I said to her when he came back. "Jason, my sister, Dana."

"And there *is* lots of security in knowing the locals." Dana gave him a wide-eyed, welcome smile. "I should know, I am one."

Jason grinned back. "Have you been living in Christiansted long?"

"About a year. I work at the newspaper."

"Ahh, then we have an occupation in common. Although my job evaporated recently. Tough economic times," Jason said, using the brief explanation I'd heard him give everyone.

Dana nodded. "Not easy to make it if you're doing work that all kinds of people will do for free."

"How are things with your new landlord?" I asked.

"The man won't give an inch on the question of rent check timing. Can't be even a day late. The struggle is real." Dana turned to her piña colada for a little consolation.

"Weren't you looking for something new?"

"Yeah, and I'm getting close."

"The Moko Jumbies must be getting close." Jason pointed down the street where we could see the outliers of the parade. Chelsea's three little kids started jumping up and down in their excitement and all of us adults couldn't help smiling at them.

"I'm sure it will be good, but I gotta say I was expecting a bit more of a scene," Sam commented.

"What do you mean, a scene?" Dana asked.

"Bigger crowd, more action, more things for sale, more things to do, more music, more art, more architecture. It just seems a bit low-key."

Jason scanned the pitted concrete of the street, the small buildings and the dozen or so people strolling by. "It's not Times Square, you're right, but that can be a good thing, if you're not in the mood for a million people all competing for the same square foot of sidewalk space. And yes, you're not seeing skyscrapers or a New York City Thanksgiving Day Parade, but you take a different flight, if you want that."

Sam put his hands up in surrender. "Alright, alright, you got me, Jason."

"Hey, got an extra spot to spare?" This was going to be an evening for seeing everybody from Pitaya Beach out on the town at Jump Up. Park Lee was wearing a tight, short navy blazer over a small check pattern shirt in blue with white linen pants and white-sole shoes. He was carrying a small, wrought iron black Parisienne café side chair with a white velveteen seat.

"Yes, of course." Jason moved over to make room, then reached out to take the chair from Park and set it down beside him. I noticed a thin cuff on Jason's wrist. Nice. I like a guy confident enough to wear jewelry. What is that, silver? No, I think it's pewter, maybe. I wonder if he has a tattoo anywhere?

"Did you just get here, Park?"

"I rode in with the Harmons, thank you again, Devon and Bree, for making room for me in the back seat," he said, nodding to the family. "I've been over there, browsing through the local crafts. I figured it wouldn't hurt to take a break from the resort. Lots of people there to meet Liz, if she turns up tonight. I won't be gone long, and if there is any news, the police have my numbers."

I found the whole situation awkward—what do you say to somebody whose boss had disappeared and might have been murdered?

Dana had no self-consciousness about it, none at all. About anything.

"Do you have any idea about where she might have gone?" she asked Park.

"None. I'm quite worried about her, actually."

"I'm sure she'll show up," I said with what I hoped was confidence.

"Any idea why a big shot like her would check

into a laidback kind of place like the Hotel St. Croix Pitaya Beach?" Sam took a gulp of his smoothie and beamed a big smile at Park to take the edge off his nosy question.

"She flies under the radar in a lot of different ways," Park replied. " 'Hide in plain sight' can be a good technique for well-known people. Sometimes she goes places where only other famous people go, then everybody leaves everybody alone. Sometimes she rents a villa or stays with friends. And sometimes she just goes to a quiet, ordinary place that is far enough away from the mainstream that we don't have to go to a lot of effort or expense to protect her privacy."

"Hey, Nola."

We all looked up at the arrival of my friend, Malik. I saw Jason and Sam's eyes go wide as they took in the sheer size of the guy. He had been an Olympic athlete in some year gone by and had maintained his strength and fitness. His black dreads were about two feet long, gathered up at the back of his head in a black clip. He was an electrician and I had met him when I hired him to do some repair work at the resort. Nice guy. And very wise.

"Join us, Malik, would you?"

He grinned and sat down next to one of the Harmon children. "Good day to all. Just a few more minutes till the parade, are you excited?" Little Devon gave him a serious nod; it almost looked as though he had hypnotized her, and I'll bet if he asked for it she would have handed him her ice cream cone, no complaint, no protest.

"We were just talking about the Alhambra West," I said to Malik. "You've been all over the island, working. Have you ever been there?"

"Oh yeah." He raised a hand to signal the waiter, who seemed to know him. Ten seconds later a Red Stripe appeared on the table in front of Malik. "What you wanna know?"

"What's it like inside?" Colby was on the edge of his seat.

"Flowers everywhere, paintings, statues, big workout gym with four ellipticals, twelve bathrooms…"

Colby cut him off. "Nah, what about good stuff?"

Malik laughed. "Well, I thought the training equipment was rad. But what would be good, to your mind, man?"

"Lots of places to climb and run, maybe play hide and seek," Colby was working hard to impress this new arrival.

"Maybe some ghosts?" This from tiny Bree, who was sitting in her mother's lap.

Malik laughed again. "No, I didn't see any ghosts. But yah, it's a big enough place, they might be all over and I just didn't notice." He started to tap his foot to the music, a butter-smooth calypso rhythm that was getting louder.

"Here they come!" Dana announced.

"It's awesome." I had seen them about a hundred times but I was still impressed, every new time.

The six Moko Jumbies were suddenly in front of us, like magic. One minute not there, next minute towering above us. The first one was quite impressive, looming up there, dancing with moves a hundred times cooler than I can manage, even with no stilts. This was a large group, and no two costumes were the same. They all wore white gloves, though, and they all worked those stilts as though they were extensions of their own legs. Colby's jaw was almost on the table, his ice cream cone forgotten and melting down onto his fist.

"How do they do that?" he breathed, not taking his eyes away from the dancers.

"They've been learning since they was about the size of you," Malik replied. "They ask the young ones, 'Do you ride the bicycle? Are you scared of heights? Do you like the sports?' Yes, no, yes—and they have the one who wants to learn to walk stilts."

Everyone at the table was swaying in time to the music, which seemed to fill the street and the glossy night sky above. The Moko Jumbies danced, showing us all what joy might look like, and the people relaxed. That's what the Caribbean is, the people relaxed. I inhaled deeply and noticed Malik watching me. He reached up toward his own forehead and stroked the spot in between his eyebrows where, I knew, he must be seeing about a dozen frown and worry lines on mine. Nobody recognizes a frazzled person better than a mellow one.

"Nola, you let go," he said. "When you en got horse, ride cow."

# CHAPTER TEN

The next morning I was feeling a bit rough after all that rum. Not that I'd had all that many, really, but I don't drink very often. I sat behind my desk, answering the phone, waiting to help guests who needed anything, and appreciating the Ice Age air-conditioning.

At coffee break time, I went out on the patio to soak up a little sun and feel the ocean breeze. Members of a family getting ready for a destination wedding were having brunch; everyone looked excited, happy, and ready to spend far too much money trying to impress one another. The brunette had one of our special banners hanging over the back of her chair, proclaiming her as the bride. She and what looked to be her three bridesmaids were treating themselves to mimosas.

Maybe it's just me, but I would want to take off with my new husband to a private, undisclosed place right after the ceremony. I wouldn't be interested in hanging out, not even with my closest friends, and certainly not with my mother and father, for days afterward, maybe not even for hours. Grandma Ruby says in olden times the bride changed clothes during the ceremony into what was called a "going-away outfit." And then that's what they did! *Went away*, with people throwing rice and confetti on them, in a car decorated with paper flowers, to a hotel, or a cabin, sometimes even just a camping tent. Went away to a new life together. Plenty of time for others to see them in years to come, only one time to be a newlywed of just one day.

Oh, I get it, that the other way to look at it is 'plenty of married years ahead, but only these last few hours to see your friends at the beach, with lots to eat and drink. Nobody caring about the high cost. Everybody on vacation.'

That's the other way to look at it, alright. Somebody should invent a warning sign with flashing lights and a siren for this occasion, this fork in the road. Mother and father arrived at the table, looking large and in charge. Big hugs all around and more orders for mimosas. No sign of bridegroom or best man or groomsmen— maybe they were all off snorkeling together somewhere down the beach?

Or maybe he was in the doghouse already for something or other. Grandma Ruby said that young men these days seemed to have a lot of rules to follow and control to give up if they want forever love. She still hooted with laughter when she recalled a recent wedding she'd attended where the vows the bride and groom wrote themselves included only one promise from the bride: *I promise to consult you, if I can.*

Is that as romantic and heartfelt as it gets?

I hope not.

Speaking of romance, Bjorn and Natalya Vester came limping in next, noticeably wilted from the heat. Nice to see they were still together—that was quite a fight. Not the biggest I'd ever seen at the hotel, though. That would have to be the Shadborgs, about a year ago. Him a little, bitty man and her the size of a brick house. Pretty sure they weren't together any more.

"Excuse me, but do you know when the spa will be opening? We need a massage." Natalya spoke to me, but her eyes were fixed on a spot somewhere over my head.

I smiled. "Every day, 10 a.m. to 5 p.m."

"It's almost noon now. We went there and the door is locked."

"No sign?" Timing and attendance on St. Croix can be unpredictable, but there was always a sign.

"No sign. No answer when you phone, no answer when you email."

"I will look into it for you, Mrs. Vester."

Some hotel staff would be annoyed by this, but as Dana told people, it was the kind of stuff I lived for. Problem-solving, helping out, taking care of things—that's what I like, it's what I'm all about.

Today, these two didn't give me a chance. Just as I was jumping up to go down the hall to the spa door, they waved me off.

"Never mind, the moment has passed," the mister said. "We'll have lunch in the bar instead."

After they left, I took out my own bag lunch and set up for my break. I gazed out to the horizon, trying to write. A handsome, silver-haired, executive type walked out onto the patio, put his hands in his jeans pockets and looked around. Nice jacket, shirt made out of some kind of expensive-looking fabric, boots that would work if he were on a motorcycle. Looked a little older, a little better off and a little less approachable than most of our guests. I saw Rico walk out from behind the bar and offer to show the newcomer to a table by the railing, one of the best ones with the unobstructed view to the sea.

I had only been out on the patio for five minutes when my boss walked in. But of course, he didn't know that and if he was inclined, he might conclude that I sat at the desk the company provided, typing on the computer the company provided, for hours and hours of company time, working on my own stuff.

But that was not what was bothering him today.

"Ms. Stewart, we have a problem, do you know what it is?"

Crap, I hate old people who ask those kinds of questions. Socrates died about a million years ago.

"No Mr. Winter, I don't."

Emerson Winter was a man in his fifties who'd let himself go sometime in his teens. If he had ever had anything to let go. Obviously he ate far more breaded, fried, and buttery things than were good for him or could be processed by his system, and unlike too much drinking or too many drugs, this bad habit couldn't be concealed and didn't look cool, ever. Not that I think alcohol can't turn into a problem, but it takes longer than overeating.

Maybe this sounds a little unsympathetic. I like to eat a lot myself—why shouldn't he? But the thing was I didn't eat way more than my metabolism and exercise habit could accommodate, like he did. Imagine it's spending money, rather than eating food. Too much will sink you. Unfortunately, your mouth and your body don't always call you out on overdoing the food, the way your wallet and your credit card limits do on the money.

Mr. Winter wore the stock middle-manager dark blazer, gray pants, white shirt and dark shoes. If he was feeling really edgy one day, he put on khakis and a polo shirt. His expression rarely changed, though, when he was speaking to me. It was a look that said 'How did a little flea like you get in front of my face?' Many times he's shaken his head at me and signed deeply, as though I was too stupid to be believed. He'd often shaken a finger and once or twice, when I was doing something too slow, snapped them.

A piece of work, Mr. Winter.

"Ms. Stewart, these front-page newspaper articles from your sister have to stop."

"I can't do anything about that, Mr. Winter."

"Of course, you can, she's your sister."

"I can't," I said as firmly as I knew how. "I am not involved in her getting the stories in any way, I promise you. Nobody that I know of here at the hotel is answering any of her questions. She's getting the information somewhere else. I can't convince her not to write the article and I can't tell her what page to put it on. I don't think even she can control what page they put it on."

He stared at me as if he wanted to set my hair on fire with just an un-dead look, like they do in the TV shows. "Is she calling you and asking you to confirm information she's heard elsewhere?"

"No, she is not."

"Nola. She's your sister. Beg her or threaten her or manipulate her or do whatever it is you women do to get other women to do what you want."

What planet was he living on? I don't beg or threaten or manipulate my sister. I wonder if he has sisters?

"Mr. Winter, I can't take responsibility for what is written in the newspapers, no matter who writes it. I can take responsibility for all sorts of things happening here at the resort, where I work, but not at the paper, where I don't." I took a deep breath. "I like working here, and in fact I'd like to take more responsibility in the future. Could I please speak to you about some opportunities I've come across?"

He shook his head impatiently. "Another time, Ms. Stewart." He picked up his phone and started scrolling his messages. Evil, ugly thumb. I bet he's never been right-swiped.

My lunch was still intact, even if my self-confidence was not, and eating seemed like absolutely the best thing to do in this moment. I had packed a carefully curated sequence of mango shrimp in endive leaves, sesame crab cakes with chili mayo, crab and chive devilled eggs, plus empanadas with lime sour cream. My lunches were the best. Some of my friends and co-workers insisted I should become a chef but I didn't want to create and assemble for dozens or hundreds of people in some restaurant. I wanted to eat. I like to eat, not cook. The cooking is just something I have to do in order to get to eat, and some day, if I have enough success to eat out every day, or hire my own personal chef, that's what I'll do.

The man who appeared next in my windshield was a contrast to Mr. Winter like a Nicky Minaj rap is a contrast to a sonata played at low volume. Just wipes out the recent past completely. He was tall, husky in a hockey-player way, and although his face looked tanned and outdoorsy, he still had some sort of indoors, sophisticated feel about him.

He smiled at me. "Hello."

Hello.

"Do you work here? I thought I'd seen you in the main office."

"Yes, I do, I'm just on a short break, Mr.—?"

"Taylor. Boniface Taylor, but everybody calls me Buzz. I'm here from Montreal to cook in your KweeZeenArtZ competition." Ah, Canadian. Of course. With those looks. "I was in a vacation apartment that my assistant set up, but I don't like it much, and I'd rather be in a solid, normal hotel. Like yours, here." He smiled at me again and I was la beurre fondu. They speak French in Canada, right?

"Come with me, Mr. Taylor. We'll get you registered right away."

After Chef Taylor was registered in our best waterfront suite and on his way with his luggage, I sat down at my desk again and found the file I'd left open when I left on Friday afternoon to go downtown for Jump Up. "Scholarship application."

*In 1000 words or less, describe why you are the best selection for these funds.*

Oww. Not going to pour that out in a short lunch break. Don't even know how to begin what to say.

*Describe your long-term goals, in 500 words or less.*

I was agonizing over that one when my computer rescued me with a Skype incoming message. My mother.

"Nola! You look so pretty today. Every day, I'll bet!" I looked at the screen to see her beaming at me.

My mother had had her glory days in the 80s and 90s and sometimes sounded like she was still trying to recapture them. Dana and I joked that if we heard her say "as if" one more time we'd start screaming 'hasta la vista, baby!' at her. She'd been a wonderful mother, back in Seattle, when I was growing up. I could remember her always being there after school, at my plays, my sports events, my piano lessons and my science fairs. Cuddling me under a blanket on the couch when I was sick, watching cartoons together when I was little, then MTV when I got older.

But somehow when I turned 14 she got annoying. My 600 friends became more important than she was and we had a major conflict over whether I wanted her creeping my Facebook profile. Things between us weren't quite the same. Then my desire to see the world and be my own person took over. I was never the girl who would grow up five minutes away from her mother's kitchen and then spend the rest of my life hanging around there, trying to be best friends with a parent. I was lucky, compared to some of my friends, whose mothers were still trying to run their lives ten years after high school graduation. Mine was chill. The door was open but nobody was pushing.

"I'm in Miami, cookie, and I'll be arriving in St. Croix in about three hours. Delta."

"I'll be there. Mom."

"Awesome."

"But after I pick you up, I have to go back to work."

Her smile drooped for just a second. "Of course, Nolie. I get it. We'll have lots of time to catch up tomorrow. Can't wait to see you!"

I couldn't wait to see her, too.

# CHAPTER ELEVEN

The St. Croix International Airport is usually quite calm and charming, a low-rise, one-runway terminal with not too many people and just enough space to move between them. I've heard from guests who travel a lot more than I do that it's one of the best small airports they've seen—easy to get around, rental cars nearby, baggage out fast, lots of that Caribbean atmosphere.

Every generalization has its exceptions, and today happened to be one of them. The place was jammed, every seat occupied, lineups near the café, the souvenir store filled with people. I went up to the desk agent at the gate where Mom's plane was scheduled to land and asked why the crowd.

"I heard something about three late flights and everything getting backed up," she said with a weary smile. "Weather, it was."

I said no more. It never pays in the Caribbean to show your irritation or impatience about waits, fees or any kind of hassle; everybody does their best and everything happens in its own time.

I had asked Eleni to cover for me while I was away from the hotel. It just wouldn't work to be seen to be doing less than 110% and then ask Mr. Winter for a recommendation on my scholarship application. Shorter term than that, I also wanted to ask him for a green light for an exciting new promotions project based on the

KweeZeenArtZ festival coming up. I needed to be the star around there right now.

This trip to the airport wouldn't take long.

Through the windows that looked out to the tarmac, I could see a plane coming in for a landing. Probably Mom's—at least, according to the clock, it would be, but I wouldn't know for sure until I saw her. As the plane taxied toward the terminal, a couple of guys rolled out the passenger boarding stairs; I watched as St. Croix's newest visitors and returning residents emerged from the plane one by one. Most were wearing brightly colored shirts, shorts and flip flops. A gusty wind was whipping hair and ruffling blouses.

There she was. Average height, average build, average, even personality. No amount of wind ruffled my mother, usually. It seemed the older I got the more distinct her personality became, but I think I could say for sure—and could have said even when I was 12—is that the main thing about her is that she is a gazpacho rather than a five-alarm chili.

Mom was 55 but she still had it goin' on. I had to admit that, even though it's weird to think of your mother that way. Not that she dressed outrageously or spent a fortune on her clothes or makeup, but I had been told by more than a few of my friends, who were pretty much experts on the subject, that she was hot.

I heard it back in high school in Seattle, I'd heard it from people who'd seen her picture over the years. She looked her age but she kept up, you know? Long-ish, well-cut, well-colored dark hair, slender thanks to the same jet-fuel metabolism she'd handed down to me, about 5 foot 10 in the heels she was still wearing all the time. From a distance, through the airport windows, she could have passed for 35. Up close, as she kissed me on the cheek, I could see the smile lines beside her mouth and the worry lines between her eyebrows.

"Nola, baby." She squeezed me in a short hug. Smelled like oranges and cinnamon.

"Hey, mom. It's nice to see you." And it was.

"Where's your sister?" Not so nice.

"She got held up at work and couldn't come out to the airport today. She'll see us later at dinner."

"Is she cooking?"

We both started roaring. "Okay, mom, good to see you still have your sense of humor."

"Don't tell her I said that." Mom settled her huge bag more firmly over her shoulder, shoved her hands into her pockets and leaned against a wall. "So, tell me all the latest with you."

Mom liked to be wherever she was, at any moment, and sometimes it was difficult to get her moving. "I'll tell you everything after we get your luggage and get out of here."

"Alright, I'll just figure out which way we go to the baggage claim." She tried to read the overhead signs and tried to pick up on the flow of people-traffic from the plane she'd just left. Even though I'd been an adult for nearly ten years, she still seemed to feel that she had to take charge and figure things out whenever we got together.

"I've got it, Mom. Just follow me." But, maybe I was being too sensitive. I'd better get a handle on that—otherwise, it was going to be a long week.

The group around the baggage carousel was already starting to scatter when we got there. She pointed out her travel bag, a sleek, two-tone green and tan hardside that she probably could have carried on board, but ever since she'd broken an arm skiing a few years ago she cut back on the amount of heavy lifting that she did. I hauled it off the belt and we headed for the parking lot.

"How's it going, Nola, is everything good?" She pulled a massive pair of sunglasses out of her purse and put them on before we reached the exit door.

"So-so."

"What's the good part?" She made a half-hearted move to take the rollerboard handle from me, then relaxed and let me pull it.

"Friends are good, apartment's good, running's good."

"How about work?"

I made a face. "It would be a lot better if I could get a promotion, but I think it's going to have to do an education upgrade before I'll get anywhere."

"Good boss?"

Another face. "Nice co-workers, though."

"That's good to hear. That awful Chanterelle is gone?"

"Yeah, she only lasted a month."

"As predicted!"

"Yeah, toxic." Mom laughed and already I was feeling better.

"How about dating?"

"Nobody new. You?"

"Ha. Last thing on my mind." We had reached my dusty old toy auto, parked in the lot near the exit. Mom pulled open the passenger door to climb in. "Dana says she has her eye on someone nice."

"Really? She didn't tell me." I concentrated on making my right turn out of the lot and into the highway traffic.

"Hmm. She told me it's someone you introduced her to. A journalist, like her. Jeremy? John?"

"Jason."

"Jason! Yes, that's it."

Well done Dana. I clenched the steering wheel and tried to avoid chewing my bottom lip to bits.

I dropped Mom off at my place with a blanket and a pillow on the couch and a promise that she would try to catch a nap before dinnertime. Going from Seattle to St. Croix means you cross four time zones (I can never get the vocabulary straight, who's ahead and who's behind, who's earlier, who's late). But I knew she'd been on and off airplanes all day long and I didn't want her falling asleep facedown in the amazing conch fritters I planned to put in front of her at the very special restaurant I planned on showing her later tonight.

Everything was quiet in the resort front office when I walked in. I had my scholarship application underway and if the opportunity came up I was going to ask Mr. Winter to sign off on giving me the recommendation. It would soothe the sting of hearing that my younger sister planned to hang out with the man I was attracted to if I could distract myself with a giant career step forward or upward or something.

"Good evening, Nola."

Jean-Claude Legrande was at the edge of my desk. Sofrania was over by the tourist brochures stand, and she gave me a wave.

"We have a few new questions, can you spare us ten minutes?"

"Sure, what's up?"

"Just want to go over a few of the things we heard from guests right after the Pirates' Feast last week. Some things we aren't sure are factual, you know?"

"Absolutely. You know I'll help however I can. Things like what?"

Jean-Claude consulted his notes. "Things like we got Mr. and Mrs. Vester saying the spa isn't open at all right now."

"It's open. What I mean is, it's open right now, these are normal operating hours. It wouldn't have been open at 8 o'clock on a Friday night."

"No, they seem to be under the impression that it's never open, that it's closed for renovations or because the hotel isn't offering spa services for some reason, or…"

"No, it's open. I don't know where they would have got that idea. I'll speak to them about it."

Sofrania walked over to join us and looked at her notes on her phone. "The gift store clerk told us she saw Liz Barga browsing there shortly before the Feast started but her assistant says she was taking a nap before dinner. Says Liz was complaining that there weren't enough books to choose from."

"She might have done both the shopping and the nap," I commented, and Jean-Claude nodded encouragingly, the small earring in his left ear catching the light, just briefly. I was sidetracked—"Is that a diamond?"

Now, that might have seemed a bit too direct, for any other person talking with cops in a similar situation, but Jean-Claude and I go back a ways, too. I didn't have a hobby in common with him, like running with Sofe, but I had met him socially though Malik and had shared a few slices of rum cake here and there.

"Nah, it's moissanite." He put a finger up behind his right ear lobe and wiggled the tiny stone. "Probably as close as I'll get."

"Now, Jean-Claude, you don't know that." Sofe smiled at him in that kindly way she did with everybody. "If you actually want to put a diamond on you, somewhere, and you want it bad enough, you'll get it."

"With all respect, Miss Sofrania, that's just dreaming."

"Keep thinking that way and that's all it will be."

I felt like somebody had to get in between these two and mediate, a little bit. Change the subject. "Jean-Claude, have you come across anything that might be a motive for her to disappear?"

He shook his head as though he had to clear his vision. "Well, yeah. If you're reading the news online about her, or even the rags on the magazine racks at the supermarket, it's simple to figure out. She's been in some big trouble with the SEC and the FDA on the mainland and she might lose her job."

Sofrania stared off into the distance, in a way she had of looking as though she were gazing into the distant future. "But she also has a very wealthy boyfriend—not a good reason for disappearing, I'd be thinking."

This conversation seemed to have taken on an after-hours feel and I have to say I was ready to kick back a little. "A wealthy anything would be a good reason to stick around, to my mind. Wealthy boyfriend, wealthy cousin, wealthy neighbor, wealthy boss, wealthy uncle." The rhythm had me almost singing.

Jean-Claude laughed. "Wealthy friends, wealthy cats, wealthy dog."

"You're all being too silly." But Sofrania was laughing, too.

"What would you do, if you became wealthy, Miss Nola?"

"Get more education. You?"

"Leave this island and see more of the world."

Sofe went down to the parking lot to get the car and Jean-Claude stood waiting with me by the front door. He flipped through the newspaper he'd picked up earlier.

"Anything in there about your investigation?" I asked.

"Not that I'm seeing so far. I'm just checking my lottery numbers right now. Going to be my only road to those wealthy people we were talking about." He grinned, then started to read out the headlines: *"Road Projects Underway. Elections Board Holds Emergency Meeting. Free Flu Shots Next Week."*

"Man, that's dull. Don't you think so, Nola? I bet there's nowhere in the world as dull as this. If I had a wealthy girlfriend, I'd be out of here so fast..."

"Why?"

"You know, it's dull, it's too hot, there's too much traffic and not enough to do."

"Jean-Claude, you've been complaining about St. Croix for as long as I've known you. And I met you the second week I got here. Other people think it's paradise, but you..."

"Me, I'd like to leave. I just need the bills."

"Right? There's a lot of things I could do if I just had a little more money."

"Like what, Nola? What would you do?"

"Like I said. Go to school. Get my master's."

"So you would leave as well!"

"Yes, but not to get away from St. Croix. To get to some place else. Some thing else. A future."

"You don't think there's any future for you here, Nola?"

Neither of us had heard Mr. Winter sneak up behind us.

"That wasn't what I was saying, Mr. Winter." Did even his wife get to call him by his first name? Was there even a wife? I'd known him a year and all of my efforts to establish some casual, personal communication had gone nowhere. The more I thought about it the more I thought that it was a really good thing that he wasn't on-site all day, every day.

"Good evening, officer. I assume you are getting the assistance you need from us?"

"Yes, thank you, Mr. Winter. We're all finished here for tonight."

The three of us watched as Sofe pulled up to the door. Then Jean-Claude finished the quick scan of the Lottery page he'd been doing when my boss arrived, and stopped mid-read. His eyes opened wide. "Mine!" He mouthed the word, and then leaped forward to grab the passenger door handle on Sofe's car.

I could see him waving his arms as they drove away.

Really?

I turned to ask Mr. Winter if he'd seen the same thing I had but he had other topics on his mind.

"Ms. Stewart, it would be best if you only speak with the police when I am present."

"Of course, Mr. Winter." It was easy to say yes, but there was a 'but' coming. "But—"

"But?"

"They are personal friends of mine, Mr. Winter. I assume you mean that I can't speak with them about the hotel when they are here in an official capacity, investigating Ms. Barga's disappearance, or something like that."

He looked at me, but he looked right through me. "I mean only when I am present. At all."

The gentle night breeze stirred the bit of hair below his bald spot and behind his ears, growing long over his collar, and I let myself be distracted by that, rather than look at his face.

"In fact, I think it would be best, Ms. Stewart, if you didn't discuss anything about the hotel with them or anybody else, ever." He headed back into the hotel. "And that includes your reporter sister."

*Don't discuss the hotel with anybody else, ever, about anything, any time.* I was fuming when I got back to my desk.

How could I follow those orders? It was impossible.

"Hey pretty lady."

He was short, maybe half a foot over five, well-dressed in some Barney's clerk's idea of what the wealthy male wears on a Caribbean vacation, and smiling in an outgoing way that took the edge off his dorky line. He was over fifty or so, I was guessing, so maybe that's appropriate in that age group?

"Yes, sir, what can I do for you? Are you checking in?"

"Yes, ma'am." He pulled out a silver business card holder, took one out, and tossed it across the desk to me. *Simon Humberton, CEO, ELT Technologies.*

"My, um, how do I say this? My girlfriend is the woman who disappeared here a few days ago. I'd like to be checked into her suite—I was on my way to meet her here when I got the news. I would have been in her room anyway, once I got here, so…"

I read the card. "It's a bit awkward, Mr.—Humberton. We are holding the room for her and I'm afraid I can't just release it to you or let you check into it, without authorization." I bent over my computer and pretended to be studying screens of beautiful hotel rooms. "We have some other lovely suites available, and I can arrange to upgrade you to one of them … or do a discount for you on this waterfront suite I have open?"

He huffed and puffed a bit but in the end, took the key and went off, towing a basic black canvas rollerboard.

Mom was dressed and ready to go when I got back to the apartment. I was so ready, myself: it had been a crappy day.

"What's the best restaurant on the island, Nola?" Mom asked. "I'm buying."

"I feel like it's either Kojo's or VIB."

"Well, you pick. You've never steered me wrong."

The atmosphere at VIB was the perfect mix of casual, cozy, welcoming and upscale. Dining out was one of Mom's favorite things to do and I knew she'd be enchanted with this Caribbean classic spot. Wouldn't hurt that the chef, Paige Fleming, was also a member of my Saturday running group and could be counted on to come over to the table and make a bit of a fuss over us.

"No kidding, Mom, it was the strangest day. We had more friends and associates of Liz Barga popping up... her boyfriend, her boss, and we already had her assistant. Next maybe we'll get her next-door neighbors!"

Mom laughed. "They say it's variety but I'd say it's coincidence! That is the spice of life, I mean." She looked over the cocktail menu. "But you know, it's not really surprising that a lot of people would come into town if someone disappeared. I know I'd go, if anything happened to you."

"Thanks, Mom." I smiled.

"But her boss, what boss? I thought she was this super-achiever CEO, entrepreneur celebrity person."

"The chairman of the board of her company."

"What's he like?"

"Gorgeous, I have to say. In that 'older guy, has his own dining room and 80-square-foot executive washroom in his office' kind of way."

"What about the boyfriend, what's he like?"

"Same vintage, looks pretty prosperous, but a little bizarre, you know?"

She shook her head, rejecting the word, and I searched for better communication. "Remember Mr. Mulligan when I was in middle school?"

"The one who wore gloves all the time, the kind with the fingers cut out? And a scarf and a beret?"

"Both cashmere, don't forget we had to know

they were cashmere." I laughed. "And he always called you 'Keem-ber-lee.' "

"And he bowed to people all the time."

"Including the students!"

"I haven't thought of Mr. Mulligan in years, but I get what you mean." She said. "Harmless but just not quite conforming enough, somehow."

"Lots of money, but just no idea," I agreed. "Did you pick a drink?"

"This is the best place in the world for rum, they tell me."

The server was so gorgeous she could have been a super-model. Maybe would be, one day. After she took our drink orders, I leaned over to Mom.

"She's in my running group, too."

"Well, really, Nola. Your running group seems to be the in crowd on St. Croix."

"It's the cool kids' table, what can I say?" I grinned and passed her the massive menu. "This is a great place for outstanding cuisine. Maybe not Michelin-starred, but Paige is a certified executive chef and has experience all over the Caribbean. She's very consistent and the dishes are always great here."

Mom sipped at her rum punch. "You have so much interest in food, Nola, I've often wondered whether you might decide to become a chef."

"I'd rather be a professional eater, Mom. Although that might ruin a perfectly wonderful hobby. What are we going to have?"

We discussed our way through a lengthy list that was heavy on seafood and local specialties, finally settling on jerk chicken for her, roti for me. We had some guidance from our server, who went through the dishes one by one, describing the local ingredients in them and the special touches to the way they were prepared. After we placed our order, Mom leaned back in her chair and looked around. "Nice seats. The best in here, I'd say."

"It's certainly not Siberia," I agreed. "What's the worst seat you ever had in a restaurant?"

"It was kind of a restaurant, kind of a club, a private room for a special occasion. Somebody's birthday or something. They put us at a table behind the band and during the speeches we got to watch the drummer looking at his phone messages. All we could see. Oh—once in a while, we caught a glimpse of the back of the MC's jacket. We missed the toasts, the jokes, the stories, everything. By the time they brought out the birthday cake we were ready to hang ourselves from boredom and hurt feelings."

"Ha. There was a message in that, I guess."

"So true. What was your worst?"

"Once I was in a place that was so popular and so crowded they actually put a table inside the hallway to the restrooms. They denied it was eating in the can but it really was."

Mom laughed. "Is St. Croix big for foodies?"

"It's great. Everybody seems to know how to cook. They have some terrific food festivals, too. There's one called A Taste of St. Croix and another one called Food and Wine Experience, there's a VI Restaurant Week, there's a bunch of events called Dine VI and there's KweeZeenArtz, coming up really soon."

Our server appeared with a basket of bread, a grater, a beautiful glass bottle of oil and a wedge of cheese in hand. She prepared the side plates, added a sprinkle of ground pepper, and disappeared. I tasted—yes, asiago. Perfect.

"That makes me think of this restaurant name. Why VIB?"

Our server had returned with our appetizers— some sizzling mushrooms, fried in butter and covered in

Emmental cheese. "Virgin Islands Bread," she said. "Or maybe Bites. Or maybe Best. Chef Paige picked it."

"Virgin Islands Bliss." The voice behind my head had a smile between the tones. "My favorite song when I opened this place."

"Good evening, Paige." I was thrilled that she'd come out of the kitchen so that we could thank her directly and praise her for the meal.

"Good evening, Nola. And good evening, Nola's mother?" When I nodded, she pretended to pat herself on the back for her accurate guess. "Are you enjoying everything?"

"Absolutely." Mom smiled at her.

"My mom is quite a cook herself," I told Paige. "When we were little and we were sick, she would make crab cake in tomato bisque and then crème caramel, once we were feeling a bit better."

"Wow." Paige tucked a stray piece of her hair back into her topknot. "You must have plotted to stay sick forever."

I laughed. "It was tempting."

Paige's face turned serious. "Quite the news, over there at your resort, Nola."

"About Liz Barga?"

"You know, she was just in here a couple of days before she went missing. We had a wonderful talk. She told me all about her start at Portrush, what it takes to get a Michelin star, her dog—she's got a dog and she calls him Saffron—and her signature dish, *Mushrooms Dhaniya*. I tried to get her to tell me the secret, but she wouldn't. I've got one of her books, though, and it's in there. It's the tomato chutney. And the coriander, of course."

"Mom, Paige is one of the chefs in the international competition we're having here soon," I said.

"Not quite sure how that happened," Paige said

modestly. I didn't quite believe her; I'd never met a chef who wasn't self-confident, some of them aggressively so.

"What are you going to cook for the competition?" Mom asked.

"Oh Mom, I don't think Paige would—"

"A family recipe, using fresh fish, rum, sugar, mango, guava, figs, sea grapes, and carambolas."

Well, I guess Paige would. And Mom knew.

A loud voice came from the window that opened from the dining room to the kitchen and we all looked in that direction. The shouting persisted. "Excuse me," Paige said. We heard her name called and a moment later two of the servers burst from the kitchen door.

"There's been an accident. Is anyone here a doctor?"

My jaw dropped when my mom jumped to her feet. "I was trained as a nurse and my first-aid certification is up to date. Let me help until anyone else comes forward. Has the ambulance been called?"

"Yes, ma'am."

"What is it?" I heard her ask as she followed the servers toward the kitchen.

"One of the cooks ate something poisonous." The one who answered was almost crying. The other was so upset she was speechless. "She started throwing up right away and there's white foam all over her mouth."

# CHAPTER TWELVE

The pool area was busy when Jason got back from Cane Bay the next morning. His scuba diving plans had gone to hell when the dive shop refused to take his credit card. He'd had 12 emails from the car rental company just yesterday, pointing out that he was a day past his original return date and asking him to call right away if he wanted to extend. Oh yeah, he wanted to extend, all right. He wanted to extend his rental car contract, his stay at the resort, his bank account, his escape from his real life, his flight under the radar and he wanted to extend his chances. He was pretty much at the end of Anthony's reward points and apparently his credit card was redlined now. Looked like he was going to have to stay close to the resort from now on. Find a good book. Or borrow one. Ridiculous situation for a man his age.

Bondi was up and around early this morning. "How ya goin', Jason?"

"Hey there."

"What's on for today?"

"Well, I was hoping to do some diving or at least go snorkeling but I'm having a bit of trouble getting equipped." Jason tried not to sound like a spoiled brat, but he was disappointed, he couldn't deny it.

"Come along with me. Day off, and I don't have to teach anybody anything, just please myself—and I'd love the company."

Sweet. Maybe his luck was turning.

They were pulling the tanks and masks from the shelves in the dive shop when Jason heard a short knock on the doorframe. Park Lee was there, in swim shorts and a T-shirt. "Hey, can I join you boys?"

"Yep." Bondi pulled out another tank and started to organize all the gear. "Are you new?"

"I'd say yeah." Park pitched in to help. "Not my first time but not my tenth."

"Good. Jason, you?"

"Same."

A half hour later they were exploring beneath the waves off Davis Beach. Jason relaxed into that feeling of weightlessness and tried to clear his mind of all of his worries, particularly the money ones. The Liz Barga thoughts needed banishing, too. He moved his hands slowly back and forth, watching the bright colors of the tropical fish as they darted around in their world, seeing them magnified three times or so. When he first started it had taken him a while to get used to the way the mask and regulator interfered with his peripheral vision but now that it seemed normal, he enjoyed the startling way a fish would suddenly appear in front of his nose.

Park swam in front of him and motioned toward a school of fish a few feet away. Bondi caught up with them as they swam toward it and they surrounded the tiny group.

When they surfaced, it was all Park wanted to talk about. "Were those triggerfish?"

The dude was definitely excited. "Yep, they were." Bondi grinned. "Cool, yeah?"

"Oh yeah." Park was almost vibrating.

Jason had to grin, too. Nice to see the guy having some fun after all the hassle he'd been through since his boss went missing. Not to mention what it must have been like to work with her every day. He slid the tank down off his shoulders to the ground and took a good look at his left wrist. His waterproof watch was still there but his cuff was missing.

"What's up, mate?" Bondi saw him hunting around the surface of the sand.

"Dropped something—that pewter cuff I was wearing."

Bondi and Park helped him look for a few minutes, then lost interest. "It'll turn up somewhere," Bondi said. "Stop by the office and ask Nola to ask our maintenance staff to keep a lookout for it."

When Jason got to the office, Nola was on the phone. "That's wonderful news. Thanks for letting us know." She put her phone down and looked over at four curious pairs of eyes. "The sous-chef at VIB who got sick while my mom and I were there last night is going to be all right."

"What happened to him?" Eleni asked.

"Her," Nola said. "They think it was a toxic mushroom, of all things. They have a really good supplier but somehow something poisonous got in there."

"Good thing it turned up in the kitchen, not on some customer's plate," Chelsea Harmon made the comment a bit slowly, her nose wrinkling as she spoke.

"Yuh-huh, you think?" Nola was a bit embarrassed about laughing, but couldn't help it. "Not that we want staff getting sick, or being like royal tasters or something, but that sort of thing could ruin a restaurant forever, if a customer got sick."

"No kidding." Some sort of expression of something conclusive passed over Chelsea's face but Jason couldn't identify exactly what it was—a memory? An intention? A warning? He couldn't figure it out.

"What can I do for you, Mr. and Mrs. Harmon?"

Nola asked.

"We're in no rush. Take care of Mr. Palmateer first," Sam directed.

"Alright, then," Jason said, responding to Sam's wave of his hand. "It's just that I've lost a piece of jewelry, kind of a bracelet. A cuff. Made of pewter. I might have left it in one of the restaurants or dropped it on the beach somewhere. Do you have a Lost and Found?"

"We do." Nola stood up. "It's a box we keep in the back office. Let me go take a look. I'll call you if I find anything."

George Corelli crossed paths with Jason Palmateer at the door. I watched Jason's back disappear and then focused on George's face. Hell, yeah, what a handsome man that was, if you had no age stereotypes in mind, and I didn't. Silver hair, broad shoulders, artist's hands, long legs. Hot. Friendly smile but not a hint of inappropriate flirting.

"Ms. Stewart, I wonder if I could talk to you about Ms. Barga's room here at the resort?"

"Yes, of course, Mr. Corelli. What can I do for you?"

"I do understand that the police have been conducting an investigation and that a search has been done of the grounds and the common areas. Several searches, in fact, Mr. Lee has told me. But he has suggested, and I agree, that another search of her room and her possessions might turn up some clue that we've missed, so far. I could perhaps be helpful to the police, with my knowledge of her, professionally—particularly if it comes to looking at any materials she may have had with her that pertain to her position within Portrush Inc."

"I assume you've spoken with the police?"

"They're on their way over here now. But I wanted to let you know this is happening."

"Thank you, Mr. Corelli, I appreciate it."

"Please. Call me George. Nothing's been done in her suite since last week, has it?"

"No, nothing. I've been under quite a bit of pressure from a couple of the other guests who would like to move in there, though."

"Yes, Mr. Lee told me about that. A newlywed couple who want it as the Honeymoon Suite?"

"Yes, that's it," I said. "The old-timers refer to it as the Astor Room, named for some billionaire from long ago." I edited myself. "I feel like they didn't have billionaires in those days. But they had high rollers, anyways, and lots of things named after them. Our best suite was one of them."

"Why didn't you check them into it, once Ms. Barga had been gone more than a day or two?"

"Mr. Lee insisted that we not. And the account is up-to-date, so…"

We both looked toward the door as it opened. One of those weird coincidences.

"Good morning, Mr. Vester," I said.

Bjorn was a man on a mission and in a hurry. "Nola, my wife and I are seriously thinking of relocating to The Buccaneer if we can't get into the Honeymoon Suite."

"I'm on it. The police will be doing one more look around there and then I might be able to put you in there. I'll discuss it with my manager, Mr. Winter."

He seemed satisfied with that and I should have left it alone but I wasn't smart enough to do that. "We have a lot of other lovely suites, you know, if you really want to move. And the one you're in is very nice, don't you think?"

"You're missing the point. The Astor Room was

where my parents stayed when they were here ten years ago and we wanted the same room for our honeymoon. We set that up months ago, when we booked, then you let that celebrity chef come in and take it out from under us. But now that she's gone, it would be nice to get it for even part of our time here. We go home Wednesday."

Next Wednesday? Somehow I had it in my windshield that they'd be with us for another ten days. Why would he lie about something so minor? Or maybe this was his way of informing me that they were changing their reservation, checking out early?

"I'm not sure we'll be finished with the suite by Wednesday," George contributed.

"What's that mean?" Bjorn turned on me. "Have you promised the suite to somebody else? To this guy?"

"No, I'm not interested in staying in the suite. I have my own accommodations elsewhere, and they're quite satisfactory, thank you."

"Who are you?" Bjorn demanded.

"I'm George Corelli, the chairman of the board at Portrush Inc., Ms. Barga's employer. As I'm sure you can imagine, we're quite concerned about investigating her disappearance."

"And as I'm sure you can imagine, I'm quite concerned about my honeymoon!" And Bjorn Vester stormed out.


Jason was walking down the hill from the hiking path when he saw Bjorn come exploding out of the hotel entrance and right into Park Lee. In three seconds, Bjorn was up in Park's face, screaming and waving his arms around.

"Look! I've been as patient as anybody can be, waiting for you to get out of that suite! It's not my fault your boss took off or whatever happened to her happened to her, and I don't see why, on what is one of the most important vacations of my life, I should hang around waiting."

Park said something in reply but Jason couldn't hear it. He broke into a jog and managed to get there just as Bjorn made a move to shove Park.

"Whoa, whoa! Let's bring it down a notch." He put a hand on Bjorn's arm and got a shoulder into his chest in return for his peacemaker effort. Bjorn glared at him and then walked away. "You okay, man?" he said to Park, who looked a little shaken up.

"Yeah, I'm good. I guess he really wants that room," Park said with a weak laugh. "Well, he'll probably get his way soon enough. The police are going to declare Liz's disappearance 'officially suspicious', whatever that means and whether it's even an official term. Bottom line, they think she's been murdered."

Jason was stunned. "Is there some reason somebody would want to kill her, Park?"

"I don't know. Maybe no reason. Maybe it was completely random, not provoked in any way."

"That's even scarier."

Park looked past Jason's shoulder toward the hotel gate. "Cops are here."

I had my head deep in the purchasing orders for the coming month when Jean-Claude and Sofrania showed up in the front office.

"I'm surprised to see you, Jean-Claude," I said as I closed my computer. "I thought with your lottery win you'd be long gone. Or was it too small?"

"Oh, it was plenty big, I'll tell you," Jean-Claude said, eyes glowing. "But I'm still thinking over my options. Maybe I'll stay here and just get a fancy new place and stop working."

"But I thought you had about a million criticisms of St. Croix," I said. "I thought you were going to get to someplace better the first chance you got."

"Excuse me, you two, but could we get to work and leave all this for some other time, some social time?" Sofe looked grim. "We have to begin our questioning all over again, cover the ground again. We now think Liz Barga was murdered and we have a lot of work to do."

Jean-Claude put on a serious face. "Absolutely true. We're sealing her hotel suite—we'll let you know when you can let anybody in there. Her bags can stay there for now but no one is to touch anything. We've just finished another search, done more photographs. Did she leave any valuables in your safe in here?"

"We'll look. I can get maintenance to go in and open the one in her room, too."

"Right away, please."

I couldn't help myself, my curiosity was on a furious boil. "Did you find anything in her suite? Anything else, now that you're thinking something bad happened to her?"

Jean-Claude probably shouldn't be answering that kind of question, but he couldn't help himself either. "We're looking at the room with a whole new pair of eyes." He said. "Questioning every little thing."

"Jean-Claude, time to go." Sofrania said.

He held out a gloved hand, to show me a piece of jewelry. "Does this look like something that she would have worn?"

It was a slim, pewter bracelet, and no, it didn't.

# CHAPTER THIRTEEN

J ason stood up in the surf. The diving and snorkeling in the crystalline turquoise water near the reef were dope beyond belief; the crashing of the surf and the froth that you got here at Pitaya added a bit of drama that was really choice. He'd been body surfing for hours; the sun, the waves and the wind drove all of his worries out of his mind.

When he got back to his room, they were back. Money running out, cops watching him, no new job in sight. But he wasn't the type to get depressed about things. There was still a lot to enjoy—it was the Caribbean after all. And he was liking the people, too. Bondi, John the music guy, Rico the bartender, Nola… everybody except that Dana, the local newspaper reporter, the one who was Nola's sister. He wasn't sure what to make of her. She looked like she'd be quite a handful, and while he might have enjoyed a friendship or even a relationship with that sort of woman a few years back, these days he didn't have the energy or the means to play in that game.

Nola, on the other hand… Nola would be a tranquil morning, a quiet sky. He would like to have the time to get to know her better, maybe.

Who was he kidding? He had so many problems right now and he had no business approaching any woman, even one with nerves of steel, a spine like iron, and a bulletproof wallet. He'd heard from Anthony that the magazine was not about to overlook the allegations of plagiarism and the subject of his profile piece was talking legal action, too. He couldn't imagine why; this particular magazine wasn't known for defending its freelancers, and if his interview guy thought that Jason had any assets worth coming after he was very misinformed.

His short-term cash flow issue was rather severe but he thought he'd come up with a solution. An ad in a tourist brochure he'd seen in the gift shop featured the casino at the Divi Carina Bay resort and it started him thinking about a little blackjack or even some time at the slots as a way of staying one step ahead of a complete cash drought. Worth a look, maybe tomorrow.

His phone buzzed with a text and he picked it up to look. Dana Stewart. Huh.

> *You around?*
> *Yeah. What's up?*
> *Just thinking about going out to grab a drink*
> *Uh huh*
> *Wanna come with?*
> *Can't tonight. Writing on deadline*
> *Ah. Been there, done that*
> *Got the T-shirt*
> *What T-shirt? I didn't even get dinner. Lol*

Very interesting. Didn't know she had a sense of humor. What did she want with me, I wonder? We did share an occupation, and maybe she saw me as a brain to pick, a contact to mine.

Me, I could use a ride. The rental car had gone back, and I wanted to get to the Divi Carina Bay Casino.

> *Changed my mind. Screw the deadline. Pick me up?*

The sight of Jason and Dana huddled together over a slot machine, when I walked through the casino at the Divi Carina Bay Beach Resort to have a late-night drink and catch-up with my friend Beth, was pretty much the most surprising thing I'd seen in what had been a pretty surprising week.

WTF? She'd met him, what—48 hours ago? Okay, maybe a bit longer than that, but not much. I mean, yeah, I had thought I saw some chemistry between them at Jump Up, but then I decided that was just fear.

False Evidence Affecting Results.

False.

Evidence.

Maybe they'd just run into each other, complete accident, here. Maybe she was interviewing him for something for the paper. Not chemistry at all, just journalism. Business networking.

He and I clicked, I felt it. He was available, too, I could just tell. So far, anyway... although that might be a picture about to change.

But if I wanted him, I needed to start being upbeat about him. That's what Mom would say, and Beth, and Sofrania, and Dana, too, probably.

But that was the problem, I wasn't sure I did want him. Maybe any man was not what I needed right now (although there were definitely some lonesome evenings when I knew it would be nice.) But what I really needed was a career cure. Surgery, even. Money. School. Money. A plan.

They saw me and stopped, mid video-poker hand. I waved at them, in a fakey, jolly way, and they waved back, motioning that I should go over and join them. I pretended not to understand, then walked as quickly as I could out to my car.

As I dropped into the seat behind the steering wheel, my phone rang.

"Nola? Hi, it's Mom."

"Mom, hi." I smiled as I got ready to say it, and almost bit my tongue to hold it back… but somebody had to tell her. Help her, if she wanted to be in the 21st century. "You don't have to tell me it's you, I can see it on my phone."

"Oops, yes, you're right. We all can do that now," she said.

"I meant to call you. Did you hear that poor person who got sick is alright?"

"That's a relief. Was it food poisoning?"

"Yeah, mushrooms. They hydrated her big time and got her to the hospital right away. It's looking good for total recovery."

"Oh, that's good to hear." Mom's voice showed that she obviously had something on her mind. "Honey, would you meet me for lunch tomorrow? I'd like to talk about Dana."

Yeah. Me too.

The Reef is one of the nicest restaurants on St. Croix—Mom chose well. I got there first and picked out a table near the pool. Despite a busy morning at the hotel, I'd had Jason on my mind a lot and I was intending to hear what she might have to say about this situation. I had been trying to fool myself that he might actually be available, and worth the effort. It seemed pretty clear now that I had no chance. I'd reached this conclusion after four hours of insomnia, cut with occasional stretches of bad dreams.

My sister and I had been raised to be competitive and it was only natural that it spill over. Sure, there were probably families elsewhere that had sisters ten months apart in age who didn't strive to win and to keep score all the time but that wasn't us and there was no point trying to rewrite history.

I had started out to be a musician, back in Seattle. That lasted about six months and then I had to take a job in a hotel to pay the rent. I could see the potential, in hotel land, and I worked hard to end up here. Dana came to visit and then never left.

She got her newspaper job from an ad and it turned out she was really good at it. I teased her that it suited her perfectly, of course, since it called for a snoopy bystander, and she teased me that my job called for a thick-skinned servant.

Someday we might do something together but for now, we compete.

But always, before now, it had been fair. Men off-limits. Girl Code. I was working myself up into a self-righteous snit, pacing around my apartment and picturing calling my sister out, when I passed by the hallway mirror and met my own eyes. What do we do if the man has a mind of his own and doesn't want to follow Girl Code? What if he wants to make his own choice?

Well, what about Hotel Code? No dating the guests. Was that the rule at this resort? It is at most hotels, I've heard, but I've never checked it out. Never came up before. Probably a bad idea, no matter what the rules. Too many potential complications.

So for many reasons (the big one being that Jason hadn't approached me in any way anyway) he was not available to me. Why shouldn't Dana have him? Why did I care?

Mom looked nice, in her yellow shorts and white blouse. It was an outfit that would have been too sweet for me but it worked on her. I don't think she owned anything black at all.

We talked about Dana, then my job, and we were

just about to get to the dating discussion, when I became aware of someone standing by our table. It was George, Liz Barga's boss, and he obviously wanted an introduction. I helped them meet each other, and as he left he had a puzzled look on his face. Maybe he had met her somewhere before?

Mom seemed preoccupied after that encounter, too, and seemed to have lost the drive to get me talking about my social life. We passed on dessert and called for the check.

When I got back to the resort, I walked in on a small crowd standing in the hallway outside the spa. It hadn't been open in days and I had no idea where Fasia, the owner, was, most of the time. Six or seven people stood there, rapping on the door, with no result. Bjorn and Natalya were among them, and boy, did he look pissed off.

My own annoyance with Fasia went up like the wave height on a day with a named storm coming in. I had literally been chasing this woman around for days now. But I managed to keep my face under control, and promised everyone I would look into it.

I gave up on the spa and went into the Gift Shop. Collette was there, in her red ruffled dress and black shoes. She always looked like she could pinch-hit at a salsa performance if things got too slow in the shop. She was busy with a customer so I roamed around the place, looking at the books, the ancient coins from shipwrecks, various natural artifacts, and the maps. The store also had the usual shelves and racks full of ball caps, tie-dyed tops, fridge magnets, postcards and books.

The note she'd left me in the office said she wanted to discuss a "guest situation". Very mysterious.

It turned out that she wanted to tell me that she didn't think Bjorn and Natalya were the honeymooners they claimed to be. They'd been in to the shop to buy a St.

Croix hook bracelet and Natalya wanted the platinum version, the most expensive item in the entire store. Bjorn tried to talk her out of it but she resisted. Collette overheard Natalya mutter "call it my tenth wedding anniversary present" and Bjorn hiss back at her "that's what this trip is".

I thanked Collette and promised to check it out. Just before I left, she brought up the subject of Liz Barga. Murder? Really? Did I think we maybe should bring in better security at the hotel? She wasn't concerned herself, she said, but her husband and her mother were asking.

My head was buzzing, and it was time for me to take a break for half an hour. A walk on the beach usually settled me down. But that was for small worries, minor challenges. This would take more than the Caribbean sun and the ocean lullaby. As I walked toward the shore, I caught side of a vaguely familiar man walking barefoot at the water's edge. Was it that Ronald guy who'd been having lunch with Frida Axelsen? He was not a guest here, I would have made the connection. Man, I needed to talk to Isaac about security.

I was starting to feel really jittery. I hated to make this all about me. After all, Liz Barga had been missing for many days, and now it had officially been listed as a murder. This was tragic and much more serious than someone being denied a promotion, or running out of money, or being stuck in a dead-end job. Still, this was definitely a trifecta of a bummer.

The news about the cops starting up a murder investigation had spread through the resort like bread soaking up oil. Besides Collette's questions, I'd fielded about three dozen, coming in as texts on my phone. When I saw Bondi heading toward me across the sand, I could tell that he had already heard that we'd now officially had a murder at our property and that he wanted to talk about it.

"Nola, yo, wait up."

I turned and stopped for him, digging my toes into the sand, as one small defiant act of *I might have to deal with you but one part of me is still pretending I'm off on a Caribbean no-stress vacation.* I was also bracing myself.

"Hey, Bondi. What's up?"

"I saw the cops out front. Is something happening?"

"I guess everyone will know, soon enough." Somehow, eye contact seemed called for, although I usually avoided looking too directly for too long at Bondi, or anybody else with his attitudes and his testosterone level, in case he chose to imagine some communication I didn't intend to send. "They're calling it murder, now."

"Crikey."

We stood in silence for a few minutes, looking out at the sapphire Caribbean sea. It went on longer than I might have expected, if I'd given two seconds to thinking about Bondi's reaction to anything.

"Bloody hell."

His face was flushed and he was breathing hard, blinking fast. He seemed really upset.

"What is it, Bondi?"

He grabbed control of himself, but there seemed to be a wave of weakness go over him. "I knew her, Nola. Before she was here, I mean."

I was confused. "You knew her? Her who? Liz Barga? You knew her before she was a guest here?"

"Yeah. In Oz. We had a thing."

A thing. Wow. Bondi and Liz Barga.

"What happened?" I stood as still as I could, to let him gather his thoughts and talk. It felt a bit like watching a rare bird doing something incredibly private, something humans had hardly ever seen.

"She booked me as a diving guide—Great Barrier

Reef. We took her group to the North Horn—man, she saw all those sharks and she didn't bat an eyelid! She was something." Moments passed and he didn't seem ready to say anything more.

I had about a million questions but I managed to limit myself. "When was this?"

"Couple of years ago."

"How did it end?" He didn't answer and I decided I'd try to re-phrase. "Big thing? Little thing?"

"Fairly significant, I'd say. We hit it off and spent her entire vacation together. She brought me to New York and I stayed a couple of months with her. But it wasn't the right place for me, and I had to get out of there." He looked away from me and out at the horizon. "Then she turned up here."

Wow. Again, wow. Now it was my turn to be speechless, but it was like I'd caught a really big wave and Bondi wanted to talk now.

"It was so great at the beginning, you know? She was just… dishy. And not just 'for her age'. I took a shine to her right off, specially when we'd be toting up the damage in the pub at the end of the night and she pulled out that black card." He grinned and you could tell that he was bouncing back. "Although if I had to say, between her money and her knockers, I'd say it was the knockers."

Yeah, well.

"But. It didn't work out, so I left the Big Apple and came here. We were in touch for a while but then I tried to break it off and she wouldn't stop phoning me. Texting me. On and on. So I just disappeared on her ass."

I could see someone up on the restaurant patio waving a hand at me. Eleni. Yeah, I had had an unusually long break, and I needed to get back to the desk. But Bondi wasn't finished.

"Worked for a few months, but then she turned

up here."

"Was it a coincidence?"

He looked at me like I had two heads. "I wish."

Well, excuse me, but it wasn't that dumb a question. Maybe Bondi had people pursuing him halfway down the globe, but most people didn't.

"She got up in my face the very first day she was here. Problems for me… I actually have somebody serious now, the kind make you put your phone down, you know?"

TMI.

I looked over toward the patio and saw two men, walking in to take a table. Was that Mr. Winter? Damn, I hope he hasn't suddenly decided to come in on a Sunday, weekends were the only time off we could count on not seeing him. I squinted to try to see the two more clearly. No, not Mr. Winter, it looked like George Corelli and … Simon Humberton, Liz's boyfriend.

I wonder if they know about Liz and Bondi's history? Especially Simon?

I got back to the front office to find a whole lot of action. Mr. Winter *had* come in to work, in a complete change from his usual routine. Eleni was trying to answer calls from reporters, and Sofrania was sitting behind my desk waiting for me.

"Good afternoon, Sofe." I said. "I thought you guys left."

"We did, and now we're back. We checked, and just as I thought, that pewter cuff was not on the list we made when we searched Liz Barga's suite the first time."

Ah. I had refused to think about that cuff. Bondi's revelation had exploded in my brain, scorched earth for every other thought around it. But now, it was back.

And Sofe could read my face.

"What?"

Crap.

How much do I say? And in what way? And what would it mean to Jason? And would I care? Did I care? What was my responsibility in this situation?

"What is it, Nola? What do you have to tell us?"

I hadn't noticed Jean-Claude, hovering in the back of the office near the driveway. He joined Sofrania, shoulder to shoulder, when she stood and came out from behind my desk.

"Have you seen that bracelet before?"

I could just say no. That would be true. But only technically.

The door opened, with George and Simon deep in conversation as they walked in. The silence and the heavy atmosphere in the room startled them, and their conversation ended. Everybody was waiting.

I looked at Simon. Her boyfriend. I didn't like her much, didn't even know her except as a rude guest, but somebody loved her. Somebody loved her enough to fly all the way to St. Croix to try to help find out what had happened to her. Didn't matter, the way he dressed, whether he was cool or famous or had money or was tall, or what he looked like—he loved her enough to get off his ass and come here to help.

I had to say.

"Jason Palmateer was in here saying he'd lost something just like this."

# CHAPTER FOURTEEN

When I came in the next morning, after a restless night that featured dreams of jewelry boxes, tropical fish and Moko Jumbies, Chelsea and Sam Harmon were there, waiting. They were dressed up, her in a sundress, wide-brimmed hat and heels, him in a white shirt, linen pants and boat shoes, no socks.

"Good morning, Chelsea, good morning, Sam. You both look very nice," I said with a smile.

"Back atcha," Sam said, in his slightly creepy way.

"What can I do for you?" I asked.

Chelsea was scanning the room, looking everywhere but into my eyes. "Thanks, Nola. We just need a map."

I pulled out a copy of our best island map and spread it on the desk in front of them. "Ah, a little road exploring. Good for you." I pulled out a pen to mark a few locations. "This is where we are, you need to turn right, here, if you want to go toward the airport area, keep going straight if you're on your way to Christiansted. What are your plans, would you like me to recommend a few good restaurants for lunch time?"

"No, no, no restaurants," Chelsea said, in what seemed like a weird hurry. "Just the map, thanks."

Sam grabbed it and began folding. "Just a map, Miss Nola. No restaurant recommendations. There aren't any good ones here, anyway, that I saw. Everything overpriced and low quality. This trip has been a disaster. If it weren't for the amazing beaches and the palm trees, it would be a total waste of a place. Big disappointment, if you ask me."

Now, this was harsh. Out of the blue. Up to now, he'd seemed a bit immature, and the kind you were glad was some other woman's problem. But he hadn't seemed like one of those ugly mainlanders, who thought the world stopped and started at New York or L.A. Those people were welcome to take their money and go to Mexico or Hawaii, if you ask me.

"Well, Sam, you might want to try Hawaii next time."

He glared at me. "Nola, I like you. But we can't put up with this. Keep it up and I might have to mention this to your boss."

I don't respond well to bullies. Never have. Plenty of ways to get me to do what you want, but threats aren't one of them. All you have to do is ask me. Or persuade me. Or come at me with a gift of food.

But if what you bring are threats of public embarrassment, criticism, or financial pressure… If an ultimatum is your idea of negotiation… If you think you're in a position to tell me 'you've had enough time'… If you try to intimidate me with 'you have to do what I say, or else!' … If you try to call it 'a promise' or 'a warning' or 'options'— watch out. I will fight back.

"Mr. Harmon. Sam," I said. "This is not the way to get what you want. Be nice, or I might have to talk to the housekeeping staff about your room." Oh crap, too direct. Now he would report me for sure. Still, the pepper was in the stew now, and there was no taking it out. "It's just a joke, right?" I smiled at them both and Chelsea responded. Sam didn't; he was still blinded by his middle-school imagination of his own strength. He had none, acting this way, but he didn't know it. Or he did know it, but he refused to admit it. People who have to be right, no matter what, miss out on a lot of life's goodies.

Chelsea took the map from his hands and headed for the door. He followed her and I watched them go, then turned around just in time to see the door to the private office in the back open, and Mr. Winter walk out.

"I heard all that."

Well, great. "Mr. Winter, yes, I overreacted to Mr. Harmon, but I'll set it right with them when then get back from their drive."

He sniffed and turned to go. My window of opportunity for talking to him privately was about a sliver in size, and closing fast. "Mr. Winter, while you're here, I wanted to ask you something."

"Is it about the Liz Barga situation?"

"No, not that. But that is awful, I agree. Is there any news?"

"The police are coming back later this morning to interview people again." He leaned back against the desk; I don't think I've ever actually seen him sit down. "Speaking of news, I trust you're doing whatever you can to keep your reporter sister out of the loop here."

"I am, Mr. Winter, yes, I am. But that raises exactly the topic I wanted to speak with you about." I grabbed the flash drive where I'd stored the slide deck I'd prepared for my idea about the hotel participating in the KweeZeenArtZ festival contest. I held it out to him. "Please look at this, when you have a moment."

He did look at it, or at the tiny piece of computer storage anyway, as if it were something slimy. "What is it?"

"A presentation for an idea I have. For the hotel. It would generate terrific positive news, news we'd want to have reported, good news that would put the hotel top of mind for everyone on the island looking for a place to go and top of the list on all the websites people search when they're looking for a Caribbean resort." I smiled as optimistically as I was able, to try to balance the incredibly skeptical look on his face.

I waited probably a full 90 seconds before he spoke. "Why are you doing this, Nola?"

Good question. "For the good of the hotel, Mr. Winter. But for myself, too. I think I could be the one to organize our involvement, do the planning, manage the budget, write the collateral, handle the events. It would be great experience for me... and I'm looking for more responsibility."

"I see." He stared at the flash drive, in his palm now, and finally he nodded. "Alright, I'll look at it. But I'm not promising anything. You're way out of line to be asking me this, and you're already under review here, so..."

He turned and went back into his office, closing the door. I wasn't sure whether to cheer or cry.

George Corelli knew. I heard the sound of a round of applause, and turned to see him standing just inside the main door, clapping. "Congratulations! You managed to get that half-assed honcho to agree to take a look at your idea."

He was standing there, looking like the world's most interesting man, in jeans and a tropical shirt.

"Thank you, George."

"And thank you, Nola, for the introduction to your mother the other day. I just dropped in to ask you if you thought it would be appropriate for me to text or email her. If you would give me her number."

"You know what, George? I think I'd rather ask her if she wants to contact you, if you want to give me your numbers."

He nodded in a formal, classy way. "Good plan."

It was peculiar, but I was getting a preoccupied, even stressed vibe from him. "I feel like there's something going on with you," I said.

He considered whether to talk to me—considered it for quite a while, standing by the desk, looking down at the brochures and other items on it, pondering his options. Then he spoke up.

"You know that I chair the board of a company called Portrush Inc.? Started out as a restaurant chain, turned into a food production, cookbook publishing, television production company, all sorts of things. Liz was our CEO." He looked up and straight into my face. "And Jason was the journalist who wrote the articles that brought us down."

"Brought you down? How?"

"I got an email this morning. The Securities and Exchange Commission, which regulates all public companies like ours, is calling a hearing into allegations that we tampered with Food and Drug Administration test results on some of our products. We knew it might be a possibility but now it's on."

His face was carrying about ten years more than it had when I first met him a few days ago. "That can't be good."

"It's not, Nola. It's very, very bad."

When he left, I felt like it was a good time for me to grab a break. I walked around the hotel property and then saw Jason at the far end of the beach, passing the time with Rico, the bartender. As I moved toward them, Jason slipped around back and up the path toward Building 17. He saw me, I know he did. Why did he deliberately avoid me?

But then I got it. Of course. Because of Dana. You can't be too nice to one sister when it's the other one you really want. You have to make up your mind.

Rico offered me a rum punch, "heavy on the punch, weak on the rum, given that it is only 4 o'clock and you are still at work". I passed, which turned out to be a good choice. Mr. Winter was waiting for me when I returned.

"Nola, let's go get a coffee. I'm ready to discuss your hotel promotion idea."

He led the way out to a table on the restaurant patio.

"The part that interests me the most is this chef competition," he began, as soon as we sat down. "We have plenty of food festivals, wine festivals, special cuisine occasions all over the island—there's never a shortage of something to do. Or to eat." He smiled at his own joke. "But I really think you could do something with this idea of linking the competition to the hotel and with this idea of offering the chefs accommodation while they're here."

"We have one of them staying here now, as it is. Completely accidentally. A Mr. Taylor from Canada."

"Excellent. Let's contact the rest of them. I like your ideas on how to incentivize them to stay over here. Give it a shot, Nola. You'd have to work out the logistics of getting them back and forth to the restaurants and the kitchens where they're competing. I'll leave that up to you."

He drained his coffee mug, then got up to go. "Good ideas, Nola. You put them into action and if it turns out well, we can see about giving you even more responsibility."

And it it doesn't turn out well?

"One other thing, Mr. Winter. Oh, and thank you, yes, thank you. I'm thrilled to get this chance." I stood up, too. "Could I get you to endorse me for this scholarship application and to write a personal reference letter?"

"You go ahead and apply to a few schools, and if

you get accepted anywhere, you let me know, and then I'll take the time to write something down." And he was gone.

I was left to try to analyze this result. First, the green light for the food festival. Upside, I would get the experience, the freedom and the creative elbow room I wanted, while I worked on turning this 'KweeZeenArtZ Meets our Hotel' project into a home run. Downside, if it tanked, it would be all on me.

Second, his dodge on the scholarship reference. No upside there, that I could see.

I was starting to think about an early dinner and maybe a glass of wine. Some camembert, maybe, or a few slices of a dill Havarti. Crostini with a bit of pico de gallo or tomato chutney. Maybe two glasses of wine would be better; it had been a terrible night, a worse morning, and a putrid fillet of fish of an afternoon.

I started to close down my programs, and then I heard Sofrania's voice.

"Nola, I hope you don't mind but we'd like to use the private office."

"I think Mr. Winter is in there."

"Ah." She headed for the closed door. "I'll just check with him. Come on, Bondi."

He was following close behind her, looking like a four year-old who was afraid he'd lose track of his mommy in a crowd. Jean-Claude trailed the two of them, his head down and his attention completely on his phone.

Sofrania knocked on the door and got no answer. She tried the doorknob, rattled it—locked. That was odd.

She looked around. "Well, alright, we'll do this here. Nola, can you make sure we're not interrupted for ten minutes or so?"

"Of course," I said. "I'll just watch the door, and block anybody who needs blocking. There aren't usually any guests in here at this time of day. No new check-ins expected until later."

Sofrania led Bondi as far into the corner of the office as she could, and then turned to him. "Alright, Mr. Shepherd, what did you find?"

"I was about 40 feet away when I saw it. It was like a long box or a cabinet drawer or a fish locker or something. I admit I was a bit distracted, I'd seen a ray and then a shark and I was major disappointed when they swam away too fast for me and my camera. I barely noticed this box thing, but I almost got stuck on it. It was snagged under a big piece of coral right on the bottom.

"It looked like some kind of metal thing, dented in a few places, part of it peeled open. I swam over to take a closer look. Always on the outlook for treasure, right? Aren't we all? So I swim over and look behind it, and bugger me, there's a face!"

Bondi stopped to take a drink. "Haunting me bloody forever now. You guys are used to bodies—and ghosts, maybe. But I'm not." Bondi slugged back three or four swallows. Did he drink this much right after it happened, or was it the re-telling that required so much lubrication?

Sofrania took out her cell phone and called somebody, speaking low.

"Where exactly is it?" Jean-Claude asked.

"I can show you."

"You sure it was a face?"

"I am." Bondi took a breath. "A woman's face."

"Could you tell whose?"

Bondi shook his head. "No, I couldn't. This is so messed-up."

# CHAPTER FIFTEEN

If a Caribbean resort can ever be said to be frantic with excitement and hysteria, this was the closest I'd seen it. An ambulance, followed by half a dozen black vehicles, came speeding up to the entrance gate and after being waved through without stopping, pulled up past our front office door and cruised down the paved lane toward the beach.

At that moment, Sam and Chelsea Harmon came strolling in. "Whoa, what's going on here?"

I didn't want to deal with him at that moment but he was a guest, and I'd been well-coached in my duties. "Mr. Harmon—"

"Call me Sam, darlin', how many times do I have to ask yuh?"

"Alright, Sam. They think Liz has been found."

"Her body, that is," Eleni said. Technically correct, but ghoulish.

"Whoa." Sam had a few favorite words, and that was one of them. "Where?"

"In the sea. It was Bondi who found her. Bondi, our head dive instructor."

"Do they think she's been in the water all this time? Since the last time anybody saw her, what's that, about 10 days now? How could anybody recognize her?" Sam was rattling out the words like popcorn hitting the right temperature. "Did she drown? Or maybe she was already dead when somebody threw her in? Where, right there? Or did her body move? Was it totally submerged or floating up to the surface?"

Chelsea quietly put a hand on his forearm to get him to stop talking. If it were up to me, I'd probably do the same. He was making us all even jumpier than we already were.

"I don't think Nola or Eleni or anybody else here has any of those answers," Chelsea said. "The police probably don't even know, maybe won't know for weeks. Maybe it's Liz Barga, maybe it's not. We could all stand around here and speculate, and trade misinformation—" and she smiled to take the bite out of her words—"or we could just get on with our day and find something nicer than a murder or a drowning to talk about."

Sam didn't look convinced but he let her lead him out of our front office.

"It shouldn't be that big a deal! I am so frustrated right now." Bjorn and Natalya were next through the door.

"I know, right? If I want a massage, I want a massage."

At least they weren't having one of their public fights. Semi-public though, and they ran right into me like a chainsaw hitting a tree.

"What is it with your spa?" Bjorn demanded, in a voice that he might have used to drill soldiers on a parade ground. "We've been trying to get an appointment for a week!"

"Well, Fasia does double-book sometimes. She also runs a horseback riding stable on the other side of the island."

"Not my problem." Bjorn was flipping through one of the tourist magazines from the racks by the door. "Just get her here, one of these days, okay? Or get her to answer the phone."

I started to protest that it wasn't the way it worked here, that I couldn't "get" her to do anything, but he and Natalya were gone.

"Any chance the hotel manager would be willing to give a comment?"

Well, terrific. Three in a row. My sister was exactly the person I wanted to see this afternoon. Yeah, right.

"I doubt it, Dana," I said. "He's got a lot to do right now."

"That's fine, I'll just head down to the beach where everybody else is."

"They probably have it closed off. We've had a death here, or near here."

"I know, Liz Barga's body."

"How do you know that? Has there been a press release from the police?"

"Not yet, I'm a little ahead of the curve. That's why it's best to get here ASAP and get my questions happening."

Dana pulled open the door and headed outside into the open-air hallway. The change from the air-conditioned space to the hot air outside put a sheen of perspiration on my forehead almost instantly.

"I have a few questions, too, Dana. I hope you don't mind. I know you saw me the other night, at the Divi Carina Bay casino… and I saw you and Jason. What was that about?"

Dana stopped in her tracks and turned toward me. "Do you like him? You do, you like him! Well, listen, there was nothing to that, over at the casino. Really. He's been a bit short of cash and he was trying to add a little something to his wallet. I had to go there to do a feature piece for the paper and so we went over together. Nothing to it." She was looking over my head toward the crowd on the beach and I could tell she was eager to get there. "And he's a reporter, like me. I wanted to pick his brain a little, ask a few questions about the biz. He's just been involved in a major business story with the SEC and I was curious about what he knew. That's all."

Dana moved off toward the ambulance parked near the beach. I followed, still trying to talk to her. We both saw Jason at the same moment, walking toward us from his room. He turned on his heel and started to head back, but he was waylaid by Sofrania and Jean-Claude.

They looked grim, as they stood there talking to him. I couldn't hear what they said, but then Jean-Claude was reaching into his briefcase for a tablet. It looked as though he was reading something from it to Jason, then... my God, were those handcuffs?

They walked him past me. I asked him quietly whether this had to do with the SEC case that George Corelli had told me about. Jason stared at me, his eyes wide with surprise and defeat, but he shook his head. He only had time to mutter 'Liz  Barga' before Jean-Claude applied a little pressure to Jason's back and they walked off. Mr. Winter met them at the entrance and I heard him say "You remember, no commotion" to Sofrania and she nodded.

I watched them put Jason into the back seat of a police car.

OMG. Was he there because of what I'd said about his search for his bracelet?

# CHAPTER SIXTEEN

He hadn't expected to be behind bars in paradise. It wasn't a terribly intimidating prison cell, but his basis for comparison wasn't huge, right? Non-existent, really, except for binge-watching TV shows about prisons and prison breaks. Oh and that movie about the guy crawling through a canal of sewage to try to get to redemption.

The cops assured him he wouldn't be there long. Just the time it took to get booked—fingerprints, mug shots, etc. Then what? Get an attorney, son. Front bail, and he'd be out, walking, they told him.

When Sofrania came to announce that someone had delivered the bail money for him, she arrived at his cell alone.

"Where's your partner?" Jason asked.

"Jean-Claude put in his resignation," Sofrania said as they walked along the hallway toward the booking area. "He won the island lottery and he resigned."

"Wow, good for him. Any chance he was the one who put up my bail money? Cuz otherwise I have no clue who it might be."

" Ha. Not a chance. Your lawyer called and then delivered the funds," Sofrania said. "He left instructions for you to meet him off the premises in about an hour."

"I have no clue about who that is, either."

It took them about an hour to process Jason's release. He wandered out to the waterfront, exhausted, and almost fell over one of the chairs at a small café. It looked as welcome as a king-sized bed at the end of an Ironman triathlon. He dropped into the nearest seat and opened a menu. Oh yeah, no money. He sighed and settled his sunglasses as firmly as possible against his eyes. He had bigger problems than that right now.

His phone pinged and he looked at the text. That was quick. The lawyer was ready to see him or talk to him—where was he?

Yeah. Damn. Where was he?

The sun was setting over the Caribbean Sea and Pitaya Beach, and I had to stop to watch. The sunset was an event, every day, just as the sunrise was, and I was conscious that we all only get a certain number of them, a certain range of opportunities. Liz's death had made me super conscious of that. The sky turned golden, then orange, then lemon yellow, and the palm trees, in their dark silhouette against the changing colors of the lights, seemed almost to pulsate with beauty. Why is it that palm trees are so singular, each one different from its neighbor, each an individual, an entity on its own? Other trees, you had a grove or a forest; you had a choice of which way you would consider them, as a unit or as part of a group. With a palm tree, it was as if a unique creature were looming above you.

I gave myself a shake—that was enough time for that. I had so much to do, now that I had a go-ahead from Mr. Winter to craft the resort's event and sponsorship at KweeZeenArtz. It was only a week away; my first task was to find out whether we were too late.

"Nola, hold on a minute!" Park was coming toward me, his expensive dock shoes littered with sand

and his zippered jacket totally out of place amidst the bathing trunks and bikinis on the beach.

I waited for him to catch up. "Hey, Park, what can I do for you today?"

"I wanted to know what you have heard from the police about finding Liz's body."

*Whoosh. Man. I so do not want this conversation right now. Here comes George Corelli. Rescued.*

"Nola, Park, hello. Looks like a lovely time for a long stroll along the beach. May I join you both?"

*Not.*

"Yes, of course, Mr. Corelli," Park said. "I was just asking Nola if she had any update on the investigation about Liz."

"Please call me George," the older man smiled at his CEO's assistant. "It seems weird to be so formal on an island so far from home."

"George." Park seemed very pleased with the invitation. "It seems like quite a relief that we are finally getting some answers."

"I'm sure it was very stressful for you, to be the only one here when she went missing. Thank you for all you've done for Liz… and for Portrush."

Park glowed. "You are welcome."

This was good. If it went on this way, we'd be able to finish this stroll and I could get back to my office without having to say much of anything.

"Nola, what is the latest information on this investigation?" George asked.

*Not.*

"Well, as you know, a woman's body was found in the water. The police have taken Jason Palmateer in for questioning," I said.

"Have they definitely identified the body as Liz's?"

"Of course, it is Liz." Park was starting to breathe heavily from the physical exertion of walking through the soft sand. George was setting a vigorous pace for this little stroll. "Wouldn't it be too much of a coincidence, if it weren't? How many women go missing in the same week on an island this size?"

"That's logical," George agreed.

"And I can't believe Liz would have gone this long without contacting me or somebody at Portrush." Park seemed to be pretty intense about all this. Why?

"Well, there's a bit of a dispute about a rather large severance package right now, that might explain it," George commented. "Do they have much evidence against Jason?"

"He was the last one seen with her the night she disappeared," Park said. "He had been working for her, as a sort of tour guide/driver around the island. I feel safer already, knowing he is in custody."

"I've been speaking with Liz's boyfriend, Simon Humberton. Do you know Simon, Park?"

"Yes, I saw quite a bit of him, in New York and elsewhere. My job involved handling some of Liz's personal errands, in addition to her business activities."

"Really." George's tone was icy, but Park didn't seem to notice.

"They had pretty much broken up, though, before she came out to the USVI for this vacation. There were some rumors of a married boyfriend she had on the side, too." Park was warming up to this gossipy conversation. "I never saw any evidence of it but Liz could be very discreet, when she wanted. But if there was another boyfriend, and Simon knew about that, I'd be very surprised if he turned up here."

"Maybe you're not the competitive type. I heard that Simon was quite upset when he heard Liz was missing," George said. "He was one of the first ones we called, and he said she hadn't been in contact with him at all. Flew down here on his own, and yesterday when I spoke with him, all he could talk about was this fellow Bondi, at the dive shop."

"Because Bondi was the one who found the body?" I asked.

"Because Bondi was her boyfriend before Simon," Park said.

"Yes, Simon seems to think that's significant, and that Bondi should be attracting the police attention."

Park snorted. "Unlikely. Bondi Shepherd couldn't stay focused long enough to do anything to anybody. I think Simon Humberton is just being territorial. He and Liz were done but as soon as he saw that someone else was interested in her, or she was interested in someone else, he didn't want to let go. And he's blaming Bondi for everything that's ever happened, to avoid taking any responsibility himself."

*Well, he certainly seems to have it all thought out. I wonder if George agrees?*

"That could be true, Park, but maybe not. I think it's early days to have all the answers, but I assume that's the job the police are doing right now," George said.

"I assume they've figured it out, since they've got Jason in custody," Park said. "That, and the fact that he was the journalist who did the first interview with our whistleblower."

George shot him another piercing look. "Really."


Jason had managed to pick up his phone and answer the attorney's text. The man was due to meet him here any minute. With any luck, he'd buy dinner.

"Mr. Palmateer. Good evening." A short man in his mid 50s pulled back the chair opposite Jason, sat down and stuck out a hand. "Lewis DeLouis."

His clothes were something you'd see on a cowboy wannabe in Texas. Jeans, red plaid shirt, snaps instead of buttons, boots with heels. At least there was no hat. Ha.

The light was failing, as the sun was going down and Jason had to focus to try to see much of Lewis DeLouis's face. He was a good-looking man, once. Maybe. But obviously he'd decided to let it all go. His salt and pepper hair hadn't been cut in several months and he needed a shave.

"Tell me a little about yourself, Mr. Palmateer."

"You first."

Lewis laughed. "Alright. My ancestors in the USVI date back almost 300 years. After a brief stay in New England, just long enough to do my undergrad and get a Harvard law degree, I ran back to the sunshine of St. Croix. I'd rather live here, trying to scrape a living from the occasional real estate conveyance, drunk driving charge, or divorce, than trudge through the snowy slush and endless days in New York or Massachusetts.

"The tradeoff—and there always is one—is on the income side. Good thing I also have a boat that I rent to tourists, yeah?"

The waiter came by and Lewis asked for a couple of beers and a couple of burgers.

"Is that good? We're okay? Alright. Down to business. I'm a generalist, Jason. Doesn't mean I don't know my legal stuff, though. I like to think of myself as being like 'special teams' in football. I understand the game and I've played it both ways, offense and defense. I can sub in anywhere." Lewis signaled to the waiter; time for another. "But I do have a specialty, just like a kicker or a punt returner, and putting me in there is the best use of my time and skills. Once or twice, I've even done a punt return touchdown, when the other side got sloppy. Get out the way."

"How did you get my number, to text me?"

"Got a phone call at the office. I didn't talk to the guy, it was my assistant, Sherri. Told her your situation, asked that I set up a meeting with you, gave her your number, said he was going to contact the cops about paying the bail."

"Maybe my brother, Anthony," Jason said. "He's in New York."

"Did you call him?"

"No."

"Then it couldn't have been him, how would he know?"

"Good point."

"Did you call anybody, to ask?" Jason shook his head. "But you've met a few people here on the island, right? Somebody knew you'd been taken in and decided to post bail. Nice to have friends." Lewis greeted his beer with a smile.

"Nice to have friends," Jason agreed.

"This anonymous benefactor left a direct deposit retainer with Sherri, and the woman was so distracted by something or other that she didn't get his exact name or contact details. Mr. Smith, she said was all he said. Such an unusual name, yeah?"

The burgers arrived and for a few minutes they devoted their attention to the pleasure of eating. Jason felt famished, as if he hadn't eaten in weeks, and this burger tasted fantastic. Stress and emotional disaster will do that to you.

Lewis finished a mouthful and wiped his mouth with a napkin. "Alright. Jason. Let's get started. I've been paid to assist you with the procedural things over the next few days. I'll be with you when you do your first court appearance and find out what they have in mind. If necessary, I can defend you, although you're certainly free to choose your own counsel, if things proceed. Any questions?"

Jason shook his head.

"Alright. Where are you going to be staying?"

This required some thought. Jason didn't want to go back to the resort and answer any questions from his curious fellow guests, but he didn't really have any other ideas.

"There's a nice little studio apartment just around the corner from here, that you can use. The mysterious Mr. Smith also put forward money earmarked for your expenses."

Suddenly, this was all looking not so bad. Jason managed to squeeze out a small smile and Lewis caught it immediately.

"That's better, Jason. It's going to be alright. Lots to figure out, but today will be the worst day, I promise you. It will get better."

It was getting better already, just having someone kind to talk to about all this. Jason leaned forward toward his lawyer. "Thank you, I appreciate all the help. And if you can help me sort it out with the police, that would be amazing."

"Let's get started. Why did they pick you up?"

"Obvious. They think I know something about Liz Barga's disappearance."

"Murder," Lewis corrected. "And I'd say it's a little more than thinking you know something. I think they think you did it."

"Well."

"Is there any way they could prove you did it?"

"No."

"Is there any way you could prove you didn't?"

Jason scowled at him.

"Is there anyone else who might have done it? Someone who had means, motive, and opportunity?"

"Nobody even knows for sure that she was killed deliberately!" Jason was getting upset. "Opportunity? Yeah, I suppose I had it, that night of the Pirates' Feast when she was wandering around the resort. But there were dozens of other people whose paths she might have crossed."

"How about motive, Jason? Please think like a cop, for a little while, if you can. What motive might somebody say you had?"

Jason looked at him, hard. "Alright. I wrote an article, based on an interview with a very unhappy camper in her company, who wanted to tell me all sorts of things about data they fudged in order to get an FDA approval on a new food product they'd invented."

Lewis stared into his eyes for a full count of five. Maybe it was even ten. "With all that history, why did you agree to be her driver here on St. Croix?"

Jason returned the eyeball inquisition with every ounce of earnestness he possessed. "I. Needed. The. Money."

Lewis inhaled, then tipped his head back and contemplated some spot on the ceiling, while he thought. Eventually, he exhaled. "Alright. What happened with the article?"

Jason took a long pull on his beer. "Never ran. But that was the article, by the way, that got me fired and left me with no money, no friends, and a future that didn't hold much more than bankruptcy court and maybe jail. The magazine didn't stand behind me. I told her all about that, the day I was out driving her, and she insisted that she hadn't had anything to do with that, that she hadn't even known the media were investigating her."

"Who else had a motive?" Lewis's voice was calm.

Jason tried to match his attorney's self-control. "She told me she had an ex-boyfriend who might try to find her in the Caribbean and she swore me to silence about where she was, no matter who asked. She said she'd chosen this island and this beach because a former lover of hers was working here and she wanted to try to see him."

"And she told you all this when?"

"At the end of the day that I spent as her hired driver."

"Any woman with that much power has thousands of contacts and hundreds of stories," Lewis said. "What do you think this all adds up to?"

Jason finished his beer. "Someone is trying to frame me."

Lewis raised an eyebrow. "Mr. Palmateer." He leaned back and gazed out at the yachts in the harbor. "That's what they all say."

# CHAPTER SEVENTEEN

The KweeZeenArtz festival was something someone dreamed up 40 years ago, when the USVI was on the radar of almost no one. I read in a tourist brochure that six buddies got into a disagreement over what island delicacy was the best food St. Croix had to offer. The candidates were: Kallaloo soup. Pot fish and fungi. Roti. Conch fritters. Red grout. Coconut ginger shrimp. They organized a contest one Saturday and each one found a local cook to put forward his argument, in plated form. They nominated themselves as the judges, but the results were inconclusive because each one voted for his own favorite. So they had a second cook-off and conscripted a team of avid eaters from the senior citizens' home to pick the best.

Which dish was chosen was lost to the mists of memory but the festival continued year after year, and grew each time. When a New York financier who took his winter break in the USVI got bored and decided to get involved in the 80s, the KweeZeenArtZ Festival became a phenomenon, spreading through the islands, to North America, Europe and Asia. Local 'heats' were held in cities around the world, regional, and national winners were declared, and the whole thing ended with a week of exquisite food and good times in the Caribbean. One dish was named Best in Show and one chef got bragging rights for a year.

You'd think something this marquee would be more likely to have developed in a bigger place, like New York City or Paris, and you'd be right, but stranger things have happened.

When I went to my first KweeZeenArtZ three years ago, I'd spent time looking at their display of posters for each year of the festival since the mid 1970s. This year the graphic designer had decided to go with a collage of the artwork throughout the history, and as I sat and looked at the sample I'd downloaded I was enjoying the vast display of creativity. There had to be something here that would inspire me to come up with an idea for a way that our resort could participate in this international event, at the last minute, with no actual sponsorship money to contribute. Hmm.

I had contacted each of the celebrity chefs to offer a suite for the week but no one was interested and I was trying to come up with something else. The whole thing was built on the genius of the competing chefs. No teaming up with amateurs or students, like the reality TV shows. This contest was for professionals. The six I'd heard were scheduled to fly in this year, from Japan, Canada, Italy, France and New York, were all here now, according to the island grapevine. Actually, I should say the five who were scheduled to fly in were here now. My friend Paige, from VIB Restaurant, of course, was boots on the ground all the time. To say that we were excited about that, all over the islands, would be an understatement.

My phone rang and I silently cheered. I was getting nowhere, trying to think of a strategy, and I needed a distraction, or a flash of an idea, or something.

"Hello?"

"Nola, hey." My sister's voice, so much like my own, was very unexpected. "I was just wondering whether anyone had heard anything from Jason, or what happened after the police took him?"

"Are you working, or is this a personal call?"

Long pause, then—"Working."

"Then, no comment." I said.

"Alright, not working. Personal call."

"I still can't answer your question. Maybe I shouldn't even be talking to you. If you write anything at all people are going to assume I gave you the info, whether I did or not. But if I can honestly say I haven't talked to you at all…"

"So, what are you saying, that you're not going to talk to your own sister? About anything, even if it has nothing to do with a story?" She paused and I could picture her tightening her lips the way she does when she's about to do something difficult. "How about talking about the man we both want?"

"We don't both want him. You might, but I don't." I said it with quite a bit of heat—not because the opposite was true, but because I wanted her to hear me. "What I want is a job with some kind of a future. I want an advanced education. I want to live like a grownup!"

Dana was rattled by my intensity and she backed way up. We each mumbled a few more things, agreed that we should get together to take Mom out while she was here, and put down the phones.

After I blow up over something, sometimes I wish I hadn't. But not this time.

When Jason woke up after a long afternoon nap in the apartment where Lewis stowed him, he was so disoriented at first that he thought he was still in the jail cell where he'd spent last night. But the rattan furniture, well-filled bookshelf and 36-inch flat-screen TV within these four walls were definitely different than what was on offer at the island slammer.

He picked up his phone to check his texts and saw that Lewis was on the case.

*4 p.m. We meet with ur guy. I'll pick u up.*

His guy? Who was that? Jason went to splash water on his face and run his fingers through his hair. He'd find out soon enough.

The past few days had taken on such a surreal quality that Jason was starting to feel as though he was nothing more than a pinball in a machine. Or maybe a kid, blindfolded, trying to play 'Pin the Tail on the Donkey,' pushed and pulled around the room. Passive, confused, sightless, powerless. Every few moments it felt like he was in a bad dream and he had to do something to make himself wake up. The rest of the time he was barely aware. He was just bouncing, from wall to wall, from hand to hand.

Lewis led him down the boardwalk and over to a small dinghy, tied up to the dock. They climbed in and Lewis expertly guided the little craft out among the dozens of boats at anchor—quite a change from the view the day he drove Liz along the waterfront. The farther they got from shore the bigger and better the yachts became. The last one, before the open sea, was a superyacht that looked about four stories high, gleaming white with dozens of portholes, lining five or six decks. The upper deck was home to a helicopter.

Lewis slowly motored them up beside it and requested permission to come aboard. A slender man in crisp whites nodded and tossed a rope to them. He had them take off their shoes as soon as they climbed up and then showed them below to living quarters that featured seating for twelve, a separate dining room with a round table and more chairs than Jason was able to count. He had only a few seconds to look around before George Corelli joined them, hand outstretched.

"Jason Palmateer, I assume?"

Jason shook hands, glad not to be confused with the middle-aged guy dressed like a cowboy.

"And Mr. DeLouis?"

Lewis stepped forward. "Good day, Mr. Corelli. Thank you for the invitation."

"*The Alice Rose.* What do you think of her?"

"Magnificent." Lewis seemed to have fallen in love with his surroundings. He gazed around and seemed to have forgotten about Jason and George. Jason felt like he was watching someone have one of those 'time stood still' moments. "I have a boat of my own, nothing quite like this, but I do know a bit about them."

George smiled. "Yes, she's pretty impressive. My favorite. Please. Sit down. Would you like something to eat? Or drink?"

"Yes, please," Jason said.

George grinned, pushed a button beside his leather chair, and then swept a hand across the interior view, giving Jason permission to gawk.

Jason had never seen anything like it, not in a private home, a hotel lobby or a public institution, and certainly not on a boat. The walls were painted a soft white, with black lacquered stripes in the corners as accents. A stunning chandelier hanging above the dining table dominated one end of the room. At the other end, a ceiling fan drew lazy circles and Jason felt himself almost hypnotized by the motion. He'd often wondered about all the ceiling fans in the southern spaces; you found air-conditioning wherever you went, so what were the ceiling fans for? Atmosphere, maybe—or perhaps for the way they stirred up things up and kept them moving?

The seating on this yacht was all leather, the tables glass and chrome. A spiral staircase stretched upward and past its mahogany handrails Jason could see the galley, everything luxurious, shipshape and stowed away, including hundreds of bottles of wine in a cabinet that looked to be about eight feet by eight feet. One end of this room was covered by a 60-inch flat-screen, with built-in bookshelves on either side; the other was decorated with a baby grand piano.

"Wow," Jason said, and his host seemed to appreciate the lack of pretense.

"Indeed." George smiled. "My favorite is the hot tub. You can't see it from down here, it's on the aft deck. But it's truly remarkable."

"I'd say the entire *Alice Rose* is remarkable," Lewis said. He took a glass of wine from the steward, raised it toward toward George, and then got down to cases. "Could you bring us up to speed on why we are here? What's your interest in Jason's situation?"

George waited until everyone was served and the crewmember had left the room. He leaned forward, elbows on his knees, and dove in. "Alright, I will deal with that question, but first I have a few of my own. I think I'm entitled to answers, given the bail money that the USVI government now holds on our behalf."

Jason looked at Lewis and got a slight nod. "Alright, let's go. I am so ready to talk right now."

"I know that you were involved in the *Business Diurnal* coverage of the FDA and SEC investigation of Portrush Inc. I know that you met with the whistleblower and he was the unnamed source in the series. I don't know whether you wrote the articles but I think you're the one who gathered the quotes."

Jason nodded.

"I know that Liz Barga didn't cooperate with the

writing of the series, but what I don't know is whether she was the unnamed source."

The tension in the air was thicker than any ceiling fan could handle.

"Was Liz your informer?" George asked.

Jason shook his head.

George exhaled, considering this information. "Somehow, that's both good news and bad news. Part of me was hoping that she was the one who decided this problem had to be revealed to the entire world. Although, that would mean that somehow, for some reason, she felt she couldn't come to me with her doubts about the process and the mess our lab was making of the food testing trials and results reporting." George inhaled again, but this time there was a good ounce or two of a very nice Beaujolais drawn in, as well. "So. If Liz was not the whistleblower who talked to you, then she was one of the ones maintaining the cover-up."

Jason nodded again. "One of the ones, and the primary one."

"I won't ask you to reveal your source's name, but I will ask you whether you shared that information with your editor."

"Required to," Jason replied. "And I was glad to. I thought I was spreading the responsibility throughout the *Business Diurnal* organization. But it turned out they were happy to cut me loose the first chance they got."

"What do you mean?"

"They got a dynamite-level blast from Portrush. As you know. Or should know. Cease-and-desist letters from really scary lawyers. Senior editors being followed to their cars at night, suddenly finding it difficult to get their own lawyers or bankers on the phone. Emails received, containing threats of accusations that would be made of nasty activities—none of them true, but in that shady category of things that would be believed whether there was any proof or not."

George looked as though he'd been punched in the face. "None of this had my authorization. This is the first I'm hearing of it. Are you saying that Liz set all that in motion?"

"Somebody at Portrush did. I have no proof that it was her… but I have no theories about who else it might be." Jason drained his wine glass. "Anyway, I got fired over it all. They were spooked, my bosses at the magazine, and they needed somebody to hide behind, someone to relieve their guilty consciences over murdering every principle of sound journalism, fought for across two centuries." He was getting upset. "They accused me of manufacturing quotes, they terminated my contract, they reported to Portrush that they'd found a corrupt journalist who was just trying to build a career and find the limelight by writing lies."

"Did Portrush back off?" Lewis asked.

"They were pacified, yeah," Jason said. "I was absolutely shocked when Liz Barga turned up here. I still think she was… is… the only one who can clear all this up."

"You say 'is'…"

"Yes, sir," Jason said to George.

"You don't think she's dead?"

"I do not."

"But why?" Lewis asked. "And where is she?"

Jason shook his head. "No idea." He stared off into the middle distance for a few moments. "Seriously. You don't need to ask me that question. I don't know where she is or what happened to her."

"Let's unpack the questions on this," Lewis continued. "If she is not dead, what happened to her? Why? And how? If she is dead, and it wasn't you, then who? And why? So far, the police theory is that it was you, because Portrush ruined your career and left you heading for destitution. But how about this for a theory? Homeless psycho crosses paths with her on a deserted beach where she ill-advisedly went for a walk on a dark Friday evening, tries to rob her and kills her instead? Or how about this one? Business rival accidentally loses his temper while arguing with her? Or… boyfriend or ex-boyfriend or potential boyfriend, gets jealous. Crime of passion.”

"Or…” Jason got into the spirit of the conversation,“…she threatens and bullies one too many people, or the wrong people?”

"Or… she was kidnapped for ransom or to apply pressure to the global corporation she heads and when the results didn't come through, the kidnappers killed her.” George contributed.

"Did you get ransom demands?” Lewis asked.

George frowned. "None. Since the night she disappeared, there's been absolutely nothing.”

Jason turned his attention back to George. "Listen, if it's alright with you, I'm exhausted, and I think we're about done here, for now.” Something about George's expression and his air of authority had Jason revising the statement to a question. "Are we done here, George? I'd like to go back to the place where I'm staying and get some sleep.”

George stood up. "Jason, I'd like this to be the place where you are staying.” He addressed Lewis. "If it's okay with your attorney, and there would be no repercussions, I'd like to offer you one of the staterooms here on the boat, for your use to rest while you're here and to prepare for your next interview with the St. Croix police.”

From the ceiling of a jail cell to the skylight over the king-sized bed on a superyacht. Later that night Jason lay awake for hours, staring at his new view. You couldn't make this stuff up.

# CHAPTER EIGHTEEN

The sea was so still it looked as though we could walk out on it all the way to the horizon. It was a blue very close to the shade of the sky and the water was so clear we could see the tiny fish darting in and out of the crevices in the coral and the rock beneath. I'd picked the restaurant because of its fabulous location; the food was mediocre.

I pointed out the glories of the view to Dana but she had other things on her mind.

"Yeah yeah." She reached across the table to my plate and pinched a French fry. "This is going directly to my hips, you know that. Why did you order it?"

I ignored her and went to my second topic, now that I'd had my short moment to enjoy the beauty of the beach. "Mom is wondering when you're going to have a free evening for her."

Dana made a face. "Yeah, okay, gotta do that. Why didn't you invite her for lunch today?"

"Why didn't you?"

"I did talk to her on the phone last night. For about an hour. She's concerned about you, Nola. Thinks you should get a boyfriend."

I gave my attention to the few remaining fries that Dana had left me. "She's concerned about you, too."

Dana grinned. "Yeah, but she doesn't think I should get a boyfriend."

"She knows you have about a million of them." Several more of my French fries disappeared, then she said, "Hey, look over there. Isn't that those parent guests from the resort that I met the other night at Jump Up?"

Dana was motioning, as discreetly as she was capable, toward the back of the restaurant, where, sure enough, there were Sam and Chelsea Harmon, eating lunch. She was wearing her big straw hat and he had on the brightest orange shorts I'd ever seen. I think they knew it was me, but their menus went up in front of their faces. Hmm. Snobby.

Stuck-up and strange. Then, even stranger, I noticed a large round table to their left, seating about half a dozen people. One was my friend Paige Fleming from VIB Restaurant—and one was nasty Natalya Vester, from the resort. Hmm. While I watched, a man walked across from the direction of the restrooms and dropped into the seat next to Natalya. Yup, it was her evil other half, Bjorn Vester.

Dana was watching the direction of my gaze. "Definitely sus. What's up, do you think?"

"No reason to sit here and speculate."

"Come on, Nola, I'm a reporter, that's what I do." Dana grinned and followed me over to the mystery table.

The conversation at the table was loud and lively; it took a few seconds before anyone noticed us. Then— "Hey, Nola! Nice to see you." Paige was such a treat, always.

"Hi Paige. Hello, everyone." Out of the corner of my eye at the table at the back I saw Sam and Chelsea shrink even shorter behind their menus.

"We'd ask you to join us, but this is kind of an official meeting. We're getting ready for KweeZeenArtZ to start next week, meeting everybody, hearing the rules. This is Cathleen, the contest director. "

"These are the competitors?" I asked, looking over the group. Bjorn wasn't meeting my eyes.

Aside from those two, it was a totally interesting group. George Corelli, the Portrush company honcho, was sitting beside Paige. Frida Axelsen, the strange Danish aristocrat who owned the Alhambra West, was sitting beside Cathleen.

"Hello, Miss Stewart." Natalya was on her feet and in my face, no hesitating.

Backatcha. "Mrs. Vester. I had no idea you were here for KweeZeenArtZ."

"Bjorn and I are executive chef/owners of *Block* in New York," she said proudly. "We qualified for the St. Croix competition during the winter but we didn't want it known that we were entered. Didn't want the distraction while we were building our new place."

"And while we were having a wedding and a honeymoon." Bjorn looked at her with what might have been a loving look, but to me, seemed like a smirk. I just didn't like him somehow.

A crash came from the direction of the kitchen and the six chefs winced. We could hear the voice noise level rising.

I tried to divert the attention. "So, is this the entire group, then, or is it a much bigger crowd, like on *Best Chef*?"

"Six is what we do," Cathleen explained. She was dressed all in red, silk scarf to high tops. It was an outfit that could take some analyzing, but the overall effect was contrast, flash and smarts. "We have six spots and the chefs who fill them have worked their way up through a series of national and continental qualifying events."

"So, are Mr. and Mrs. Vester competing against one another?"

"We made a special arrangement for this year,

because they work together and they've entered and won all the events leading here as a team."

Silence in a glaze over the table—nobody was meeting anybody else's eyes.

I looked around the table at the others. "And is everyone okay with that?"

A roundish fellow in a brown leather jacket with a fringe spoke up. "It is unusual, to be sure." Strong Italian accent. "But I believe it is is more difficult to cook with someone else than alone and I think we will see that they pay a price for trying to be a team."

"I checked the rules and it's allowed, so what can we do?" A shrug from the tall man sitting next to Cathleen. Oh, yeah. It was that Chef Taylor who had checked into the hotel.

A Japanese man stood and reached across the table toward me, hand extended. "Pleased to meet you, Miss Stewart. Hisashi Mizuno."

Dana smiled. "So. I count five entries then." She nodded at the tall man beside Cathleen. "You're the Canadian, right? You make five, if we count Bjorn and Natalya as one entry. What happened? Did someone not show up? Or is number six the person we hear shouting in the kitchen?"

They all looked at her and I felt compelled to make an introduction. "This is my sister, Dana Stewart, by the way. She's a reporter with the *St. Croix Times.*"

Everyone sat up a little straighter and Cathleen beamed back at her. "Very nice to meet you, Ms. Stewart! We're always so pleased to have the press out to cover our festival, and we have quite a few people coming from the mainland this year, too, from Miami, from Atlanta, from New York. Food writers from all over the world, some of the top food and wine critics in the world—"

The screaming from the kitchen had become

intense and every person in the restaurant now couldn't avoid paying attention.

"Lots of people cook with bitter melon!" The voice was high-pitched and self-assured.

"It tastes like poison!" The answering tones were also shrill, and even more certain.

"What is the prize for the best dish?" Dana was working hard to stay the focus of their attention. "Or is it for a dish?"

"A menu. Three courses. And an homage to a famous Caribbean chef. Alberta Fernandina. " The Italian stared at the kitchen door, his curiosity on high heat, like everyone else's in the room. Chefs were notoriously volatile, although that might be just a stereotype. But these two, in this argument, certainly sounded passionate.

"We're fortunate this year to have two top-level sponsors, Portrush, of course, but an additional major supporter, one that has stepped forward very recently. The winner will receive the award provided by Portrush, but this year the prize will include $100,000 recently contributed by our new title sponsor, MediTek. This will all be in a press release that we're putting out first thing tomorrow morning."

"It's a bit last-minute, isn't it?" Dana pointed out. "Too short notice for most of the mainland media outlets to make arrangements to get over here to cover it."

"We'll do better next year."

Dana tried to shoot me a look, but I refused to make eye contact. MediTek? Simon Humberton's company. So maybe he wasn't in St. Croix just because his girlfriend had disappeared?

"So MediTek is the new donor of a big chunk of the prize. How does the judging work?" Dana didn't have her notebook or phone out, but I could tell she was storing up all these details for something she'd be writing later tonight.

"Four categories—appetizer, main, dessert and overall menu." Hisashi anticipated Dana's next question. "The judge is Marty Michener from *Gourmet Force* magazine."

"Marty?" Gennaro stopped halfway through a reach toward the breadbasket. "I was told it was the person who writes the Poisoned Pen column."

Cathleen lifted the wicker container and offered it in his direction. "The identity of our judge is actually confidential. Adds a little drama at the end and lets that person do their job without any distractions."

"Only one judge?" Dana asked.

"Only one judge," Cathleen confirmed.

The group shared a laugh that was lost on me, but I didn't have long to think about it. I saw Sam Harmon waving at his server, trying to get the bill. His wife had her head down, pulling her bag off the back of her chair and then pushing her phone into it.

"Did you bring Noriko with you on this trip?" Cathleen inquired of Mr. Mizuno.

"I did, but she is gone." Mr. Mizuno looked quite upset. A girlfriend?

"No, really? I'm so sorry. That is terrible for you. What happened?" Mr. Bianchi looked concerned, too.

"She disappeared after I arrived on St. Croix. We reported it to the police but there's been no solution, no help."

"What will you do, instead?" Chef Taylor asked. That was kind of a weird question.

"I'll have to get something to replace her, I suppose."

Say, what?

Chef Taylor nodded. "There's a good place in Christiansted. I saw it the other day, when I was shopping.

Near the boardwalk. Some real beauties there. How much of a curve do you like?"

Dana looked at me and even though her facial muscles didn't move, I could imagine I saw her jaw drop.

"The curve is less important to me than the steel. Mine is irreplaceable."

"Did you bring an alternative?"

Okay, now I was completely confused. Chef Taylor saw it on my face. "He's talking about a knife. He calls it 'Noriko', after his daughter."

Now I really couldn't make eye contact with Dana.

"Noriko the knife," Dana said. "Any clues about what happened to her?"

Chef Muzino was just shaking his head when the two fighting chefs came stomping out of the kitchen. Man, this was a restaurant with a lot of action.

"It's my menu tonight, Don! Mondays are mine!" The woman had a blond Mohawk, tattoos on both her forearms and a deeply wounded look on her face.

"And that kitchen is mine! No bitter melon! No poison!" The man was short and old. Both wore chef's whites and each carried a knife.

"Isn't this kind of a weird thing to hear, after what just happened at your place last week?" I whispered to Paige.

She looked at me without understanding, then the answer hit her. "Oh, I forgot! You were there for that. We thought it was toxic mushrooms, but it turned out to be a hoax, a prank. Couple of the sous-chefs just blowing off steam."

"I wondered why we didn't see anything about it on the news," I murmured to Dana.

Then the spotlight turned on Bjorn and Natalya. "How exactly are you going to cook together?" I asked.

"It is like a dance," Natalya declared.

"I thought it might be more like a scene in an American movie," the Italian chef commented. "You are tied together, like captives, and you have to move around the kitchen as one. Very slow, no running, no reaching, much shouting."

"We move as one, yes, but smoothly, quickly," Natalya said, focusing her narrow, unfriendly eyes on the man. "What is your name again, Mr.....?"

She read the paper nametag stuck to his left lapel. *Hello my name is Gennaro Bianchi.* "Mr. Bianchi." She squinted at him. "I know you! You are Gennaro Bianchi. The one who cheated in the 2014 competition in Cannes."

"I did not cheat. Not then, not ever." Mr. Bianchi seemed a bit dazed by the sudden attack. The smiles on everyone else at the table faded. Suspicion flared like a grease fire.

"You did." Natalya seemed to be one of those who fling false accusations around, leaving her victims trying to prove a negative and her associates to try to deal with her demands for backup. "Bjorn heard the same information, he knows, he can tell you."

Bjorn obliged. "It is true."

"No, it is not!" Gennaro Bianchi was on his feet. "Cathleen, this is unacceptable! She can't just ignore the facts like that!"

Cathleen tried to reduce the tension with a joke. "Oh, yes, we can, they do it in Washington, we can do that here all day long." Chef Bianchi didn't smile. Cathleen tried again. "Come now, everyone... children, let's play nice. It's going to be a long week, otherwise." She grinned as she said it and seemed to get away with calling them children; maybe it was something about the red high-top shoes.

"She is absolutely right." George's tone was

friendly but commanding. "This culinary competition has to be about making incredible food, not settling old scores. Run through it for us, Cathleen, please—timing, rules, order of things, personnel, and so on."

Cathleen nodded. "Thank you, Mr. Corelli."

"George."

"George." Again, that megawatt smile. "Mr. Bianchi from Italy is our contestant number 1. Mr. Taylor from Canada number 2. Ms. Fleming from the USVI number 3. Mr. Mizuno from Japan, number 4, and Mr. and Mrs. Vester, together, as number 5."

"And number 6?" Dana's furrowed forehead could only mean that she was memorizing details furiously.

George and Cathleen exchanged a look. "I have to walk carefully here," George said. "Our contestant number 6 goes by the name Frank Vatel. You'd know his real name if I told you, but he will be here using an alias."

"Will be here?" Dana was alert, I'll give her that.

"Any minute." George nodded confidently at her. "Yes, I know it's getting a little late but we have no concerns. He'll be here when everything gets underway at the festival."

"And why the secrecy?" Dana asked.

"He is so well-known, it's necessary."

Boniface Taylor looked up from his inspection of the menu. "Most of us are quite well-known," he said mildly.

George nodded toward Boniface in recognition. "Yes, of course, Chef Taylor. Of course you are. In your home country, Canada, and famous throughout the culinary world. But in Chef Vatel's case we're talking about a whole other pack of complications. Believe me, it's best he not identify himself. Best for him, best for the integrity of the competition, and best for all of you. We want to keep the focus on the food and on the importance of this event, this year, being held on this island."

He turned to include Frida Axelsen. "At the amazing home of Lady Axelsen, without whom we couldn't have pulled this off and to whom we are especially grateful."

"Not Lady Axelsen, please. Just call me Frida."

"We Americans aren't at our best with titles," George smiled.

"It isn't Lady, but more to the point, it's just too formal," Frida said.

"Alright, Frida. What can you tell us about your home, how it will be used for the festival, where the chefs will be cooking and so on?"

"You'll understand, I'm sure, that some areas will be off-limits," she said. "It's just too large to open up and air-condition the entire building. But the signage will be excellent and it will be very clear to the guests where they are to go. We have expanded the kitchen, which is already quite large, into a space that can accommodate six… seven…." She nodded at Bjorn and Natalya "… quite easily. And tell me, Cathleen, how early should we be ready to open up for the first activities?"

This was my opening. I had been leaning from foot to foot for almost half an hour now and no one had invited us to sit down. I think we had stayed too long, anyway. "You all have a lot to discuss and Dana and I should go. Best of luck, everyone."

After a few waves and nods, we were on our way through the restaurant front door. Dana wanted to wander back into the kitchen to interview the fighting cooks but I managed to convince her that she probably wouldn't get much cooperation. We walked down to the Frederiksted waterfront to enjoy the ocean air and the sunshine.

Ten minutes later, Bjorn and Natalya emerged from the restaurant. They spotted Dana and me, despite my effort to avoid them by bending over and pretending to tie my shoe. That's what the detectives do in the movies, right? Except they usually aren't wearing an open-toed, sling back pump.

"Nola!" No question, I never would have made it as a spy.

I didn't want to talk to them but apparently it couldn't be avoided. They wanted to talk to me.

"Nola, you need to know more about Chef Bianchi, what kind of person he is!" Natalya's face was about six inches from mine and I had an insane urge to punch it.

Now, I am not a violent person and not one who takes a dislike to very many people. But for some reason there were quite a few in this bunch who should be on the naughty list, IMO. And not in the good way.

This one seemed to think that bullying and threatening me would get her her way. Maybe because it worked with her husband? (If he even was her husband. I'd heard so much exaggeration and so many lies presented as fact from this woman that I didn't believe anything from or about her.) Maybe because she enjoyed bullying people? Whatever. I wasn't interested.

"Nola, something has to be done about this! You know the island, you know the people, what's the way to go on this? Gennaro Bianchi can't be allowed to participate in this competition!"

"I'm sure the organizers have checked everything out and have everything under control," I said with as much ice as I could.

I could feel Dana shifting beside me, suppressing every nosy journalist bone in her body. *Keep quiet, don't ask any questions,* I silently ordered her. *This is my world and if you stomp around in it, you'll mess it up for me.*

"I'm not so sure of that," Bjorn said. "We sent an email about him to Cathleen Piper and we got no reply."

"When was this?" I asked.

"Yesterday, when we saw his name listed for this competition," Natalya answered.

"Maybe Ms. Piper is still thinking about her reply."

"For 24 hours?!" Natalya was exasperated. "She's had enough time!"

"Says who?" asked Dana.

"Did you tell Miss Cathleen you sent the email? And who you were?"

She looked slightly uncomfortable. "No, but she knows now. Everyone will know that we are here now." She looked Dana in the eye. "But that's alright. The time for people to know is now. Look. We are the underdogs in this contest. We are up against wealthy, famous people who will leave us starving if they can. The best defense is a good offense, and that's what we have going on. If we don't defend ourselves, no one else will."

Dana's skepticism could have filled a moat. "Don't you think you're taking this way too far? This is a cooking competition, for Heaven's sake. It's not war."

Natalya's intensity got weirder. "They just better watch their step, that's what I'm saying. We know things about Gennaro Bianchi and we know things about Boniface Taylor and we won't hesitate to tell."

Dana was uncomfortable and I was downright creeped out. "This has nothing to do with me, Natalya. But I will give you my opinion—making unfounded, unproven accusations is a crime. It's called defamation and it can get you in a lot of trouble." I stood up. "This is all way above my pay grade. We have to go now. Come on, Dana."

She didn't need to be invited twice, and in minutes we were on our way out of Frederiksted.

# CHAPTER NINETEEN

Jason could see the sun setting from his lounge chair on the *Alice Rose's* deck and the moon promised to be a glorious replacement in a very short time. For about two hours, he had been rethinking his decision to stay there and take George's help. He'd had a brief chance to talk it over with Lewis, his new best friend. Yes, there was wisdom in Lewis's explanation of the reason for George's invitation—"better to have you inside the tent, making trouble for people on the outside, than have you outside the tent, making trouble for me in here."

But was that the way George thought?

When his host joined him topside, Jason had decided that the best idea was just to outright confront him.

"George, why am I here?" Jason asked, accepting the glass of brandy that George held out to him.

George ignored the question. "It's not that easy to build a company," he said. "I started Portrush Inc. in the 1970s, and the biggest jump for me was learning to manage teams, rather than individuals. I had no trouble with vision, mission, desire. Risk was my middle name, and I could borrow money, spend and invest without staring obsessively into the rear-view mirror, like most people do."

They sipped their brandies for a few minutes and Jason thought about George's words. He did try to avoid the regrets and the rear-view mirror but sometimes it was hard to do.

"I've spent millions over the years," George continued. "We call it an investment, but it's only an investment if there's a return on it. If there isn't, it's just one more expenditure. Yes, there might be a lag time after you spend the money while you wait to see the return. But that can't be too many years. Maybe not even too many months. You can go bankrupt, waiting for an expense to turn into an investment. Going bankrupt might be a sexy thing to talk about, once you're up on a pile of billions again, but believe me, you'd rather talk about it than actually do it."

They sat in a silence that felt companionable, somehow. Jason had no idea what this had to do with anything, but he had a feeling things would become clear, eventually. He was feeling just so happy to have a break from all the screwed-up emotions of the past few days. He was past the initial chaos and blinding fear that followed the false accusation made against him. Those first few hours he'd been in some sort of shock, he was sure of it. Now that he was calmer and not so terrified, he had a million questions: why hadn't he denied everything, screamed out his innocence, over and over? Why was he so frozen? Why had he let Liz speak to him at all, that night at the Pirates' Feast? Why had he taken the job, driving her around? He wasn't guilty, why did he feel guilty, in some way? Because he hadn't protected her, because he was supposed to protect everybody? God, he'd be a banquet meal for a psychotherapist. Or a cop.

"Do you see that yacht over there, Jason?" George pointed out a catamaran brightly decorated with colored lights outlining its sails and rigging. The name *Pivot*, painted in glitter gold on the white fiberglass, stood out almost as luminously as the lights shining across the black water from the harbor entrance buoys.

"Can't miss it."

"Guess who it belongs to."

Jason hated that kind of game, but he was beholden here so he played along. "Lady Gaga? Tiger Woods? No, wait, that would be *Divot.*"

"It belongs to one of the chefs in our KweeZeenArtZ cooking competition."

"Wow. I had heard that celebrity chefs brought in a lot of dough but that's incredible."

"And your wordplay is killing me here," George grinned at him. "But at least you didn't say 'pardon the pun'."

"Yeah." Jason finished off his brandy. "That yacht must be worth—what, two million?"

George laughed. "Try 100 times that. And the yacht is just the beginning. You should see the guy's Ferrari."

"So. Who is it?"

"Frank Vatel is his name. For now. We've all been waiting for him to get here, and his boat sailed in this afternoon." George waited for a moment while a steward suddenly appeared and refilled their glasses. Damn—there must be a call button somewhere here that Jason hadn't seen.

"He's the key to everything, Jason. If your curiosity starts to open your eyes, he's the direction to look."

Jason stared at George for a few seconds; the guy certainly seemed concerned, and friendly—was he really someone to trust?

It had taken Jason all of two minutes to consider and accept George's invitation to stay on board the *Alice Rose.* Was that wise? He'd feel a lot more confident if he knew George's motivation.

Confidence was not one of Jason's go-to emotions

these days. And what did he mean by 'Frank Vatel is his name … for now'?

"I'm going to tell you a few things but I have to know that I have your full confidence and full loyalty," George continued. "From a journalist to a source, if nothing else. You cannot … and I stress… cannot!... pass along any of what I am about to tell you. You can't write about it, you can't change a few details and call it fiction, and you can't reveal my name."

Jason let a few minutes pass. This was a conversation to take totally seriously. "You have a deal."

The evening hours poolside at the resort were magical every night, with few people seeking the lounge chairs and almost no one ever in the water. Colored lights turned the deck and the water purple, then aqua green, then pink. The spotlights on the steps, the walls, and the red roofs of the resort created even more of a dreamlike quality than the bright sunshine, blue skies and palm trees delivered in the daytime. From my lounge chair, I could see Park Lee and Bondi Shepherd having dinner together on the patio, deep in conversation over their drinks. They saw me, too, and waved me over.

Sure, why not?

"So, Bondi," I said as I sat down, "have you heard anything from Jason Palmateer?"

"Not a word. Didn't really expect to. We were diving with him a few days ago," he said, indicating Park, "and we've had drinks a few times, but I wouldn't call him a mate. Not the sort you'd call to bail you out of jail, anyway."

"What do you think of them arresting him?" I asked. "I was totally shocked."

"Isn't that what people always say?" Park commented. "When the media go to interview the next-door neighbors. 'Oh, he seemed like such a nice, normal guy.' Nobody really ever knows anybody."

I shrugged. "I don't know, Park. I'd say, it varies. Jason *did* seem like a nice, normal guy. But the police know what they're doing. They must have something pretty conclusive, since they've made an arrest."

"Gives me a bit of space, I'll tell you that." Bondi stared off into the distance for a moment, as if immersing himself in a memory.

"What do you mean?" I asked.

"It's pretty much common knowledge now that Liz and I had a relationship in the past."

"So?"

"Quite a few people have been looking at me quite suspiciously lately, and I think it's because Humberton is going around telling them that I treated her badly."

"And did you?"

"Not likely!" Bondi slammed back the rest of his beer. "We had our ups and downs, like anybody, but once it was more downs than ups, I called it off."

"Did she come here to see you?" I asked.

"That's what Humberton is insinuating. I don't think that's true. I think it was just one of those cosmic coincidences, you know? "Of all the gin joints in all the world..." We both turned up in St. Croix for different reasons. Paths cross, you know?"

"What did she say when she saw you?"

"That she had a few things she wanted to say to me, you know that kind of stuff. But I stayed out of her way."

He was becoming quite heated. It sounded a lot like what I could imagine him saying during the police questioning.

"I didn't see the two of them together at all either, and I was with her almost constantly that week," Park offered. "Except for that day she went off driving around the island with Jason. And for part of the evening at the Pirates' Feast, when she asked him to walk her back to the suite." His mood was sinking. "And that was the last time I saw her."

"I've heard that Simon is going around pointing fingers at Jason, too," I said. "But that he thinks the police should have taken you in, too."

"If people want to start looking at Liz's old boyfriends, there's quite a few more than me to consider," Bondi continued. "Old and new. There's at least one, right now, so I'm told."

"Yeah, Simon Humberton."

"He's the official one. But I hear there's another guy, too, somebody really famous, going by an alias."

"Sounds like she was a complicated woman," I commented.

"Oh, yes, she was," Park agreed.

"Did all this stuff about Liz's death come up at the chefs' meeting you dropped by in Frederiksted?" Park asked.

"No." *How had Park heard about that?*

"I guess things are going to start to pop around here, with the cooking competition coming up and all these celebrity chefs arriving in town," Bondi said. "Might make it hard for the cops to keep their eye on the ball."

"I think Frida Axelsen will keep a lid on everything," I commented. Park and Bondi exchanged looks.

Park cleared his throat. "Frida was responsible for

Liz and Bondi breaking up, Nola. She disapproved, thought Bondi was too young or something, so she arranged to put someone new in his path."

"The decision to leave New York kinda got made for me," Bondi added.

Park rolled his eyes. "Well, not really. You did have a choice. We all, always, have a choice."

George and Jason had been talking for hours and Jason still had not run out of questions. He was not regretting his pledge of confidentiality, but man, this was some story. He wasn't one of those reporters who got into the game in the first place because he loved to pass on the information that he dug up or stumbled on. He was content to know the story for himself, and for its own sake—but man, this was some story.

"So, how is he going to participate in the competition without being identified?" he asked as he sipped at the third brandy George had so kindly supplied.

"Disguise. Maybe just a mask or maybe something complete, in case somebody there recognizes his walk, or his build, or his style or something."

"The KweeZeenArtz people are all on board with this?"

George smiled. "Cathleen Piper is very cool. She's making everything happen."

"And she's cool with the reasons for all this?"

"She wants a smooth competition. And she wants the four hundred grand that Portrush is putting up for the prize."

"Whoa. Lotta cash. I had no idea a cooking contest could have that much at stake."

"You should get out more. It's not that much, either. The big league is baking. You can go for a million there." George's eyes went as round as Jason's. "Yeah, I know. Shaking my head."

"Literally."

"So. We have a guy who's an incredibly big international deal coming to compete here, and he wants to win, legit."

"Does he want the prize money, by the way?"

"He doesn't need it, but who wouldn't want it?" George grinned.

"What does any of this have to do with me?"

"I don't think Frank Vatel is the only one competing in this contest incognito."

# CHAPTER TWENTY

When Dana called me to talk about her evening, I thought I was in for another in a long series of sister narratives about party times. And it started out that way. She'd been at the Parched Pirate lounge in Frederiksted. As she was leaving she saw one of the visitor competitor chefs climbing up out of the water. Looked like he'd swum in from a boat. Why would he do that?

After I finished talking to her, I drove down the road to Rainbow Beach, one of my favorite places when I feel like crap—or when I feel good, too. It's just a prime place to be. I spread out my beach blanket, a cold drink and a good book. The sun was strong and warm, and when its rays were suddenly blocked, I was surprised by the arrival of a cloud. The weather forecast for today hadn't said anything about anything but clear skies.

But it wasn't the advent of a cloud, it was the arrival of Park Lee. He towered above me, blocking my light.

"Mr. Lee," I said, trying to make a joke of it, "are you following me?"

"Yeah, call me Stan," he joked back. "No, I've been meaning to visit this beach since the day we got here. I read about it in one of the brochures. Nice, huh?" he said, looking around.

"Very nice," I agreed. "One of my favorites. Are you here to dive?"

"No, just hanging out. Trying to process all this new information about Liz."

I nodded. "It's a lot to take in."

He dropped to sit beside me on my beach blanket.

I smiled at him, with what I hoped was a comforting look. "Do you think she might have committed suicide, Park? Over the embarrassment of being exposed? Maybe the prospect of even more bad news to come?"

"Maybe," he said. "I mean, I was her assistant, not her therapist or her boyfriend. I don't know." He stared out at the horizon. "But I have to say…she was not a nice lady, let's face it. I think it's more likely that someone decided it was time for her to say good-bye, permanently."

When my mother arrived at my apartment later that morning, the first order of business was to pass along to her George Corelli's request for her phone number or her email. She ducked. I told her it might be good for her; she ducked again. She started to roam around my apartment, restlessly. Obviously, the topic made her nervous.

I tried to keep an eye on Mom but it wasn't easy. She had a way of gliding from spot to spot, picking things up and setting them down, examining them, touching them. My laptop, my mongoose figurine, a wine glass, a book. All the while talking and all the while giving off an attitude of authority that was hard to challenge. She had an expression of wide-eyed guiltlessness that I was just too exhausted to defend against. I tried glaring fiercely at her each time she touched something and got that "Who, me?" look every time.

"Mom! Sit. Relax. Could I make you some tea?"

"That would be nice, sweetie. Tea and a bowl of ice cream."

I went off into the kitchen to make the snack. When I returned she was hovering over my desk and she jumped when she saw me.

She'd brought a magazine with her—*Gourmet Force*. I picked it up from the coffee table, and shoved it into her hands, trying to distract her. For a while, it kept her occupied.

"Have you read this "Poisoned Pen" column? She's quite hilarious, this writer. Hard to tell whether she likes cooking, particularly, or restaurants, or even eating. But she's entertaining as hell," she said.

"Yes, I read it all the time. Mom, I want to talk to you again about Mr. Corelli. He seems really nice, just right for you. You should give him your contact info." Her eye contact had me fading a bit. "I'm just sayin'."

"So you've said. Let's go out," she replied.

So, that was a no. I started to ask her why, and what was wrong with him, but stopped when I realized how grouchy I would be if she asked me the same questions.

We found a lovely table at an outdoor café on the boardwalk, and within minutes of settling in, I noticed Sam Harmon facing the harbor on a bench nearby, alternating between reading the magazine in his left hand and putting something up to his face with his right. Every few seconds he would look over his shoulder, like some sort of low-rent detective. Was he spying on somebody? Chelsea, maybe?

I had to know more. I excused myself to Mom, telling her I was going to say hello to someone and asking her to order me a piña colada when the server showed up. Strolling in Sam's direction but a little back of him, I could see that he was reading the foodie magazine *Gourmet Force*. I didn't intend for him to notice me, but that didn't work out.

"Nola! Well, aren't you a sight for sore eyes!"

Why did that saying sound okay when my grandpa used to use it, but sound dorky coming from Sam Harmon? Dorky and very forced.

"Hello, Sam. What are you doing in Christiansted today? Such a gorgeous day, isn't it?"

"It is. Perfect day, and perfect place to take it in."

I could see something dark and metallic in his lap, partially covered by the magazine. A camera? No—binoculars. Hmm.

He saw the direction of my gaze and tried to redirect it. "Great place to sit and read. Do you know this magazine? Terrific magazine."

"Yes, I read it all the time. Love the photography," I said. "Not so fond of their main columnist, though. "The Poisoned Pen", do you read it?"

"All the time," Sam said. "What's wrong with it?"

I shrugged. "Meh. I don't know… it's just kind of nasty, I think."

"I don't think I'd call it that. The writing is crisp, of course. I think it's very well done." His chin was up in a 'don't mess with me' pose. Hey, okay. Tact and diplomacy, with the guests. Walk away, walk away.

"Yes, the writer definitely knows his stuff."

"What else are you doing, Sam?" I asked, motioning toward his binoculars. "Shorebird watching? Or checking out the yachts?"

"They are jaw-dropping, some of them, aren't they?"

I heard the woman's voice behind me and turned around. "Chelsea! Hi!" Why did she make me feel flustered, as though I'd been caught at something?

"Well, hello," she said, with a smile. "When I left to find the restroom, Sam was by himself, checking out the harbor. How nice to come back and see you, Nola."

"I'm down here for lunch with my mother." I pointed toward the café and Mom waved back.

"May we join you?" Chelsea asked.

How could I say no? I led them back to our table, where Mom was immersed in a menu the size of an old-fashioned road map.

We all nodded, smiled, made a little small talk. Chelsea had arrived in time to save her husband from the barrage of questions about the binoculars I might have sent at him, but once the preliminary comments about the Caribbean sun and the beautiful yachts in the harbor had been made, the questions did begin. They weren't flowing from me to Sam, though.

"So. Nola. Interesting group you were with the last time I saw you." Sam said.

"They were the celebrity chefs here for the KweeZeenArtZ contest. Most of them are staying at The Buccaneer or at private homes. One or two on yachts, I heard."

Sam and Chelsea exchanged a look. Why do people do that? And why do they never seem to realize that people see them do it?

"Not all chefs, though," Sam commented. "I saw that Lady Axelsen, the quirky artistocrat one."

"Yes, Frida Axelsen was there. And Cathleen Piper, the organizer of the competition."

"She's very well-regarded, I've heard," Chelsea observed. "Or is she?"

Yeah, no. Not really in the gossip girl mood today.

"Very well-regarded," I said.

"And there was a distinguished-looking man who almost looked as if he were hosting everything." Sam had taken the menu my mother offered and was looking it over.

"That's the owner of the sugar factory," Chelsea

put in.

"No, I don't think so, I've seen photos online. I think he's the one who is the owner of the new boat-building facility they're planning."

Neither, of course, was even remotely accurate, but they gave off such a clumsy good-cop, bad-cop hum that I just wasn't going to sing along.

"Lot of questions today, Sam." I stared at the menu, too, and didn't make eye contact with him.

"What do you mean?" The confrontational tone in his voice was unmistakable. "Is that a problem?"

What was it with him?

I was getting quite rattled by all of this and Mom was staring at me pretty closely, picking up on all my anxiety. Relief arrived in the form of that Canadian chef, the one from Montreal, who came strolling along the boardwalk in our direction.

I stood up. "Chef Taylor!" I called out.

He looked startled, but cooperative enough. "Miss … Stewart, is it? Hello."

I pulled over a chair for him. "Yes, Nola Stewart from the resort on Pitaya Beach. Are you enjoying St. Croix?"

"The people are very friendly, I've noticed," he said.

I laughed, and made the introductions. "My mother, Kim Stewart. Sam Harmon, Chelsea Harmon, guests at the resort this week."

"Boniface Taylor," he said, shaking hands all around and then picking up the menu. "How is the food here?"

"This is quite a casual place," I said. "They give you lunch in a paper bag in case you want to take it back to the boat."

"Ah yes, the boats," Chelsea said. "Lots of very

interesting boats."

"Do we call you 'Boniface'?" I asked. He seemed like an approachable, nice guy.

He grinned. "A mouthful, isn't it? A family name, and I'm proud to use it. It's memorable in chef world, too. But when I was a kid, it was a liability. I got nicknamed Buzz and that stuck. I go by Buzz, with my friends."

The next hour rolled by pleasantly, as we chatted about the islands, about food, about Canada. I felt an odd vibe in the air, though, and started to notice that Chef Taylor was examining Chelsea Harmon in a strange, considering way. Finally, he spoke up.

"You know, I don't mean to be rude…"

"Canadians never do," Sam jumped in.

"Precisely," the chef continued smoothly. "But I have to say, I'm recognizing you from somewhere, madam."

"Oh, I doubt it," Chelsea replied. "Unless your habits take you past the Carstairs Elementary School or the grocery store on 57th. And please… call me Chelsea."

His mouth was twitching and tensing as he gazed at her. "Do you cook, professionally?"

Sam laughed. "No, she doesn't. But she could!" He regarded his wife fondly. She smiled modestly. Why did it all seem so phony?

Buzz Taylor thought for a few more seconds, then shook it off. "Je ne sais pas. Maybe it's your voice, reminds me of somebody else. Or your hands." He grinned at us all. "I look at people's hands a lot. Chef thing, I think. Maybe piano players do the same?"

Chelsea smiled. "I'm not a professional chef, Buzz. Just a mom." The ripples around her were very subtle, but there, unmistakably.

What was it with her?

Jason had been snoozing for an hour. What was it about strong emotion that left you craving extra sleep? He made his way topside and found George there, enjoying the evening sights and sounds.

"May I join you?" he asked.

"Please do," George replied.

"What's on your mind tonight?" Jason asked. It was one of his best interviewer questions.

"You know, weirdly enough, it's a woman I met here. From Seattle, visiting here."

"Nola's mother?"

"You know her?"

"Met her. Seems nice."

They smiled and then sat companionably in silence for a while.

"It's heavy that Liz Barga's love life might have something to do with all this." Jason said.

"I doubt it, you know?" George commented. "The whole thing is business. Money. Maybe there's a ransom demand coming."

That stopped Jason. "Wait, what? You don't think she's dead."

George shook his head slowly.

"Whose body, then?"

"No idea," George said.

"But not hers." Jason persisted.

"That's why you're here with me on the yacht," George said.

"You don't think I did it."

"I know you didn't." George took a swallow of his drink, his mouth open to take a big slug of it, in a confident, in-charge sort of way. "I was able to get your cell phone records, thanks to a friend of mine, and I know you were texting a woman in NYC every 30 seconds all night, while you were at the Pirates' Feast and later on, from your room."

Really? George could do that?

I was in no hurry to get home and neither, it seemed, was my mother. Park, Sam and Chelsea had all drifted away but Chef Buzz Taylor was still hanging in, too. Those Canadians have stamina, I've always heard that. Across the harbor, we could see the small island hotel; with binoculars, we'd probably be able to see guests on the patios with bottles of wine and happy friends. For now, we just had our imaginations.

"Nola! Hey." It was Beth, my card dealer friend from the casino.

"Hey, Beth, what's up?"

She was laughing. "I just can't get over it. I was up on Company Street and I stumbled into a new restaurant. *The Cooking Cop.* Do you know Jean-Claude Legrande?"

"I do."

"He's the one who won the lottery a few weeks ago. Apparently, he's taken the money and used it to set up his own restaurant."

"Gee, makes you wonder about the policing around here."

"Yah think?" Beth said. "Distractions much?"

"No kidding." Mom said. "A Shot in the Dark, yeah?"

Beth and I looked at her blankly but Chef Taylor was laughing. "Right, eh?"

"I thought Jean-Claude was going to buy a boat or a first-class airplane ticket and get away from the USVI.

That's what he always said, right in the middle of complaining about everything." I was somehow just a bit disappointed that Jean-Claude hadn't run just a little bit farther than Company Street. Even to Nassau would have had him walking the talk a little more.

"Changed his mind, I guess. And still doesn't seem too happy. While I was having lunch there he was berating the staff about some shipment of killer fish that didn't show up."

"Killer fish?"

"Also called fugu. Or pufferfish. Or blowfish," Chef Taylor said. "A Japanese delicacy. Fatal to the diner, if not prepared correctly."

"Seriously?" Beth and I spoke simultaneously.

"Seriously. Used to be that a chef had to have a special license to serve it. They've loosened up on the regulations in some places… and I've heard there are some strains of fugu that have been bred to not be poisonous now. Still…" he took a long swallow of his beer, "I wouldn't eat a bite unless I knew exactly where it came from and who cooked it."

"Well." I needed beer, too. "That's definitely a new addition to the St. Croix dining scene."

"Could turn out to be like the riskier places to surf or dive. Or the overnight hiking on the north side. Bragging rights, you know?" I could feel Beth still giggling, just beneath her surface.

"There could be a T-shirt. *I survived a meal at the Cooking Cop of St. Croix.*" I'd forgotten that Mom was there, but clearly she was following along.

"Let's go take a look," Chef Taylor was on his feet.

Who could say no?

We discovered Jean-Claude and his new restaurant in a state of chaos. Only four customers were in the place but that didn't stop him from carrying on as though the sky was falling and the end was near. Beth and the chef were laughing out loud and even my mother was failing to hide her amusement.

"Nola! I don't have time to talk to you right now!" Jean-Claude was pacing from one end of the tiny restaurant to another, consulting the phone in his hand and clearly, trying to decide about something. "Unless you are here to eat? Sit, sit. Here's the menu, order something."

"Thanks, Jean-Claude, but we just came by to see how you are doing. I just heard today that you opened a place." I was doing my best to avoid letting him sweep me into a chair for a meal that I didn't want. "I thought you were leaving the island, with your big score in the lottery."

"I decided that I didn't have quite enough yet, and better to invest it in a restaurant and double my money before I head off to L.A.," he said as he thumbed away at some text message or search term.

Chef Taylor snorted. "Haven't you heard the old saying about the fastest way to lose a million bucks? Buy a restaurant and wait a month."

"You, sir, are too negative," Jean-Claude told him, but with a smile. I think he recognized the celebrity chef.

Buzz was reading Jean-Claude's menu. "They weren't kidding, you are doing fugu. Do you know how to handle it?"

"I've hired two chefs who were certified in Japan, so, yes. But I really can't imagine too many people ordering it here," Jean-Claude said. "But it's giving us some great word-of-mouth."

The door to the restaurant opened and we all looked up. The character coming through was in full Harley style: boots, leather chaps, vest, plaid shirt and gloves. It was Frida Axelsen.

"Hello, Nola, nice to see you again. Who is this?" She'd spotted my mother, also a traveler from the same era.

"My mother, Kim Stewart," I said. "Mom, this is Frida. She owns the Alhambra West."

"A beautiful home," my mother said, in her smoothest, 'let's get acquainted' manner. "I've only seen it from the outside, of course."

"We will be open to the public for KweeZeenArtZ," Frida said.

"So that's what George Corelli was talking about," my mother said, doing the math. I was still struggling with the equation. When had my mother been talking with Mr. Corelli about anything at all?

Suspicion was in the air, it seemed. While I was raising an eyebrow at my mother, Frida Axelsen was glaring at everybody. Or perhaps she just seemed sinister and accusatory to me because she was dressed like a motorcycle mama on a mission.

"When did this place open up?" she demanded. "I was just past here last week and there was nothing like this here."

All of us—Buzz Taylor, Jean-Claude, Beth, me, even Mom—opened our mouths at once to answer. Frida seemed to have that leadership effect on people.

She also seemed to be impatient. We obviously took too long to answer. "Never mind, it's irrelevant. Easy come, easy go. The classics, the contenders, the winners, they stick around. For years. For decades." She headed for the door, then stopped. "Like KweeZeenArtZ, that's a classic. This year will be the best yet, you'll see."

# CHAPTER TWENTY-ONE

For about an hour I felt inspired by Frida's optimism. While Mom and I strolled around and explored Christiansted I enjoyed thinking about all of the benefits that would be coming to St. Croix after the big KweeZeenArtZ triumph this year. My hotel had been accepted as a last-minute participant, thanks to Cathleen Piper's easygoing nature, and Mr. Winter was giving "Nola and Nola's network" the credit. They'd given us the responsibility for setting up and provisioning a water supply. That table would be dressed with some fantastic signs, brochures and giveaways to next week's Pirates' Feast. All of this was going on my résumé faster than syrup goes on pancakes.

"Let's go in here." Mom was waving at a small bookstore with a window full of coffee table books with glorious photos of wide white beaches and palm trees. "I want to send your grandmother something from St. Croix."

The store was full of more nautical souvenirs than I'd ever seen in one place, interspersed with kitchenware, soaps, stationery and a few books, here and there. I left Mom happily shopping and went searching for a nice, beach-ey novel. I was standing behind a life-sized cardboard cutout of an action hero whose name anyone would recognize in a second if I said it, when I heard a voice with a familiar irritated tone.

"Come on, Sluggo. I want to get out of here."

Bjorn Vester. He calls his wife *Sluggo?!* Wow, last of the romantics.

"You won't find anything worthwhile in a bookstore. Let's walk around and find some Wi-Fi somewhere."

"I have to find something about this Alberta Caribbean chef we're supposed to design the menu around." Natalya was exasperated. "God, I wish you had a better way of getting ready for this cooking competition than wandering around the town looking for Wi-Fi. How about a hot tub? Or a massage?"

"Have you forgotten we can't seem to get in to the spa at our hotel?"

"Bjorn. Your anxiety about this is nuts. We have it under control. "

"You're sure?"

"Baby, I am so sure. We've done everything we were asked. The money will come through and the mortgage will be paid."

"I don't want to lose the restaurant, Sluggo."

"We won't."

They moved out of earshot and toward the back of the store and I grabbed the opportunity to get away without being noticed. I barely heard Mom when she spoke to me on the way out and when Jason came up to us on the street to say a brief 'hello', Mom was the one who answered him.

What the hell had I just heard, in that bookstore? Was it real or did I imagine it? After Jason passed by, I tried to answer Mom's questions about the island, the weather and the book she'd bought for Grandma, but finally, her curiosity got to her (not to mention her desire to communicate) and she asked "Don't you want to know what I think?"

"About what?"

"About Jason."

"Alright, but take your time."

She thought it over while we walked, the June sunshine kissing my face. She thought all the way through the parking lot to the car, the drive to the restaurant, and our seats at the table. You'd think restaurants were all we could think of to do, in St. Croix, and you'd be right.

"Okay," she said. "He's nice. But not ready."

"For what?"

"For knowing somebody else. He doesn't know himself yet."

"Mom, he's over 30. He's not a kid."

"Chronological age means nothing."

The waiter arrived and we discussed the small bites plates.

"What would you call this kind of cuisine?" Mom wondered. "Fusion?"

"Pretty much." I said. "Mediterranean/Asian. Sushi and prosciutto and pesto on the same plate? That's a lot going on."

"Here's one... prosciutto, ricotta, dates and scallions."

"How about this? Ribs, gorgonzola, hazelnut and applesauce."

"Yum," she agreed. "Let's try the salmon tartar with pesto, arugula, shallots and capers."

"Is that a salad?"

"What is a salad, really? Does anybody know anymore?"

"If it's vegetables or fruit all smushed together, it's a salad. But if it's a work of art on a plate, it's more than a salad."

Mom agreed. "I've seen so many lately that look like abstract paintings."

"It's the taste, too, though."

"What's the taste?" Dana dropped into the chair across from Mom. "Man, I thought I'd never get out of there. How can one short article take so long to finish? Thanks for waiting for me, you guys. I'm starving! Lunch is long overdue."

"We've had lunch. This is second lunch—maybe even third lunch? I've lost track," Mom said, grinning.

"A plate of onion rings," Dana said to the server. Mom and I both shuddered. "Fry 'em deep and fry 'em silly," she instructed. "Rum on the side, yeah?"

"Cocktail?" the server inquired.

"Surprise me," Dana requested. "So what's new, ladies?"

"Mom is giving me her views on Jason Palmateer." I enjoyed the look of surprise and wariness on my sister's face. "And whether he's the right type for me."

"I'll evaluate him for you, too," Mom said. Dana looked thrilled. "I'll cut right to it, and jump over the first and most important question."

Dana and I looked at each other helplessly, then both asked, "Which is?"

"Is he you? And I don't mean, do you have things in common? You have to go deeper than that. And never, never, toward 'opposites attract'. That's just bogus."

"Thanks, Mom, got it," Dana said. "What about Jason, then?"

"Not right for either one of you," she announced. "For you, Nola, he'd be a romantic dream come true, but you'd be living in self-delusion land. All the time. And for you, Dana, he'd be a bedroom dream come true but you'd pay. Too much, in my opinion."

"Mom, when you know so much, you really should use some of all this knowledge to help yourself," Dana said.

"In fact," I said, piling on, "we have a current situation for you right now. Mr. Corelli has been asking and asking me for your number or your email."

"Let me think about it." That sentence could mean 12 to 18 months of waiting. She didn't procrastinate, exactly, because procrastination is nothing more or less than your heart telling you it's not ready.  But she did think. "Let's talk about something else."

"I've got something for you." Dana almost leaped from her chair. She'd been waiting. "There was an item in the news just before I left that the Securities and Exchange Commission has changed its reporting rules for packaged food production companies and the experiments they're doing. Would change everything for Liz Barga and the fuss she's facing."

"Was facing," I amended.

"Was facing," Dana agreed.

"Except that she'd still have had to face it," Mom commented. "And spend about a million dollars to pay the attorneys and PR consultants she'd need to take it all the way through, and clear her name."

Good point.

My phone buzzed and I read the text from Park. *Can we go together to the food festival tomorrow? I need to talk*

# CHAPTER TWENTY-TWO

Even though I had sworn I wouldn't help him anymore, there I was, in a car with him. Just inches away from his tanned right forearm, speeding along the highway toward the Alhambra West, we were listening to alternative music and just seizing the day. I hadn't seen much of him lately, probably not nearly as much as Dana had. She was the one, after all, who'd told me that he was staying aboard the *Alice Rose*. But it was the quality of time that mattered, not the small quantity, and I could catch up. I closed my eyes and leaned my head against the passenger door window.

*"Jason, have you been over to Buck Island yet?"*

*"No, Nola, I haven't, but I'd love to go with you. We could take a picnic, walk on the beach, maybe make love on a blanket in the sand…"*

*"That would be a new experience, but I'd love to try…"*

"…Nola, for the third time, is the turn to the food festival venue coming up any time soon? I feel like we've gone by this stretch of road a bunch of times already!"

This was a different voice. I gave my head a shake and opened my eyes to see Park Lee to my left, with a very unhappy look on his face. "Yes, soon. Right after the last farm and then the crafts store."

*Get a grip, girl. Fantasize about people you don't know.*

The day of the KweeZeenArtZ Food Festival had dawned with a blistering sun, just as the previous three days had done. The papers and the radio stations were full of chatter for the tourists about the dangers of heat stroke, and we were carrying about a dozen bottles of water in the trunk of Park's rental car. We also had coolers filled with ingredients that could be thrown together in various combinations for lunch, and for dinner if the competition went on that long. Usually, the judges declared a clear winner within minutes of the final tasting, but it was always possible that a tie would be declared. Then we'd be in for more hours of waiting, surrounded by delicious aromas. Food everywhere, and not a bite to eat. Experienced food festival-goers brought their own supplies, odd as that seemed. Of course, there were several temporary cafés set up at the venue but the prices were so high you should be buying an entire garden, rather than just a cucumber or a pepper.

The venue this year was a big part of the high level of the excitement. The KweeZeenArtZ competition had a different location every year, and we'd seen it at almost every major restaurant and resort on the island. Last year, right after it wrapped up in the courtyard of the Fort in Christiansted, Frida Axelsen had contacted the organizers and invited them to consider the Alhambra West as the site for the next one. She changed her mind four times over the next twelve months, but people in St. Croix just waited to find out what decision she would finally alight on, like a bee going from flower to flower or a bird from perch to perch. It was worth the wait and the uncertainty, because we all wanted to see inside the Alhambra West, and when she announced, finally! that she had decided that yes! the annual KweeZeenArtZ chefs' competition would go ahead at her estate, we all cheered.

The mood at the backup venue, the Cruzan Conquistador, was gloomy, but too bad for them. Maybe next year. This year, we were driving through the front gate of the most majestic building on St. Croix and my eyes were taking it all in, the way they would have if we'd been talking a five-course meal at L'Arpège in Paris.

I'd asked Park about his text message about five times and he hadn't shed any light. Just muttered something about bringing a friend back with us to the hotel after the competition and needing to book another room. Said we could talk about it more later. He seemed very jumpy, and I have to admit I was looking forward to his exit from the island. He'd been around long enough.

Stopping in the temporary lot set up to the east of the main structure, I saw Chelsea and Sam Harmon getting out of their rental car. He waved at me enthusiastically, but she ducked her head and turned her back. WTF?

I walked toward them to say hello but Chelsea headed off toward the back of the palace. I could have sworn that I saw him touch her right shoulder and give her a push.

"Nola! Hello! Isn't this marvelous, to be here in this amazing place with such an amazing day in front of us?" The lower half of Sam's face was covered in a smile but above it, his brown eyes were cold. What was it with me lately, that almost every man I saw seemed sinister and shady?

"Sam! Nola!" Crap. Almost every woman, too. It was Natalya Vester.

"Good morning, Natalya. Sam." I wanted to escape but I couldn't. Park was right behind me.

"Hello, Sam! How are you?" Park's hand was extended and it looked like Sam was just as trapped as I. "Did I see Chelsea with you a moment ago?"

"You did, but she's had to go back to the resort. Something going on with one of the kids, apparently."

"Why don't you hang with us?" Park suggested. "Let's go in, okay?"

I turned to speak to Natalya but she had slipped away. The advance billing of the Alhambra West had undersold the place. I had never seen anything like it—and I'd seen quite a few of the more upscale constructions in St. Croix. There aren't a lot, and there are many areas that are filled with whatever the extreme opposite of 'upscale' might be, but I'd had the opportunity to see a good-sized slice of the expensive ones. None of them compared to this, not one.

The foyer was 18 feet high, easily, with an enormous crystal chandelier dominating the upper space. Beautiful floral arrangements set off antique tables and oil paintings that looked to be museum quality filled almost every square inch of wall space. A table that looked as though it didn't belong there had been set up perpendicular to the mahogany door and two women were checking credentials. We had to show identification, be checked off against the invitation list, hand over our purses for a physical search and walk through a scanner. I was just getting ready to take off my shoes when one of the staff shook her head at me: that won't be necessary, ma'am.

We were directed toward a hallway at the back of the entrance area. The ceiling dropped to seven feet, the wall color transitioned into a dark, warm chocolate, and rattan dominated the furniture choice for the side chairs and sofas scattered along the way. We walked for what seemed like a block or two, and then suddenly we were in what I guessed was the main living room. From a snug, dark, low-height passageway, we emerged into a glorious, brightly lit room the size of my high school gym. I couldn't begin to take in the details of the décor but the overall impression was elegance, glamor and expense—with a little bit of edge, even hip-hop thrown in. Obviously, many layers to this Frida Axelsen.

We weren't allowed to linger in the main salon; uniformed security staff, wearing white gloves and bright smiles kept all of us guests moving toward a doorway at the back. Velvet ropes blocked access to the artwork and the antique furniture, and clearly, we weren't invited to sit down or step up close to inspect the paintings and sculpture. There was a lot of rubbernecking anyway, and the river of people heading for wherever we were going had slowed to a trickle. I managed to look at a stunning Escher original for a few seconds before the people behind me got impatient; we all moved forward toward a double French door.

An immense ballroom with a stage, spotlights and an orchestra pit awaited us on the door's other side. But music and dancing were not the intended use today; it was going to be all about cuisine. Going from least important to most, three-quarters of the room had been set up theater-style with well-padded chairs filling rows from wall to wall. That was for us spectators. At the south end of the room, an astonishing kitchen had been constructed, with gleaming stainless steel ovens, ranges, sinks, refrigerators and acres of countertop dominating the space. That was the competitors' turf. Then, up on the stage, a single table, set with a milky white cloth and one yellow hibiscus flower in a turquoise vase.

"Do you think that's where they're putting the judges?" I said to Park. Why was I whispering? Something about the place made me feel too young.

"The judge." Sam answered. "I saw something about that in the program."

"Only one judge? Is that all they could get?" Park's tone went with his body language. He didn't seem to be nearly as impressed with the Alhambra West as I was.

"I don't think that's it," I said. " But it does seem unfair, only one judge."

"Seems like life," Sam commented. "Hey, there's three seats over there, let's snag 'em." He headed toward the second row and we followed. I didn't really want to sit with him but the place was filling up and if I waited too long or spent too much time looking for Dana or Jason or anybody else I might prefer, I could end up sitting nowhere.

The buzz in the room was like being near a nighttime crowd of crickets at mating time. I spotted a lot of people I knew. Fasia, Collette and Pascal the chef from the resort were across the aisle, sitting together. People had claimed seats and dropped bags, programs, hats, even flip-flops on them, but no one sat down. We weren't going to be allowed to wander around the room, milling around the chefs, apparently; we had to watch from the audience area. Great for the chefs, not so great for those of us not six feet tall. But according to the program, part of the plan included samples for the guests to enjoy while the judge was tasting and evaluating each course. The catch was that to receive your precious bite you had to be in possession of a chair, and sitting. Reminded me a bit of dog training.

Malik was sitting to my right, scanning the kitchen area through binoculars. What a good idea, why hadn't I thought of that? I snapped a couple of photos with my smartphone, pinching and swiping the screen to get a better look at what was going on, but that didn't work.

He took pity on me. "Do you want to borrow my binoculars for a while?"

Thank you! This was ideal. I scrutinized each of the six set ups. Gennaro Bianchi was already hard at work at Station 1. At Station 2, it was the Canadian culinary king, Boniface Taylor. I fiddled with the focusing knob and zoomed in on his hands. He was holding a skillet and a spoon; something was frying and if I concentrated, I was sure I could smell the Vidalia onions. Did I know for a fact that they were Vidalia? No, but those are my favorite, and these smelled so good, that's what they must be, yes?

My friend Paige was bent over a chopping board at Station 3. Her knife was pounding at the speed of a Usain Bolt sprint and those carrots were toast.

Hisashi Mizuno, at Station 4, had dozens of tiny tubs looking like exquisite bento boxes covering his counter surface. I had heard from Dana that the pre-check on this competition was super-strict, so the contents every one of those tubs would have been examined before Hisashi was allowed to set them out for his prep. Nobody wanted any sort of repeat of the horrendous experience at a contest back in the mists of time—in the 90s or so, I think—when a winning contestant was revealed to have brought in and used a supply of pre-packaged ingredients.

At Station 5, Bjorn and Natalya were fronting what had to be the most stylish of the stations. Beautiful utensils, knives that gleamed beyond belief, signage that announced their names and showed their commitment to brand-building. I was excited about seeing whether their food presentation was as slick as their personal. Natalya wore an outfit that looked as if it belonged on a Paris runway—feathers, flash, and skin— and Bjorn had on a tuxedo. But wouldn't they have to change into the traditional chef's jacket at some point? Wasn't that a rule?

I turned to ask Park or Sam or somebody, and found Malik holding out his hand to get his binoculars back.

"Hey, thanks," I said. "Park, do you know, are the Vesters allowed to dress like that?"

Park shrugged. "Don't know. I didn't know they'd be allowed to enter as a couple, but there they are."

"The rules are flexible, apparently." The voice behind me had that familiar, ironic tone. "Hey, Nola."

"Hey, Dana. What do you think?"

"Smart money says Bianchi, the Italian. But there's lots of interest in the two of them, team-cooking." Dana stared through her own binoculars. "They sure do mingle, those two. They're roaming up and down the kitchen, saying hello and hanging out with everyone as though they're the hosts or something." Dana stood right beside my chair. Territorial... or maybe protective?

"I heard a rumor, too, that the Japanese is going to do some toxic, poisonous fish. That's pulling in a lot of attention—it's trending on Twitter."

"At some point, don't we think it's all getting very gimmicky?" Park asked. "I mean, so what if your diner could die from eating something not prepared properly? Why would that make you the better chef?"

"It would make you not the killer chef, anyway." Dana continued to scan the action. "It's actually quite cool, the way Bjorn and Natalya cook together. It's sort of like a dance. In a very small space."

"Will she go between his legs, like with the Moko Jumbie?" I wondered. Dana laughed. "Do you know, Dana, what's happening with Station 6?"

All we could see there was a stainless steel range, a stool, a sink and an oven. No contestant there, no flag, no cards from well-wishers.

"Speaking of gimmicky," Dana said. "Whoever it is, they're keeping it dark right up to the last minute. Along with the identity of the judge."

For an hour, we watched the chefs work their magic with their ingredients, chopping, stirring, pan-frying, blending, sprinkling and mixing. No one gave us any information about the dishes being cooked and we had a lot of fun taking guesses, with the help of Dana's binoculars. Each chef had complete creative license to interpret the challenge of the competition in any way he or she chose. Over the years I'd heard of lots of intriguing and unusual forms of competition. My favorite so far was the one where they're given a mystery bottle of wine, $1000 and four hours to plan the perfect dish to pair with the wine, source the ingredients, then prepare and present the plate.

For KweeZeenArtZ, the six of them had been allowed to plan their recipes and acquire their ingredients in advance, but the challenge was to present a fine-dining, updated version of a three-course island meal that in some way integrated the flavors of their own country's unique cuisine with the fish, fowl, and flavors of the Caribbean, while honoring Alberta Fernandina. Within three hours. Without being pretentious. Or predictable. Or bland. Or poisoning anybody.

Each of the chefs hunched over the plate on his or her patch of stainless steel countertop like a dog mesmerized by a slab of meat. It was hard to define the precise contents of each dish without a description, but each plate was a symphony of color, shape and texture, cut into unique forms and arranged with precision.

"Service!" barked Chef Bianchi when he was finished with his creation, forgetting that this was a competition, not the dinner run at a three-starred restaurant. No one was allowed any assistance so we were spared the sight of a diva chef abusing anybody, but we all knew we were just inches away from it. Each chef had carried in his or her knives in a slotted cloth. None brought in any notes—recipes and menus belonged in their heads, only. Secrets. The one thing they would all have in common was a drive toward perfection.

"Hey, listen to this!" Dana read from the program. "This competition was set up in honor of Alberta

Fernandina, one of the Virgin Islands' most famous cooks. A hundred years ago she opened a small café with a kitchen that delivered such amazing meals that people traveled miles in all directions for them. By land and by sea. Eventually lineups became a regular sight, a good business manager kept her on track and she was able to grow and prosper. A granddaughter helped her write and publish a cookbook. A son and daughter-in-law took over the restaurant when Alberta became too elderly to handle things any more.

"She died before the downturn came. Guests to the islands began to want service, menus and glamor like they were used to, back home in New York or L.A. or wherever, and for a long time, Alberta's brand of Caribbean cuisine was out of favor. People wanted fusion, they wanted penne alla vodka, they wanted tofurkey, they wanted raw. Her children and grandchildren patiently waited it out and when the trend drafted back, they were ready. *Alberta's Restaurant* expanded and trained dozens of chefs, who went off to take jobs and open restaurants all over the islands, Florida, Central and South America. Her cookbooks became textbooks and her recipes the standard for classic Caribbean dishes. During the dot-com boom, an appreciative St. John diner endowed a fellowship in her name at a university culinary arts program and now, almost 20 years later, MediTek and Portrush Inc. have teamed up to put forward a half million dollar prize for the best chef in this competition."

As Dana was reading this aloud from the program, I saw my mother across the ballroom, taking a seat beside George Corelli. My, my. A third man who looked vaguely familiar sat down on George's left. Oh yes—Simon, the one from the big software company that was putting up the other part of the prize money. That was almost as intriguing as seeing Jason walk in with Bondi Shepherd. I was about to wave at them both when there suddenly was some action on the stage. Cathleen Piper walked up to the microphone.

"I'd like to let you all know that our sixth contestant—Chef Frank Vatel—has been given permission to do most of his preparation off-stage. We can assure you he will be supervised and the rules of the contest will be maintained. His dishes will be presented and tasted by our judge at the same time as everyone else. The finish time and the total time for cooking is the same for him as for everyone else."

# CHAPTER TWENTY-THREE

The room erupted and Cathleen seemed to decide more information was needed. "It is a security matter."

Well. What did *that* mean?

I turned to discuss it with Sam and anybody else nearby who might be interested, but he was gone. Sofrania had slipped into his seat, and smiled a silent greeting at me. Park was gone, too; Dana had taken his chair while she waited for me to return her binoculars.

It was too entertaining to give them back yet. Natalya and Bjorn had decided it was time to turn the spotlight their way. It could have been, though, that they were just so self-centered they didn't care about the lack of discipline, not to mention the lack of class that was coming across. I was sitting a long way from their kitchen space and couldn't hear their words, but there was no mistaking their actions. He waved a saucepan toward her and she shook a mixing spoon at him. He picked up the frying pan that she'd been tending on the stove and dumped the contents into the sink. She stood solid-still, like a tiger just about to attack, then picked up a chopping board covered in prepared vegetables and flung it at his head. Bjorn ducked, then grabbed a mixing bowl and in one continuous motion flung part of the contents at her and dumped the rest on her shoes.

Looked like a sauce of some kind—remoulade? Maybe cake batter?

"Ladies and gentlemen." My attention—the attention of everybody in the room—swung over to the podium and the chef standing there, holding the microphone.

"Something has come to my attention and I feel it needs to be announced to you." Gennaro Bianchi had now lost his mind, just like Bjorn and Natalya Vester.

Dana had her phone out, recording everything in sight and sound. Sofrania sat intently staring at the podium, with an expression on her face that I had never seen. Sam had returned, from the restroom probably, and was loitering nearby, trying to look as though he was in the right place.

"The two so-called cooks at Station 5 have called my integrity into question, in public, and so, here today, in public, I will answer them. I say 'them', but really it is her..." and Chef Bianchi pointed in Natalya's direction. She responded by gesturing back, wagging her pointer finger at him, and then lifting a middle one in a motion that Corey Morrison told me in third grade was a sign of respect that should be used frequently.

Gennaro glared at her. "Just so that you all know, I have not ever cheated at anything. Ever. I have not copied recipes, I have not stolen ideas. All that she is saying is a lie, I am innocent, and she will have to prove the things she is saying. Or pay."

He stalked down the stairs toward the empty orchestra pit. But he didn't go back to Station 1, to his various dishes in various stages of preparation. He walked right out the door. We all sat in a state of shock, then someone in a staff uniform darted toward his stovetop, with four frying pans in action, and turned off the power.

It was if all sound had been sucked from the room. I looked toward Bjorn and Natalya at Station 5 and was amazed to see them back at work, as if nothing had happened. Bjorn was chopping vegetables at a furious rate while Natalya stood over a range fully loaded with saucepans and skillets. I reached toward Dana for her binoculars and taking a closer look, I saw them smile at one another.

A normal atmosphere gradually took hold, despite the unoccupied spaces at Stations 1 and 6. Chef Taylor hovered over an extra-large pasta pot on his stove, adding so many seasonings that I lost count. At Station 3, Chef Fleming (aka my friend Paige) bustled back and forth between her prep surface and her refrigerator, a happy look on her face.

Chef Mizuno, however, was anything but happy. He was trying to concoct a fish entrée but he was having trouble getting cooperation from his knives, somehow; as I watched through the binoculars, he came at the fillet four different ways, only to shake his head in frustration after each, then try another. He pinched the blade more firmly but it just wasn't working for him. Finally, he threw the tool down in a clatter of irritation and walked away from his kitchen. Sometimes you just need to take a break.

Ten minutes later he was back—and it looked as though they were all almost finished. Each had chopped, stirred, fried, baked, sautéed and bent over dishes and plates to add final flourishes of color and design. The clock ticked down to the final half hour and suddenly, there was action on two fronts.

A figure in a white chef's jacket, white pants, short white gloves, a hat, and a blue scarf that covered all of a face but the eyes, appeared in front of the Station 6 stove and set to work. Meanwhile, another figure, this one in a long cloak and full-face mask, was wheeled across the stage in a chair and seated in front of the table.

"Dramatic much." Dana commented as she reached for the binoculars. I held on and we had a mild struggle for a moment, until Malik reached over to hand his to Dana. He got her best smile of appreciation.

We watched as Bjorn and Natalya followed the servers carrying trays with their finished plates up to the judge. He looked them over, slipped forkfuls of samples through an opening in the mask, dictated notes into a recorder, and then nodded at the two chefs. Numbers went up up on a digital scoreboard above the stage: Appearance 10; Aroma 10; Taste 10; Creativity 9; Homage to Alberta Fernandina's legacy 9.

48/50.

The audience applauded but I couldn't tell whether that was for the score, the competitors, or the servers who showed up at the end of each row with a tray of small bites for us to pass around.

Next up was Chef Taylor, and I saw the judge nod with what I imagined was appreciation when he saw the plates. He carefully tasted each of the three courses, looked back and forth over the tray to take in the full menu and its subtleties. Suddenly we heard a nasty coughing. The judge motioned desperately toward the server standing attentively next to his table and the woman jumped forward to grab the water jug and pour a glass. The judge downed half of it in a gulp.

Chef Taylor backed away slowly, as if anticipating landmines with each step.

"What was that all about?" Dana whispered to me.

From my other side, Sofrania answered. "I'd say, an unexpected flavor sensation."

The numbers went up on the digital scoreboard: 40/50. Whatever that was that had choked up the judge had strangled Boniface Taylor's shot at the prize.

Chef Mizuno was on his way up the steps, looking somewhat better for his walk outside in the tropical air. His body language was quite reserved, in an odd sort of way. He hung back while the judge gazed at the presentation. After a few a moments, the judge's eyes met Hisashi's and they each bowed to one another in a very formal way. The judge inhaled, tasted and pondered, then nodded once more. Hisashi withdrew, walked down the steps, past his kitchen station, and right out through the back doors of the ballroom.

Scores: Appearance 2; Aroma 10; Taste 10; Creativity 10; Homage 10. 42/50.

Paige Fleming was up next and I could see by the bounce in her step as she walked toward the judge, head high, that she was feeling this. She stood at attention while the judge looked over her plates, and then sampled the three courses. I peered through the binoculars and focused as sharply as I could on the judge's face, behind the mask. I was probably imagining it but I thought I could see a smile, maybe even a delighted expression. He forked second samples of each course.

Cathleen approached the judge's table and leaned down to speak into his ear. He stopped mid-bite, set down his fork, and turned to give Cathleen his full attention. I watched him lean back in his chair, nod, and look down at his gloved hands. I could tell that Paige had no more idea than we did about what was happening.

Cathleen approached the podium microphone. "We are making a change in the line-up of chef contestants," she announced. "USVI Chef Paige Fleming has been disqualified."

Paige took a step backward, as if punched. The spectators in the first few rows stood up, perhaps the better to see her distress, and so we all had to rise, to see the stage at all. Cathleen hesitated at the microphone, as if she wanted to say more, then headed backstage. I turned to Dana.

"I'm on it," she said, turning to push her way to the center aisle.

What was going on? That was Gennaro quit, Hisashi turning in a low score, Chef Taylor semi-poisoning the judge with something horrible, and now Paige kicked out. Who was left?

The commotion around me was picking up energy and volume, but in the midst of it, the judge sat at his table, silent and still like the center of a hurricane. Something about him was bothering me, and I wished I had Dana's binoculars. I pulled out my smartphone and took a couple of photos of him.

The zoomed-in version gave me my answer. Beneath the hem of the cloak disguise, you could see another hem, a brighter one, a patterned one—looked like flowers, in orange and yellow—a sundress hem.

Chelsea Harmon. Well.

"Sam!" I grabbed his arm and pulled. "Come over here and talk to me!"

He was startled into obedience. "What's up, Nola?"

"Is that Chelsea up there at the table, judging this competition?" I demanded.

He inhaled deeply several times, his bushy moustache rising and falling as he stalled for time. I jerked at his arm again.

"Alright, alright. Yes, it is. But you have to help me keep it quiet!" He was looking over my shoulder and turning around to look over his own as if we were trapped in a sketchy part of town.

"I don't have to do anything! What's going on?"

"Chelsea is an international food critic. We keep her identity secret so that chefs and restaurants can't anticipate her visits or her reviews. Her column is anonymous and her reputation is as clean as that tablecloth. She doesn't really want to do these in-person judging gigs but KweeZeenArtZ made it an offer that *Gourmet Force* couldn't refuse."

"Wait, what?" We had been whispering and hissing at each other but I almost shouted now. "Is Chelsea the Poisoned Pen?"

Sam didn't answer but I didn't need him to. Wow, they straight-up fooled everybody. I thought he might even be responsible for Liz's's disappearance, he was that strange. Eleni just thought he was kinda creepy, vaguely coming on all the time, and Dana had been trying various spellings of his name online, trying to get some 411.

And now it turns out it's his wife who has the story!

I needed a drink. I let go of Sam's arm and he took instant advantage, heading toward the stage where Chelsea sat in her cloak and mask. He didn't quite get there fast enough, though; three servers, carrying plates prepared by Chef #6, were in front of him, placing them on the table. The show must go on.

"I found out why they cut Paige." Dana was out of breath but glowing. She did love to chase a story. "They found a stash of prepared, pre-packaged food at her station—instant mashed potatoes, frozen creole sauce, fish sticks, stuff like that."

"Frozen fish sticks? Are you kidding me?"

Dana shook her head. "I know, I know. But she's out… unless she can prove somebody framed her."

"This place is overflowing with 'guilty until proven innocent'."

"So's the world." Dana handed me her binoculars. "Here, take these. Keep an eye on things for me. I have to go get a statement from Cathleen and some reaction from Paige. Hey, Jason." She brushed past him, eyes on a different prize, and left him for me. "Lots of excitement, yeah?"

"Looks like they're just about to score our mystery contestant."

"Do we know anything about Chef #6?"

"That they let him in at the last minute, that they let him do three-quarters of his cooking backstage, under heavy surveillance, so he wouldn't be distracted, or bothered, or something. That he's some big-time, world-famous chef."

He, or she?

The scoreboard lit up with the results of Chef #6's entry. Appearance 10. Aroma 10. Taste 10. Homage to Alberta Fernandina's legacy 10. Creativity 10.

The place went nuts.

"I think it's Liz Barga, Jason!" I shouted to him, over the noise of the crowd.

"No, it's some guy going by a fake name. 'Frank Vatel'. George told me." Jason started to move toward the kitchen area and I followed him.

"Maybe not." And I pointed toward Station 5, where the tiny blonde woman with the red lipstick, wearing a chef's jacket, was all up in Bjorn and Natalya's faces.

"No kidding," he breathed, and we both realized that any expectations of his future dining experiences with the USVI official prison cook could be laid to rest now.

When we got up close, we could hear her screaming. "You frickin' blew it, you screwed everything up!"

Even bitchy Natalya looked intimidated.

"The job was simple—keep 'em distracted and neutralize the competition while I cook the meal of a lifetime! I did my part, the half mill was won, and then you guys screwed it up!"

"Liz, how were we to know there would be a Chef #6 who could really cook?" Bjorn cowered by the refrigerator, keeping an eye on the stovetop where four cast-iron frying pans sat within reach of Liz's angry hand. "We thought it was just a gimmick, to raise interest in the contest, you know? Mystery contestant, super-famous chef about to arrive…"

"Yeah, like half a million dollars won't draw a crowd," Liz said.

"We did our job!" Natalya was as irate as a hotel guest not getting the upgrade to a suite that he was sure he'd been promised. "We smeared the Italian's reputation and pissed him off, we stole the Japanese guy's precious cleaver—Noriko the Knife or whatever he called her—and threw it in the harbor, we put the bitter melon in the Canadian guy's Nanaimo coconut bars, and we planted the prepackaged stuff on the local chef. While we pretended to cook. While we substituted your plates. We did our job, Liz!"

She was screaming by the time she got to the end; Liz looked ready to catch fire, like some flashy dessert. In fact, I could see a culinary torch on the counter and I could see Natalya edging away from it.

"Ms. Barga."

Sofrania's voice was firm and authoritative, and we all paid attention. Liz stopped shouting and turned to face her.

"Ms. Barga, we have been investigating your disappearance as a murder. What is going on?"

"You can't have been investigating very hard… or very well," Liz said. "Somehow you managed to misidentify some body as mine. Not sure how that happened or how I got that lovely red herring of a gift— probably has to do with your officers' preoccupation with the lottery—but I'll take it." She smiled, and managed to look as mean as any horrible woman I've ever seen.

"We'll have a lot of questions for you, Ms. Barga, as you can imagine," Sofrania said, equally calmly. "But for now, the main thing—if all you wanted was to disappear, why did you have somebody resorting to murder... even a fake one?"

"That wasn't in the plan." Park had joined the flock swarming around the picnic lunch that was Liz. Sam, Chelsea, Dana, Mom, Frida, Bondi, Malik, Fasia, Collette, Pascal, Paige and the other two chefs.

Wait, was that that Ronald guy I'd seen picking up Frida in the Reef a few days back?

Park was desperate to defend himself. "The plan was simply to have her go underground for a few weeks before the half-million dollar chefs' competition, win the thing, and take the money home to fight off the SEC. We should have stepped forward as soon as the word 'murder' started being flung around, we should have explained."

"Park, you wuss! I had no idea when I hired you that you'd be such a crybaby. Explaining wouldn't have got us anywhere, nobody would have listened. Nobody was listening to us in New York and nobody would have listened to us here." Liz looked around the crowd of onlookers and spotted Jason. "They only want to listen to the press, to the ones who are digging up all the dirt."

"Is that why you framed him? For a murder that hadn't even really happened?" George Corelli had joined the conversation now. Wait, why was he wearing a white chef's jacket and a blue scarf knotted around his neck? And why was he carrying a knife?

"I didn't frame him, Park framed him."

Park had to be restrained from leaping at her throat. "You told me to! You told me to get Jason's pewter bracelet while we dove and then hide it in your hotel room for these cops to find." He looked at Jason. "Sorry, man."

"Sorry, man? Sorry, man? That's what you've got to say?" Apparently, Bondi was with us now, too. "We trusted you, Park. We hung out with you and we trusted you. Why on earth would you do something like that? For her? She can't have been paying you *that* much!"

Bondi stared at Liz's assistant and Park couldn't meet his eyes. I was wondering whether this was going to boil over, when suddenly we heard another voice.

"Hello, Liz."

"Hello, Simon."

"Still the same games, I see." Her boyfriend had his arms crossed; with his right hand, he played with a set of car keys. He turned to look at Park and Bondi. "The players change, gentlemen, but the game remains the same. She didn't come here to try to see you again"—to Bondi—"and she didn't get you"—to Park—"to frame Jason Palmateer to put him away in prison and protect herself from his reporting."

"It was only about the money." George stepped up to stand beside Simon.

Jason stared at George. "Are you 'Frank Vatel'? Chef #6?"

"For today," George replied. "I couldn't let her have the money."

Liz bowed from the waist, in what might have been intended as an attempt at respect. Or sarcasm. "And you won, fair and square. It came down to our two menus, our six plates, and the judge chose you. The prize money is yours, George, and I'll just be on my way."

"Uh…no." Sofrania had a hand on Liz's arm. "Worked out very conveniently for you, body turning up and all. Was that part of the plan?"

"It was not!" Liz made no effort to take a physical way out. "It started out very simply. We came here to try to enter the contest and win it. I had to go underground because of all the publicity and after I went to stay at my friend Frida's house, some unfortunate homeless woman or drug addict or drunk fell into the harbor and your department was in too much of a hurry to solve the case of 'the missing celebrity CEO'." She looked at me—my God, was that a wink? "What did you think of my Moko Jumbie disguise in Frida's jeep at Jump Up?"

Sofrania had been consulting her smartphone, checking notes, maybe, or files. "We did have a report of a missing person from the old folks' home near the boardwalk," she said. "We'll check to see if there's a match."

"The wandering Esther, " Bondi said. "My cousin told me about her."

"We met her!" Jason recalled. "That day I drove Liz around the island." He noticed Sofrania watching him and rushed to answer her unspoken question. "We walked by a group of elderly people on the boardwalk. There was an old woman bragging about getting out at night alone and the others didn't believe her."

George turned to Sofrania. "I can supply your department with any information you need to put the pieces together. Ms. Barga was let go by our company very recently and we believe she came here to hide out from a federal investigation. The material is on a computer on one of my boats."

"*One* of your boats?" Dana's eyes were wide. Then she looked at Mom and raised her eyebrows to her hairline.

George grinned.

Dana was on the trail, her nose twitching. "Did you swim to the shore from one of them earlier this week?"

"Back and forth. Had to get around unnoticed." He nodded to Jason. "Got tougher once I had a guest aboard."

Everyone gazed at George as if they couldn't quite process the data. Finally, Fasia spoke. "If you had two boats, why did you pay me to keep the spa locked up for you to use exclusively? You weren't having facials or a massage."

George laughed. "No, but lots of confidential phone calls. I needed the privacy." He nodded at Ronald. "Thanks, Ronald. We're done now."

Ronald nodded back. "Thanks, boss. See you back in New York."

Sofrania, Dana and Chelsea seemed to be competing with one another over whose thumbs could flash faster over their phone touch screens. Dana even lifted hers for a second, now and then, to snap a photo.

"Is the whole competition a wash-out, then?" I wondered aloud. "With all that cheating and disqualifying and withdrawing, is there a fair winner?"

"Good question." Paige spoke up. George grinned at me. Cathleen tried to run and hide.

"I've already donated the prize money back to St. Croix," George revealed. "It'll be back in the KweeZeenArtZ bank account for next year's pot."

Paige was satisfied.

"How about double or nothing?" She raised the bar.

George and Simon exchanged looks, then George nodded. "Double or nothing."

# CHAPTER TWENTY-FOUR

Jason pulled his backpack from the trunk of Nola's car and settled it over his right shoulder. It would be weeks before he could get over the fear he'd felt while sitting in that jail cell, maybe months before he'd get back the confidence he used to have. How could he be good for anybody else when he wasn't good for himself? He hadn't even found his right place yet, so he really wasn't ready for his right person. Nola got this; Dana had been a little less understanding. She had thrown an antique typewriter, kept on display at the newspaper office, at him. Very dramatic. Usually much harder to put on a show, in these days of digital content.

But really, how could he stay in St. Croix? How could she expect him to? They'd tossed him in the jail here, and even though it had turned out all right in the end, it was a closer call than he cared to have. He'd had enough of the Caribbean. At first he thought that he'd go back to New York, even if it did mean digging out after six blizzards in six weeks, and even if he knew that he'd been miserable there, would continue to be miserable there, and had nothing, really, to return to. No, New York wasn't it. He had to keep looking, it was impossible to avoid that conclusion. St. Croix wasn't it, either—would Australia be any better?

Bondi had set him up with a friend in Sydney and George had insisted on backstopping him for a little longer. Said it was good karma.

Nola handed him a package. "Open it once you're wheels up," she said. "Just a little something to keep you going until you get on the longer flight and they give you a real meal."

"Let me guess. Not bitter melon."

She laughed. "No, not bitter melon. Not fugu or frozen fish sticks, either."

Jason tucked the container into his backpack. "Thanks, Nola. Thanks for the ride to the airport, thanks for listening to me, thanks for everything."

She smiled at him. "Will it be the right fit for you, Australia?"

"I guess I'll find out when I get there," he said.

I didn't have any idea why, but I was looking at him and feeling no regret. That was a new one. I was very familiar with the experience of wishing things were different. Usually, when I hit a dead end with some guy I'd been attracted to big-time, I wallowed in disappointment. What went wrong, why didn't it take off, what might have been. I almost always decided it was my fault—but not totally always. There was that golf pro jerk from last year. But that's a different story.

I could see that Jason was having a little trouble getting himself moving toward the door and the airplane waiting outside on the tarmac. Some mixed feelings, maybe, after all that he'd been through on St. Croix? I felt no mixed feelings at all. My path for the next few months was nicely set, thanks to my mother, who had sent in those scholarship and school applications for me. In another lifetime, I would have been furious at her interference, but now I was just wondering if she'd have time to join me in a celebration when the good news came through, given that George Corelli was taking up so much of her time these days.

I was aware that I was due back at the front desk in less than an hour and I wanted to get on with it, this saying good-bye. Probably another sign that I was over him. My farewell hug had just the slightest bit of a push at the end of it.

"Have a fantastic time in Australia, Jason. And come back and visit us, one of these days."

*Park Lee* was fired by George Corelli before the plane took off from the St. Croix airport. Today he is in charge of the loyalty program at Puerto Rico Taxi.

*Bjorn + Natalya aka Chef #5* broke up soon after the KweeZeenArtZ Festival. Today he is sous-chef at a six-seater in Siberia. She writes headlines for a yellow rag newspaper in London and has been sued 12 times.

*Bondi Shepherd* kicked himself for two years for not seeing that Park Lee was out to frame Jason Palmateer. Today, he reads detective novels and spends 80% of his time diving.

*Lewis DeLouis* discovered politics and ran for Governor, campaigning on a pledge to ban bitter melon from the island. Today he counts the days until his retirement to the golf course.

*Jean-Claude Legrande* gave the rest of his lottery winnings away after his restaurant failed and the challenge of spending four million dollars nearly exploded his head. The police department wouldn't give him his job back, so today he reads detective novels and keeps a notebook.

*Sofrania Butler* cleaned up the St. Croix crime scene once and for all. Today she dates Governor Lewis DeLouis and never writes anything down.

*Emerson Winter* came to work one day to find out that Nola Stewart had become his boss.

# Acknowledgements

Seeing the Caribbean was one of my dreams for many years and the times I've been there have lived up to every detail in my imagination. The sun, the sea, the wildlife, the trees, the flowers, the food and the people are inspiring.

Thank you to my beta readers, Alice Hulnick, Laurie Lafortune and Christina Galbraith who gave their time to read the story before anyone else and to offer their reactions and comments. I don't think I could have finished it without you.

To the professors and the other students in my University of British Columbia MFA/Creative Writing classes who taught me so much about story, character and language—thank you.

To the farmers, the growers and the chefs of St. Croix who are such an important part of everything that makes the island so memorable—thank you.

And to my husband David Stone who encouraged me to "have fun with it" and who gives me reason, every day, to keep writing.

Turn the page!
For a sneak peek at Gail Hulnick's next mystery novel

# RESORTING

# TO

# LARCENY

*Three couples join forces to create a new and unusual car rally, intended to provide them with affordable adventure in the U.S. Southeast. As the sports cars shimmy and speed through Florida, Georgia and South Carolina, scratches on the chrome start to show up and a hotel valet parker with a dream, an attitude, and a six-figure credit card debt is the only one who can get them back on the road.*

*Chapter 1*

## *Roy*

*I-95, North Florida*

Roy and Raeanne had been cooped up together in their BMW 3 Series for six hours and they'd been at each other's throats for five. Now that was an exaggeration but even a low-level irritation with each other, like this one, felt to Roy like an attack by pit bulls.

It all started with their decision to wait until late morning to leave home in Atlanta to head for the resort on Amelia Island. Roy wanted to get an early start but Raeanne wouldn't be rushed. After the first half hour or so, it was clear that heading to a beach community on the Saturday afternoon of a long weekend would be slow going. Then a five-hour drive (and one that Roy insisted he could do in four) had expanded 50 per cent because of two traffic accidents and a stalled semi near Macon.

The trip extended into the afternoon like an oil leak spreading across a ceramic garage floor. Roy needed to eat regularly and to be stuck on the I-95 with his meal still an hour or more away was enough provocation for him to start snarling (quietly) at the love of his life.

If Roy had heard her say it once, he'd heard it a thousand times. "It's all about the destination, not the journey. This wouldn't be so bad if we were going somewhere we even wanted to go and having a good time getting there," she said. "No offense, but your company's annual golf tournament stopped being fun about a dozen years ago."

His reply was to fiddle with the radio dial. "We're losing reception."

"I've been to Florida sixty million times. Let's go somewhere new, see someplace else."

"Costs a lot of money to travel, Raeanne."

"Costs a lot of money to golf."

This argument had stalled many times before and they weren't really expecting its motor to perform any better today. Just going through the motions, really. All in all, one of the most boring days of all time, Roy thought, with no relief to look forward to at the end of the road.

Until the driver of the F-Type in the lane in front of them slammed on the brakes.